BENT TOWARD JUSTICE

BENT TOWARD JUSTICE

a novel inspired by true stories

STEVEN R. FELDMAN

Rand-Smith Books

Rand-Smith Books
www.RandSmithBooks.com
USA

First Printing, 2024

Contents

I

Passover

Murray Schwartzman

Light. Dark. Light. Dark.

He only saw shadows. For days on end. Squares of light shining through the tiny rectangular holes in this train car meant to take cattle to market—and then to their deaths. In an otherwise tight, black space, darker than any cave, young Murray could only view obscurities through the one tiny lattice-barred window, no matter how much he tried. He was hungry, oh so hungry. The smell of death, which he'd thought at first remained from transported cattle, now hung in the air, nearly covering the other physical smells in this train car bound for where, hell?

In the deep dark of night, even the shadows were lost, but by day, the sun trickled through the iron latticework, creating a shadow play of light, a trick almost, overhead, giving him an elusive hope that this might end, that they might be allowed to join the land of the living. Instead of reminding him of a jail cell or a cage, the light and dark became a checkerboard, then a chess board, and he spent the hours he was forced to stand, crushed between other humans, other bodies, playing games, mastering his chess moves.

Yet the black night always fell like a shroud, and he heard a voice cry out, "My father is dead!" or when his throat ached, rubbed raw from days of thirst, or when his legs spasmed from standing, he'd want to cry. And *that* is when Uncle would squeeze his hand and tell him they were almost there. And then, worst of all, the bright blinding light assaulted him when they opened the doors, the light that led to more death.

The shadows returned to him more often since Miriam passed. She'd brought a routine cheer to his life that vanquished the memories to his dreams, but now, nearly a year had passed since his wife's death, and the shadows were lurking again, chipping away at his soul. It was as if it were happening all over again.

That's one reason he'd agreed to get out of the house more, to help the rabbi. Plus, he loved kids, so he was almost looking forward to today.

"Mr. Schwartzman," a voice said, bringing Murray out of the shadows of his daydream. He rubbed his eyes. He stared at the multi-colored Legos in the bin in front of him. Reaching in and taking a handful, he stared at his fingers, weathered and gnarled by over eighty-eight years of life. "Mr. Schwartzman," the voice repeated.

"Yes?"

"I'm sorry to wake you."

"I wasn't asleep. Just..." He thought he'd better not tell the rabbi he'd been lost in memories. They might take him to the funny farm. "Just resting my eyes."

"Oh, well, sorry to disturb you, then. It's nearly time for us to go in. But have you heard the news?" the rabbi asked. Tall and thin, Rabbi Matt wore a small, rainbow-colored, knitted yarmulke over his thick locks of red hair, a feature that often gave people the impression he was younger than he actually was. Normally, his freckled face held a bright, wide smile, and his cheerful eyes put people at ease. But now, his expression was flat and serious, and his eyes creased with worry.

Murray shook his head. No, he had not heard the news. He sighed. He wasn't ready to hear *any* news, especially if it was bad news.

"I don't want you to worry—no one was killed," the rabbi said, "but there was a rocket attack in Sderot last night. The Palestinians rained 150 rockets down on innocent Israelis."

Rabbi Matt appeared to be waiting to see the impact this news would have. At first, Murray felt numb as the sudden image of rockets echoed with his memories. He pinched the flesh on his forearm to bring himself back fully into the room. Within a few seconds, though, he experienced a toxic wave of emotions as more childhood memories rushed over him.

"These are innocent Jews," the rabbi continued quietly as if talking to himself. "Why would anyone want to hurt them? We've never done anything to hurt anyone. When will people stop attacking us? When will the world understand the terror Palestinians inflict on us?"

"You're certain no one was killed?" Murray asked when he found his voice. He wanted to close his eyes again, felt the need to blink away tears, but he didn't dare. Closing his eyes might produce more shadowy memories.

"Yes, thank goodness. Some were injured. Children will have nightmares for weeks. There will be no peace, not now, not after what the Palestinians have done. But no one was killed."

Murray rubbed his temples. He thought about his own fear-laden past. He remembered the people lined up as they waited to board disgusting cattle cars. The explosions. The putrid smells. The fear of not being able to find his mother. Of anyone. The terror of the unknown. He'd been only nine years old.

When he spoke, anger built with every word. "Yes, thankfully, no one was killed. But that trauma *will* kill some of those poor children on the inside. Some things that are taken away from us cannot be returned. You and I will forget about this attack in a few weeks or months, but those children will never forget."

"I'm sorry if I upset you," Rabbi Matt said, wincing.

Murray waved his hand. "No, no. I have seen it all before. The world is not a safe place for the Jews. We have always been the target. Always..." His voice trailed off.

"But it must stop," Rabbi Matt said in a firm voice. "We must defend our homeland from those terrorists."

"Yes, yes, of course," Murray said, his memories still clinging to him, threatening to return full force. He brushed his hand through the air, as if brushing them all away. If only it were that easy. Yes, he knew what it was like to be a child under attack.

A teacher entered the room. "We're ready to begin," she said, her gentle voice easing the tension-filled room.

Rabbi Matt reached out his hand to Murray, who waved off the assistance. He stood up from his chair—leaning on his old, worn, simple wooden cane—and followed Rabbi Matt through the school's halls, paying little mind to the children's art tacked to the walls as he shuffled his feet quickly to keep up. He followed the rabbi into one of the classrooms of the Montessori school they were visiting, and the two men walked to the front. It was filled to bursting with exuberant children. When Murray came in, they quieted, staring at him.

Murray knew the children of the temple feared him. They saw him as a stern, dour man with a grim look on his face, fearsome beaten-wooden cane in hand, but the rabbi was helping to change that image, and Murray begrudgingly accepted the help. He even started carrying hard candies in his pockets to give to the children, but even then, it took courage for them to approach him and ask for it. Maybe that would change with time.

"Children," Rabbi Matt said. "Today, we are talking about Passover. Are you ready?"

"Yes!" the nine- and ten-year-old children said, nearly in unison. Some of them scooted closer to the front. It was a chattering, laughing, loud group, and Murray couldn't help smiling. He felt an intense joy whenever he was around children and their infectious energy. But just as soon as that joy surged, he remembered the recent rocket attacks in Sderot. What kind of a future would these children have, and all children for that matter? Could they live a more peaceful life than he had lived? Or would the violence in the world find its way to them, too?

"Joining us today is our friend, Mr. Schwartzman," the rabbi said. "Can you say hello to Mr. Schwartzman?"

"Hello, Mr. Schwartzman!" the children shouted together.

"Hello, children," Murray said in a quiet, gravelly voice.

The rabbi continued, "Passover is only a few weeks away, so this is an especially important lesson. To help us better understand this important holiday, I brought some things you might like." Rabbi Matt reached behind him and brought forward a large bin of Legos and other small toys. "As we discuss Passover, we will build things with these blocks."

The children gave out a small cheer, crowding around the bin.

"But wait! Not yet! First, let us say a blessing."

Rabbi Matt paused, and the young children grew surprisingly quiet as a stack of paper made its way through the group, each child taking a sheet.

"This is how we always begin Passover:

'Blessed is the maker of the fruit of the vine! *Baruch ata adonai eloheinu melech haolam, borei pri hagafen.* Thanks to God for giving us these festivals and times we can rejoice, and today, we thank you for this Festival of Matzot to mark the Exodus from Egypt!'"

The children smiled. One of them mouthed the words along with the rabbi. They seemed lulled, intrigued by the cadence of the rabbi's voice.

"Can someone read the next line on your paper?" Rabbi Matt asked.

Twenty hands shot into the air.

"Yes?" he said, pointing to a small boy at the front of the pack.

"Thank you, God, for bringing us to this time and place," said the little voice.

Murray found himself smiling again. He was much more comfortable at home, in his armchair, reading or working out the newspaper's daily crossword puzzle. But the rabbi had insisted, and of course, he could be very persuasive. How would the Jewish people gain more allies if they did not spend time outside of their Jewish environments? If he had been home that day, he would only be reading the news of the rocket attack and getting more frustrated.

"Yes! Yes. Thank you for reading that," replied the rabbi. "Passover is a holiday of family get-togethers, where we eat special foods and share a grand meal, the Seder. How many of you have heard of this?"

Hands shot up into the air.

"How many of you have family traditions at Passover?"

A cacophony of voices rang out, each with a tradition unique to their family but in keeping tradition with the Jewish faith.

"Very good. Yes. Blessings are part of the Seder leading up to the call, 'Next year in Jerusalem!'"

"Next year in Jerusalem!" the young voices echoed.

"This represents the hope that the exile of the Jewish people will end and also that *all* people under bondage will be freed."

Because Murray knew his friend the rabbi well, he knew exactly what the rabbi meant by 'all people'—the LGBTQ community and Black people in Winston-Salem. These groups had always faced oppression that only seemed to intensify. Rabbi Matt had a soft spot for people who were different.

As Rabbi Matt brought out Lego characters to represent the Jewish people and GI Joes as Egyptians, Murray noticed that he had used different colored plastics, a subtle choice likely not lost on the attentive children. "Does anyone know why we celebrate Passover?"

The children looked back without response. "Moses?" a boy in front finally said.

"Yes, Moses! Anyone know what Moses has to do with it?"

Again, the children looked back without words. Murray could almost feel the gears turning in their heads. The rabbi continued.

"The first Passover took place in a time of famine. The Pharoah believed that there weren't enough crops for the Egyptians. He feared that the Jews, whom he'd enslaved, were starting to outnumber his own people. The Egyptians were becoming the minority. So he decided to rid his country of every Jewish baby boy. But a few were saved. God gave guidance to help them stay hidden so Pharoah's troops would 'pass over' them. One of those babies was Moses. His mother saved him by hiding him. Then, Pharoah's own daughter found him floating in a basket down the river, and she adopted him. When Moses grew up, he demanded that Pharoah stop enslaving the Jewish people. *His* people."

"These are the Egyptians chasing the Jews," Rabbi Matt said, pointing at the green plastic soldiers he'd arranged in a crowd behind the Lego characters. Then he placed two small blue blankets in a pile, blocking the Jewish people's way. "And this is the sea."

"Just when our people thought the Egyptians would catch up to them, capture them, and take them back into slavery, God told Moses to raise his staff into the air." The rabbi moved one of the Lego people so that its small arms were uplifted. The children laughed. Even Murray chuckled.

"And then?" the rabbi asked the children.

"The Red Sea parted!" one of the children exclaimed as the rabbi pulled the two blankets apart, creating a path for the Lego people to travel through. Once he had moved them all to the far side, he arranged the green plastic army men to show they had followed the Lego people into the area between the two sections of water.

"The Egyptians chased the Israelites, coming up behind them. Even Pharaoh was there among his soldiers, between the water walls. When the Jewish people were safe on dry land, the sea reformed, crashing down on the Egyptians!" Solemnly, he moved the two blankets back together, covering all the army men.

Rabbi Matt paused. He didn't seem to find gratification in the idea of the Egyptians drowning.

"Were all the Egyptian soldiers killed in the sea, Rabbi Matt?" asked one of the students.

"Yes," Rabbi Matt replied. "Sadly, they were. We should remember that the loss of any human life is tragic. We mourn the loss of the Egyptian lives, even as we celebrate the escape of the Jewish people from slavery."

Murray grunted. He was more concerned with the freed Jewish people than the Egyptian deaths. For that matter, more than Palestinian deaths. And especially German deaths. It didn't seem a great tragedy to him that those seeking the annihilation or enslavement of Jewish people were eliminated.

"We Jews have been a minority suffering in many lands and have been mistreated throughout history," Rabbi Matt said, gazing momentarily at Schwartzman as an acknowledgment of his past. "That is why Mr. Schwartzman is here with us today. His first name is Murray, but his birth name is Moses. He's here to tell you about another time when Jewish people were hunted—a story of how he survived."

"Another Moses!" a young boy cheered.

Murray's heart quickened, but he picked up a few Lego people. "Have you heard of the Holocaust?" he asked the kids, all the while wishing they didn't need to know about it. He stuttered a moment, but the kids rescued him.

"Hitler!" one said in a loud tone.

"Nazis!" said another just as loud.

"Genocide!" said one in the middle.

"Yes, Yes," Murray answered. He pulled his sleeve up from his forearm. "I was one of the Jewish people Hitler wanted to kill."
"Just like Moses!" said a boy with intense green eyes and curly red hair.

"Well, there are similarities," Murray said. He wished the rabbi hadn't said his name was Moses. "But the key is that I survived. I am here with you all today, but many did *not* survive the Holocaust. We must protect the Jewish people, prevent this type of murder from ever happening again, and we must pray to God for His help. We can never let this happen again. Never again!"

The children echoed him. "Never again!"

"The Passover story is one of God rescuing us. The moral of our Passover, however, is not just about Jews. Just as we were slaves in Egypt and God rescued us, we all should work to redeem anyone suffering from slavery, discrimination, or injustice," Rabbi Matt said.

The children had been patient up to this point but were beginning to fidget.

"Now, before we go any further, I would like you to build something with Legos, something from the Passover story. Anything you would like."

The children pressed in toward the bin holding the Legos, but Rabbi Matt saw how chaotic it was becoming. He reached in over the children and grabbed the bin of Legos. "Would you mind, Mr. Schwartzman?"

Rabbi Matt motioned toward a chair. Murray sat down, and Rabbi Matt placed the bin on his lap.

"Now," Rabbi Matt explained, "everyone, please form a line, and you can each take out a handful of Legos when it's your turn."

Murray sat in the chair as each child reached in and scooped out some blocks. He looked up at the line of tiny people, and his thoughts shifted. After so many years dealing with the memories, he could tell when the flashbacks were about to happen, and sometimes, he'd try to intervene by focusing on happier thoughts, joyous times. Yet he didn't seem able to rid his mind of the shadows today. Maybe he'd been passed over physically, left alive, but he would never rid his life of the scars, the shadows. The light and the dark, they persecuted him, drilled into him in a way that no physical abuse had. How could he share that with an innocent child?

He turned his attention back to the innocent children and watched their eager faces as they reached into the box for a handful of colorful toys. They approached, one after the other, heights shifting, expressions changing, and he could feel the familiar tug of his memories, forcing him to revisit the pain of his past. He remembered all of the lines he had stood in while living in the concentration camps under the eyes of German soldiers, the lines for food while living among refugees, the lines he had stood in to receive permission to come to the United States, and the lines that had led him here, to Winston-Salem as a teenager so many years. So many lines.

Thirty minutes later, it was time to wrap up the activities.

"Repeat after me: 'Next year in Jerusalem!'" Rabbi Matt said.

"Next year in Jerusalem!" the young ones replied, holding their Lego creations high in the air.

The children were led back to their assigned classrooms while Murray helped Rabbi Matt clean up the toys despite the rabbi's suggestion that Murray should rest.

"I have a wonderful idea, Mr. Schwartzman," Rabbi Matt said as they left the room. "You should come with me tomorrow to meet Congressional Representative Georgia Jones."

"Are you friends with Ms. Jones?" Murray asked, surprised.

"I know, I know," Rabbi Matt said, smiling. "We disagree on virtually every issue."

He laughed, and Murray chuckled. "There is one major issue she and I remain in agreement over: the importance of supporting the Israeli state, the only democracy in the Middle East and home to the Jewish people."

Murray thought about how often he'd sat in his favorite chair, watching Fox News, when Georgia Jones would pop up, her hair dyed black and styled in a severe bob. It gave her a confident but conservative air. She'd fought against a Transgender bill that took center stage a few years ago, even holding a press conference outside the bathroom of a local department store to rail against gender-neutral restrooms. She certainly towed the Republican party line on issues like abortion and gun control, with climate change and income inequality being low on the list of political priorities. He was relatively sure she also had issues with immigration and children born in the U.S. to undocumented parents. One thing for sure, she did not seem like someone from whom the rabbi would curry favor. However, he'd been around long enough to understand how politics worked—the give and take, playing to a base, making pronouncements to achieve a desired response. It was theater, pure and simple.

Murray shrugged. "You know it is one of the few points you and I agree on as well."

Rabbi Matt laughed loudly and clapped Murray on the shoulder. "This is why you are my friend, Mr. Schwartzman. You always tell me the truth. And this is why you should come with me to the meeting. Representative Jones would be honored to meet a Holocaust survivor. Today's rocket attacks will give us a lot to talk about."

They loaded the bins into the back of Rabbi Matt's small car and climbed in. Before he turned the key, the rabbi looked over at Murray.

"So, Mr. Schwartzman, are you in?"

2

A Good Day

Murray Schwartzman

Murray spent most of the morning trying to devise excuses to get out of going with Rabbi Matt to meet Georgia Jones. He'd rather stay home than almost anything else in the world. He didn't enjoy traveling, but perhaps most of all, Murray had little use for U.S. politics. The blustering he saw on television led to no tangible outcome. He'd removed himself with a keen disinterest from Winston-Salem's political stratosphere.

He'd spent the night with the flashbacks, always alternating dim to dark to that bright light. Every time he shut his eyes, he'd see the flood of humanity pouring out of a train car that smelled of death and into the arms of death in that camp. He tried to think of something else. He'd think about his wedding day, something he never thought would happen. After such a chaotic childhood, he simply never planned to marry, didn't even entertain the idea. Why would he?

Giving the impression that he was emotionally prepared to share his life with another person felt disingenuous, almost deceitful. He couldn't, in good conscience, subject his damaged spirit on someone else. So, he resigned himself to a bachelorhood. However, somehow, his reality changed when he met Miriam. After a brief courtship and a small wedding ceremony, he did have glimpses of marital bliss, of a pleasant life. But the glimpses, like the marriage, were too fleeting. Those thoughts would always return to taunt him.

"Mo, you know you need to eat a little more," Miriam would say, nudging him out of his dark reverie. She'd touch his cheek with her palm, as if she could caress the emotional pain out, just as she wrung out his shirts out to dry.

"I have to go in to work," he'd say, not wanting to make her share his heavy burden. She had lost family, too. That's how they'd connected, searching for family members. She was always there waiting for him to return home, though, and those worry lines grew ever deeper on her forehead, gazing at him, wanting him to let her in more. As if that would've helped. But she was still there, all those years, with a hearty meal, a deep, resonant laugh that came more often than not, and keeping his home cozy, delightful, even. Coming home to Miriam after a hard day dealing with tobacco farmers who respected his business sense but never trusted him as a Jew was like coming home to a hearty fire.

And now she was gone.

Until the very end, Miriam remained steadfast and made a noble attempt at running a respectable household while Murray worked from dawn to dusk as a foreman in a tobacco plant. His job was physically taxing, but it kept his mind occupied and his body tired. Miriam even got used to the smell that permeated not only his clothes, but his skin and hair, as it did so many other workers in North Carolina in the '50s and '60s.

He'd been a good provider to her, a loyal husband, but what did it matter now? At first, he'd told her he couldn't imagine bringing children into a world that hated Jews. And when he'd finally come around, 10 years or so later, he'd found that all the trying in that sad, tragic world did not produce a child, which cemented his belief that they were meant to leave the childbearing and rearing to others. This world was not one for children. He could tell Miriam was devastated, but she always hid her sadness under that bright, lipstick-red smile.

The work left Murray and Miriam financially secure, especially after the company shares he accumulated were liquidated in a leveraged buy-out of the tobacco company. Shortly thereafter, when they finally had the financial resources to travel and enjoy life, her sudden death served as another painful reminder to Murray that happiness was short-lived.

And now, he was alone. Alone with his memories.

Going out into the community would distract him, perhaps. In fact, he could not think of one good reason *not* to go. He believed in supporting Israel, no matter how much personal discomfort it brought him. Also, despite himself, he was enjoying his newfound relationship with the rabbi. It felt good when Rabbi Matt contacted him about becoming more involved in the community and sharing his story with others. It felt good to be needed and to have a friend. Which is how he found himself standing on the sidewalk outside his house, waiting for Rabbi Matt to arrive.

Rabbi Matt stopped his eight-year-old Toyota Prius just beyond Murray and waved enthusiastically. Murray noticed the two prominent bumper stickers on the back of the rabbi's car: a 2012 Obama campaign sticker and another that read COEXIST, each letter formed by the central symbol of a different religion. When Murray didn't immediately move to get into the car, Rabbi Matt backed up and lowered the passenger-side window.

"I'm sorry I'm late," he apologized. "I'm afraid we're now in a bit of a hurry."

"You know, I'm just not sure if this is for me." He stared hard at the ground, avoiding Rabbi Matt's eyes.

"You're here now, so you might as well come along." Rabbi Matt smiled, part empathy, part focused determination. "Think of this as an opportunity to support the State of Israel. Jones can do so much in Congress. We just need to share our passion with her."

"I'm just not sure. She isn't going to want to talk with me."

Rabbi Matt reached over and pushed the door open. "Come on, Mr. Schwartzman," he said, still smiling. "You have more influence than you know. Besides, I promised Ms. Jones you were coming. She is very eager to meet someone who survived the Holocaust, someone as brave as you."

Murray snorted, stood still momentarily, sighed, climbed into the car, pulled his bad leg in last, and buckled himself in.

"Excellent," Rabbi Matt said. "Now, let's go make a new ally."

***

"These videos are just horrific," Representative Jones said to the two men from across her desk. She stared out the window for a moment. The harsh sun amplified her heavy makeup. It glistened and revealed her pale skin underneath.

She seemed passionate. Was the emotion crossing her face authentic or a way to reel Murray in?

"Why we allow this to continue is beyond me," she continued, shifting her gaze back toward the men, her voice becoming more emphatic. "Nearly everyone I know in Winston-Salem is pro-Israel. There is a strong, evangelical Christian contingent here in the city, of which I am part. But tragic attacks like this one show it's important that we keep that momentum going. We must keep this kind of thing in front of the community."

A television was on in the corner, replaying the amateur cell phone clips of the Sderot rocket attacks that Rabbi Matt had sent Rep. Jones the week before. Israelis watched arcs of light and smoke trail over the small city, slicing through the evening light, landing somewhere in the distance with loud booms. The people ran, picking up speed with each new explosion. Another video showed emergency vehicles parked around a large crater in the middle of a suburban street, an ambulance screaming into the distance. In a third, a small group of people raced from a van to a nearby bomb shelter, stopping to huddle behind a wall as explosions sounded above them. Finally, in the shelter, children, held in their parents' arms, screamed inconsolably. Nearly all of them gazed upward toward the skies, in terror, even those below ground.

Murray didn't dare close his eyes. He remembered the running. He could never forget the explosions, the bombs, and later, the sound of boots marching in step, taking away everything and everyone he'd ever loved. He'd tried to run away himself, hunting everywhere for food, but they'd corralled him in and taken him to a fate worse than starvation, a life so full of death, it became every day, but never, ever routine. Ms. Jones seemed lost in thought. Murray stared down at his hands folded in his lap. He swallowed and blinked back tears but avoided looking up. He wanted them to see his strength, not his fear.

Eventually, Rabbi Matt spoke. "Ms. Jones, I want to thank you for your efforts in support of legislation to make anti-Semitic boycotts of Israel a crime. Our community greatly appreciates your work."

Representative Jones gave a robotic nod. How many of those nods did she offer up a day? Had she even heard the rabbi?

"As you might already know, Sderot is less than a mile from Gaza and was attacked multiple times in the early 2000s, when thirteen people were killed," the rabbi continued. "The town is sometimes called the 'Bomb Shelter Capital of the World.' We must act now to prevent this from escalating."

Jones shook her head. His words seemed to have reached her. "Just awful," she said with a sympathetic smile.

"Over 20,000 people living in constant fear and uncertainty," Rabbi Matt added.

The Congresswoman looked one more time toward the television screen, then shifted her focus to her visitors. "You know I will do everything possible to support the only democracy in the Middle East. Israel is America's ally. What's going on there is deplorable. Did you see the picture I sent out?"

"Yes. Thank you," Rabbi Matt replied. "We appreciate the gesture. I was proud to stand beside you in that photo, as was the temple board."

"I was a teacher and school administrator for many years before seeking public office. Did you know that?" she asked.

"No."

"It's a fact," she said. "Seeing those children in Sderot terrified, running, injured... it has left an indelible impression on me, Rabbi."

Rabbi Matt nodded. Murray was impressed with the rabbi's instincts on when to speak and when to remain silent. It was clear that Ms.

Jones was becoming more enamored with the charismatic rabbi. *But, then again, she's a politician*, Murray thought. *Maybe she's just saying what the rabbi wants to hear.*

"I want to do whatever I can for your community, for the Israelis," Representative Jones said. "I will ensure that Congress continues to give Israel all the support its military needs to protect Israel from the Palestinian terrorists. We'll also keep pressure on the president and his administration to vote in support of Israel at the United Nations."

Despite his reservations about the politician and her motives, Murray felt a flicker of hope run down his spine.

"Thank you, Ms. Jones," Rabbi Matt said, reaching into his bag and handing her a rolled-up plastic sign.

She unrolled the sign. "'We Stand with Israel.' Can I keep it?"

"We'll send you as many as you would like."

"This is the kind of thing that will bring the community together," she said. She motioned toward the television. "We need to keep educating our constituents about the miracle of Israel, its birth, its stand for democracy," she added. "They see this news footage, but they don't know what to make of it all." Ms. Jones stared at the sign for a bit longer, then turned her attention to Murray. "And what can I do for you, Mr. Schwartzman?"

Murray, embarrassed, fumbled for some words. "I don't need anything," he mumbled.

"Rabbi Matt tells me you have lived quite a life."

"Yes, yes."

"Mr. Schwartzman, what do you think people in our area need to know about the Jewish community that they do not yet know?" the rabbi asked.

The question caught him off guard, and he stared for so long into his own lap that Rabbi Matt seemed about to speak to break the tension. At last, though, Murray found his voice. "I think people do not understand all the Jewish people have been through. People who have not lived through it cannot truly comprehend all that people like me have seen. But I can't blame them. If I hadn't been literally thrown into it, I probably wouldn't be able to comprehend the sheer horror that humanity can inflict upon itself." His voice shook.

The others waited for Murray, giving him time to maintain his composure.

When he did, his words tumbled out. "When you stand in a cattle car for days on end with no food, no water, knowing that all around you people are dying, but they cannot even die in peace, they cannot even lie down in death because there is no room on the floor..." He took a long breath. "When you see it happen over and over—groups of people spilling out of train cars into a barren area in a strange land surrounded by chain link and barbwire—all because they are Jewish. Those that have survived those first days of stench and heat and moans—and death.

"You see it written on their faces as they pass by you. They know as well as you do that they've escaped death only to face it again here, on solid ground. That's when you see some fall, only to be punched or shot dead on the spot. 'Keep moving,' the uniformed men shout at them.

"When you see children separated from their parents, families torn apart. And all of this simply because they are Jewish."

Another period of silence. Rabbi Matt appeared to be close to tears. Ms. Jones seemed to be holding her breath.

"And then you see this happening today," Murray said. "These rocket attacks. These terrorists. Against the same people, the Jewish people. Against their children, and their children's children..."

The air conditioning in the room kicked on, and a gentle hum nearly drowned out Murray's soft voice, though it trembled with passion now instead of grief.

"You just hope that someone, somehow, will stop it from happening again."

***

In the car, Rabbi Matt was ecstatic.

"You were wonderful, Mr. Schwartzman. Ms. Jones took to you immediately. I knew she would. Your story really made an impact!" Rabbi Matt's face beamed as he backed out of the parking lot.

Murray smiled a dim smile. He knew in his head and heart that

Ms. Jones would be helpful to the Jewish people in some far-off, hard-to-understand kind of way. But despite Rabbi Matt's enthusiasm, he was dubious of actual change, especially in the hands of a politician. He'd learned over the years to temper his enthusiasm for change that never comes.

"Have you ever considered a career in politics?"

"No, not politics. No politics for me," Murray murmured. His thoughts lingered on the children fleeing Sderot, of the rockets exploding in the dirt. The intense darkness inside the bomb shelters. The same darkness he had witnessed for himself inside the cattle cars so long ago. He could not escape these memories, but maybe children of the next generation could.

"This was a good day," Rabbi Matt said as they pulled away.

3

Anti-Semitism Rises

Rabbi Matt

Rabbi Matt looked down at the letter at the kitchen table.

"You'd better hurry. You don't want to be late for work, do you?" Rebecca asked over her shoulder as she disappeared down the hall in response to a child's shrill cry for attention.

The rabbi appreciated his wife's concern. The kids could be demanding, and their needs came first, yet she kept him on schedule. One of the things he'd loved about Rebecca from the beginning was her gentle nature, her compassion for others. They shared a similar outlook on life, not only for their family, but the community as well. She was just as concerned about being mindful and respectful of other maligned groups as he was. They made a great team.

Settling in North Carolina by way of Israel and California, they had become accustomed to conservative politicians spouting ideologies that were directly opposed to their own. However, they saw it as an opportunity to teach by example, to welcome opposing opinions in a respectful manner.

Less than a week after Rabbi Matt's meeting with Ms. Jones and Mr. Schwartzman, the paper in front of him bore more bad news. He had left Ms. Jones' office optimistic that the community was progressing in the right direction. Yet, there he was, running late for work and feeling depressed and angry as he stared at the paper.

The letter to the editor Rebecca had pointed out this morning felt like a direct threat to Rabbi Matt and the momentum he was creating in support of Israel. It felt personal.

The Jewish Passover holiday begins at sunset on April 14. At Passover, we Jews celebrate liberation from our bondage in Egypt. At Passover, we also pray for the return of exiled Jews to the land of Israel. But Israel today is not a Jewish state.

What is a Jewish state? Jewish religious leader, sage and scholar, and descendant of the tribes of Benjamin and David, Rabbi Hillel described the central tenet of Judaism some 2,000 years ago, around the time of Jesus. "What is hateful to you, do not do to your neighbor. That is the whole Torah. The rest is commentary," Rabbi Hillel said.

Israel was created by expelling hundreds of thousands of peaceful Palestinian men, women, and children from their homes and villages, an act completely inconsistent with the foundation of our Jewish beliefs. Palestinian Muslim and Christian families, people who had peacefully coexisted with Palestinian Jews, were neither spared terrorism by the Irgun, a Zionist paramilitary organization, nor violent expulsion by the Haganah, the Zionist army. The Haganah war plans (Haganah Plan D) explicitly called for the expulsion of entire villages of Palestinian families, the destruction of their homes, and the mining of the remains of those villages. We watch today as Israel continues to rain terror down on the people of Gaza, our brothers and sisters, dropping American-made bombs with American support, killing thousands of men, women, and children. It is horrific, and it must be stopped!

At Passover this year, I will pray for the peaceful return of all refugees to their homes in the Holy Land—whether Jewish, Christian, or Muslim. While we Jews pray at Passover "Next year in Jerusalem!" we don't pray "Next year in Jerusalem by making peaceful non-Jewish families refugees!" None of us believes expelling peaceful non-Jewish families from their homes is okay. Only when we repatriate all the refugee families to live in peace together will Israel become a truly Jewish state consistent with our Jewish values.

Dr. Joseph Friedman, Winston-Salem, NC

The rabbi hoped Murray hadn't come across the letter. He'd only just successfully recruited Mr. Schwartzman to venture out and effect change. This was the kind of thing that would enrage him, if not totally dismay and deter him, and Rabbi Matt hoped for nothing but peace for his friend. But it was highly unlikely Schwartzman would miss it, considering how much time he spent alone at home, reading the newspaper as a daily ritual.

The rabbi's cell phone rang. It was Sarah, his administrative assistant.

"Good morning, Rabbi," she said.

"Hi, Sarah. How can I—wait, before I continue, I must ask, have you seen this letter that's been floating around? The one about Sderot written by a Joseph Friedman?"

"Um, yes, Rabbi, I have seen it."

"I wonder how many others have," he said, but it wasn't a question.

"Rabbi, did you forget about your 10 o'clock meeting?"

"The Israel trip," Rabbi Matt said, groaning.

"Everyone is already in the conference room."

"Thank you for the reminder, Sarah. I'll be over as soon as I can." He paused. "Sarah?"

"Yes?"

"Do you know anything about this Joseph Friedman?"

"No, I'm sorry, Rabbi. I can ask around."

"Such a Jewish name," he said. "But he's not part of our temple. If he ever attended, I don't remember him. No true Jew would make such anti-Semitic comments, especially right when Palestinian terrorists are attacking Jews in Israel."

"You never can tell these days," Sarah said. "Maybe he's just a troll, pretending to have a Jewish name. Maybe he thinks that helps make him sound more credible."

"Very true, Sarah. That's probably what's happening." For some reason, this made the rabbi feel much better, this idea that Joseph Friedman was not actually Jewish, but some online provocateur trying to stir up trouble. "Please tell everyone I'll be right over for the meeting. I'm afraid this editorial sent me off track."

He was still fuming as he approached the temple parking lot and passed the large "We Stand with Israel" banner placed prominently by the road. It made him proud to see the fruits of his labor spread.

Rabbi Matt parked in his designated spot and entered the temple office. A few years earlier, this building had housed the temple's main sanctuary, but as the rabbi succeeded in growing the congregation, adding young families, he'd led a building fund campaign. With its lucrative yield, the congregation had erected a new sanctuary, leaving the old space available for more offices and school use. This new sanctuary had been fitted with the latest in comfort and technology, all the bells and whistles needed to make it attractive to both young families who enjoyed Rabbi Matt's guitar playing projected on the big screen and older donors who appreciated having well-padded pews.

To protect the sanctuary against vandals or worse, the front doors were thick, see-through glass and nearly always locked. The temple hired one lone security guard to watch over the entrance when the sanctuary was in use. Rabbi Matt, along with the rest of his advisory board, felt that they couldn't be too careful, not in these days when attacks on places of worship, regardless of denomination, seemed to be on the rise. The recent horrific Jewish temple killings in Pittsburgh sent shivers through him.

Rabbi Matt scanned his ID card, passed through the security door, and dropped off a few things in his office before going to the meeting about the Israel trip. Another uncertainty. Rebecca had been arranging the annual trip to Israel for their young people, but with the recent attacks, many parents were growing uncertain about sending their children into a potential war zone. He wasn't sure if he and Rebecca would want to send their own children into a place of conflict. The odds of being killed by a rocket attack were remote, but the perception of the risk of attack was a difficult obstacle to overcome, even for Rabbi Matt.

His rainbow-colored tallit hung from a peg in the wall, and below it, his guitar leaned on a stand. Dozens of newspaper clippings lined the other wall, including one describing the rabbi's movement to block legislation that prevented gay marriage and limited transsexual use of public bathrooms. Public facilities should be unisex anyway. Rabbi Matt lived the temple's credo, which he had enlisted someone to write in calligraphy above his office door:

"All human beings are created in God's image.
Tikun Olam – repairing the world – is a hallmark of Judaism,
and we strive to bring peace and justice to all people."

"Peace and justice for all people." That was the phrase constantly moving through the rabbi's mind. He smiled, then remembered the editorial and its supposed author, Joseph Friedman. Nothing peaceful about that man.

Just as he was about to rush to the meeting, he heard a gentle knock on his door. He turned to find two men looking in, both senior temple members.

"Rabbi Matt," one of the men said loudly with a grim look. "Did you see the letter the *Winston-Salem Journal* published online this morning?"

The rabbi sighed and nodded. This was Sam Weisblatt, a blue-eyed, middle-aged attorney whose firm did civil litigation defense work for the tobacco industry in Winston-Salem. One of Rabbi Matt's close friends on the temple board, Sam was also one of the temple's most consistent financial supporters. It wasn't at all like Sam to be in such a state. He was a devoted parent and spent time coaching children in baseball and basketball YMCA youth leagues. Besides his work for the temple, he once chaired Winston-Salem's United Way campaign. He and his wife had once been named national American Heart Association volunteers of the year.

Having Sam, a representative of Reynolds Tobacco and all its tentacles, as a temple board member was extremely helpful in the small town. Tobacco had built Winston-Salem. Cigarette brands Winston and Salem were named after the town. The cartoon character Joe Camel had helped make Reynolds' Camel brands popular, and the Camel brand explained why so many of the city's businesses used Camel in their names: Camel City Dry Cleaners, Camel City Pawn Shop, Camel City Tattoo Parlor. In earlier days, trains would leave town loaded with cigarettes and return full of money; that money supported churches, hospitals, the arts... and the temple. Every aspect of the city had been infused with tobacco in one way or another.

But, after a leveraged buyout of Reynolds Tobacco that took the Reynolds' administrative headquarters out of Winston-Salem, tobacco's influence on the city had gradually faded, though every now and then you would still see "Pride in Tobacco" bumper stickers on pickup trucks in and around town. California-bred Rabbi Matt would roll his eyes in disbelief and disgust every time he saw one of those symbols of support for a product that took people's lives. How anyone could display and take pride in such a thing was a complete mystery to Rabbi Matt. Having grown up in Northern California, Matt couldn't appreciate what it was like to be raised in a culture steeped in tobacco. But he appreciated Sam.

Before the rabbi could respond to Sam, he saw Jon Lerner following behind. Jon had headed the temple's successful building fund campaign and was now working on fundraisers to support Israel. Under Jon's leadership, the temple made generous donations to the Jewish National Fund each year; the Fund bought land to support more Jewish communities in the Holy Land. Jon also organized a fundraiser done by the children of the temple. This year, the children had collected enough quarters to plant a record 200 trees in Israel, twice as many as last year. Jon shared his passion for Tikun Olam, for healing the world.

"Yes, Sam, I saw it," Rabbi Matt said. "I knew we'd have to deal with it, but I didn't expect you so early in the day." The three men smiled ruefully at each other.

"What are you going to do about it?" Sam asked, his smile vanishing. "Someone, maybe a group of us, needs to respond. I can't believe our local paper would print an anti-Semitic letter like that."

"Yes. It's distressing," the rabbi said, trying to keep his tone calm. He could see Sam's anger growing, and modulating his voice served to cool his own temper.

"'Distressing' is an understatement," Sam fumed. "Supporting terrorists and the destruction of Israel? In our local paper, of all places! Why would they allow it? I don't understand."

Rabbi Matt turned to Jon and asked, "And what do you think about it?"

Jon glanced over at Sam and then back at the rabbi. "It's terrible; that's what I think," Jon said. "Offensive. Here we are with terrorist organizations attacking Israel, and then this traitor in our midst attacks Israel in our newspaper. I've talked to several temple members about it, and they want to know what we can do. The only good thing is that the letter seems to have galvanized the congregation around our upcoming fundraiser for American political action to support Israel."

"I checked on this Friedman guy," Sam said. "He works at the Methodist Hospital. Maybe we can get them to fire him to show the community that his views aren't acceptable in our town."

So, Joseph Friedman is a real man.

"Hold on now, Sam," the rabbi said, holding up his hands. "This is just one person's opinion. Let's not try to get anyone fired just yet. Perhaps I could try talking to him."

Rabbi Matt wasn't really excited about the idea of talking to the man, but it seemed like the rational thing to do. Matt was, after all, a peacemaker and problem solver.

"Talk?" Sam practically spit the word out. "Talk? To an anti-Semite? To a self-hating Jew? You can't talk with terrorists!"

"You could try contacting the medical school dean," Jon suggested. "The two of you have a great relationship, Rabbi."

Jon had also worked with the dean, helping with several of the medical school's fundraising projects, the largest of which was the Nadab Children's Hospital.

"I'm sure the dean has seen this by now. He must be embarrassed and likely furious that one of his faculty published this kind of garbage," Sam said.

The rabbi's telephone buzzed. "Yes?"

"Rabbi Matt, Mr. Schwartzman is here. Should I send him in?"

The rabbi sighed. His day was not going as planned, and he wasn't seeing any possibility of getting it back on track.

"Yes, of course." He paused. "And please give my apologies to those waiting at the meeting. Let Rebecca go ahead and get started without me. I'll be there in just a little bit."

4

A Seed

Rabbi Matt

Mr. Schwartzman pushed between Sam and Jon without a word, entering the rabbi's office like a storm, cane in one hand, newspaper in the other. "Rabbi Rabinowitz," Mr. Schwartzman began, "the seeds of anti-Semitism start with letters like this. Full of lies. Evil, hateful lies full of slander against the Jewish people. I have seen what these sentiments can lead to. I have lived through it. What can we do?"

He nodded and motioned Murray to sit down. He couldn't help but notice again the small tattoo on the man's forearm, a series of numbers that had been his identity in the German concentration camps.

Clearly, the letter took Mr. Schwartzman back to his days in those camps. He'd never seen the formidable rage simmering just beneath the surface of the man's steady composure. It was more than justified, but intimidating, nonetheless.

"I'll draft a response," the rabbi said in a firm voice. "I'm sure they'll publish it. Sam and I have also discussed speaking with Dean Jacobs at the medical school. I'm open to other suggestions."

Sam looked at his watch. "That's a good start," he said. "I'm afraid I have to go, but let's check in after your rebuttal gets published."

"Sounds good to me," Jon said, and the two men said their farewells.

The rabbi could sense Mr. Schwartzman's deep respect for him, buried as it was in the moment under anger and frustration. Rabbi Matt viewed Mr. Schwartzman as a Jewish icon, someone who had suffered for being Jewish and survived. Yet, recently, they'd become friends. With the rabbi's spirit and gentle guidance, Mr. Schwartzman seemed to eventually agree (or at least not openly disagree) with most of the rabbi's progressive positions.

At the last Black Lives Matter march, he'd taken Murray with him to the very front of the march alongside other of the more liberal-leaning clergy of the town. Murray had at first resisted, saying he would rather blend in with the large group. But the rabbi reminded him that a position at the front was not only an honor Schwartzman deserved because of how he had survived the Holocaust, but that he represented all Jews, the survivors and the lost. He served as a symbol of the shared struggle of Jews and Blacks against oppression.

When Rabbi Matt had wanted to officiate the first gay wedding ever held in Temple Shalom, even though Mr. Schwartzman thought it was a crazy idea, he had vocally supported the rabbi in the presence of some of the older members of the congregation, effectively silencing their opposition. Murray Schwartzman's support gave the rabbi a sense of invincibility and the confidence that he could, and should, continue to follow his convictions.

Rabbi Matt stood and walked around the desk, putting his hand on Mr. Schwartzman's shoulder. "Murray, I'm upset about this, too. We will not let this pass unchallenged; do you understand? You can rest assured. You have other things to be concerned about right now, like the youth trip to the Holocaust Museum in D.C. It's only two weeks away. How are the preparations coming along for that?" The diversion might lower Mr. Schwartzman's blood pressure.

"Yes, yes," Mr. Schwartzman replied. "I'll do my best to calm down. The trip will help them see why letters like this happen—and why we must stand strong against such evil."

"I appreciate you going with us," the rabbi said. "I know it won't be easy for you, but it wouldn't be the same with anyone else leading those conversations. Now, you get on with your day. I have a meeting to attend, and then I'll write a letter to the editor in response."

"Thank you," Mr. Schwartzman said, rising like his legs might give way. "You're a good man, Rabbi. You give me hope."

The rabbi tried to imagine the trauma Friedman's letter could cause someone like Schwartzman, someone who had been through such hell simply because he was Jewish. Matt hoped he could ease Murray's burden.

"Murray, come to our house tonight," he said. "The kids would love to see you. We could go out for dinner together, too."

"I don't like to impose, Rabbi," Murray said.

The rabbi knew that Murray relished spending time with his and Rebecca's children, who had seen beyond his tough exterior and were clearly smitten with him. "You're not imposing! The children would love to see you again."

"Thank you. In that case, I will see you tonight."

The rabbi patiently watched as Mr. Schwartzman left, then threw together some things for the meeting and dashed through the building.

Rebecca was in complete control when he entered the meeting. She'd already coordinated transportation, reservations, and contact information.

"We want this to work, even if there is a slight risk," said Ruth, a mom of three boys sitting in the back. Other parents joined in assent, and he closed the meeting feeling upbeat. They'd not only go to Israel this summer but to D.C. This would be a year to remember.

The rabbi's heart quickened again as soon as he returned to his office. He re-read the letter.

"This mamzer hides behind a façade of Judaism to defame Israel," he mumbled. "He claims to be a Winston-Salem Jew. He's not even a member of our temple."

The way this letter had hurt Mr. Schwartzman added to his fury. He began to craft a rebuttal but put it aside. Perhaps he should first talk with this Dr. Friedman. If the man was as Jewish as he claimed to be, the rabbi might even be able to convince him to write his own retraction letter, correcting his errors. That would be a win in every respect. Surely, if Friedman could see the damage he was doing to their Jewish community, he would be willing to do such a small thing.

The rabbi sat back and smiled, feeling much better. Yes. That would be the best way forward. But it couldn't hurt to talk to the dean, too.

Rabbi Matt picked up the phone.

* * *

Rabbi Matt glanced over at Murray Schwartzman. They'd barely said a word during the ride from Murray's house to the rabbi's house. The man had an uncanny knack for appearing unfazed by silence. They hadn't even discussed Joseph Friedman, something the rabbi was happy about. He rarely had trouble leaving work at work, coming home without the weight of the day's problems. Even after most of the funerals he officiated, he returned home with a feeling of closure, ready to spend time with those he loved.

But the issue of Friedman's letter continued to gnaw at him, down to his bones. To distract himself, he focused on what a nice time they'd have. Asher was 13, a bright, quiet, thoughtful child who was preparing, along with his friends, for his upcoming Bar Mitzvah. His daughter, Miri, was 8 going on 18, Matt and Rebecca's little hippie, always dressing in loose, colorful layers. She was energetic and free-spirited, with long blond hair she refused to cut.

"Well, here we are," he said, exiting the parked car and waiting for Mr. Schwartzman to walk around and join him. "The kids will be so pleased to see you."

They walked by the hand-crafted mezuzah on the frame of the front door. It had the word *Shalom* artfully written on it, welcoming guests. Two prominently placed candlesticks greeted visitors in the living room entryway. Rebecca and Miri lit candles here every Friday night, welcoming the beginning of the Sabbath. A clay hanukkiah stood in the corner, one Asher had made in first grade at the suggestion of his teacher when the rest of his class was making Christmas tree ornaments. But it was almost Passover, not Hanukkah season. Rebecca had the home even tidier than usual, and they'd already rid the cupboards of leavened products. All that was needed was a good sweep with a duster. Matt would do it if Rebecca allowed him to. He could already taste the matzo.

Rebecca and Matt's 1940s bungalow was ample for their needs, and they had made necessary updates. The kitchen renovation was a blessing, as the new cabinetry gave them room for the four sets of dishes required for keeping kosher: two sets of everyday dishware, one for milk and one for meat meals, and two sets of fine china that they used only when entertaining guests. Like so many other Jewish homes, whether more or less religious, whether they had one set of dishes or four, Rabbi Matt's home exuded a sense of family—of warmth, friendliness, and love—that Schwartzman seemed to appreciate.

Tonight, Asher sat reading a book, and Miri played with dolls while watching television. Rabbi Matt could hear his wife talking on the phone in another room. He couldn't hear her words, but her tone was irate. She must be talking to someone about Joseph Friedman.

On seeing Schwartzman, Miri rushed to him and gave him a big hug. Schwartzman returned the hug along with a huge smile.

For some magical reason, the children never saw Murray as grim and scary the way many others did. They approached him respectfully but playfully, as if he were a giant teddy bear. Murray's demeanor changed every time he saw them, the light in his eyes, the ease of his smile.

On Murray's last visit, Matt and Rebecca told him they had met in a kibbutz, a communal settlement in Israel, 16 years before. Rebecca's family was one of the few religious families in the kibbutz. Her parents, Mr. and Mrs. Levinsohn, who had also survived the Holocaust, were proud founding members of the kibbutz.

Rebecca entered the room. "Oh, hello, Mr. Schwartzman, I'm so glad to see you."

"It's nice to see you, too, Rebbetzin Rebecca." He nodded. "Thank you for having me over. I haven't been having the best day. Seeing you and the children always seems to pick me up."

Rebecca sat down across the room from them and said, "Oh, I'm so angry about that letter, too. The author knows nothing about Israel. You know I grew up there. I know what it is really like. You have to live there to know. To be trying to build a better world for your family while being surrounded by Arab terrorists."

Murray hadn't lived in Israel, but he had survived the Holocaust. "I know about terror," he said. Then, more warmly, "Rebbetzin, what was it like growing up in Israel?"

"Well, it was mostly a glorious childhood—one big close family, with everyone caring for everyone else. But to be honest, some other kibbutz members weren't religious like us. They had come from so many countries, trying to make our God-given land bloom again."

"We are all Jews, of course," Murray said, raising his thick eyebrows.

"Oh, they thought of themselves as Jews, and we were all bound together by our former oppression, no matter what foreign land we came from. Yet, many other families didn't attend synagogue on the Sabbath, much less put tefillin on in the morning. They even ate pork! It seemed ironic that this land, given to the Jews by God, was inhabited by atheist Jews who didn't seem to believe in God."

"That is surprising," Murray agreed.

Rabbi Matt jumped in. "Because of that, Rebecca felt out of place on the kibbutz, and I don't think it was difficult for her to agree to join me in America when the time came. I had grown up in a Jewish community in Northern California but had spent two years after college living in the same kibbutz. That's how we met."

"I don't mean to make it sound unpleasant at all," Rebecca interjected. "I adored the farming life, raising chickens, cattle, dairy cows. Harvesting tomatoes, cucumbers, and lots of avocados."

"The climate of the Golan Hills, where the kibbutz was located, turned out to be perfect for avocados; we exported much of what we grew to places like France, Italy, and even Germany. It was quite an enterprise," Matt said.

"Until we found out about the pesticides," Rebecca said, shaking her head. "What a shame."

"I happily worked long hours and accepted all of the jobs the kibbutz had to offer, except one: supervising the application of pesticides to the fields. I learned the pesticides were harmful, hazardous chemicals, and years before, several kibbutz members had fallen ill after applying them."

Murray nodded, following the conversation intently. "I know about exposure to chemicals," he said. "What happened then? Someone had to work the fields."

Rabbi Matt continued. "I didn't even know Arabs were working on the kibbutz until one night when I received the job of supervising the pesticide application. There wasn't much to it – just watch the Arab workers through the gate, keep an eye on them while they applied the pesticides to the trees and fields, and then make sure they all left when the work was completed. No one wanted a rogue Arab wandering around the kibbutz at night.

"However, several days into my job as a supervisor, I read the warning labels on the pesticide containers and realized that the pesticides should only be applied while wearing protective gear—something the Arab workers were not provided. It didn't feel right. If a member of the kibbutz had been given the pesticide application job, surely, he or she would have been given protective gear to wear."

"I can't imagine you remained quiet," Murray said.

Rabbi Matt smiled. "Ah, you know me so well. I complained to the kibbutz leaders, arguing anyone applying pesticides should wear protective gear. But rather than argue with me, the leaders simply took me off the job. I gladly returned to the physical work of farming and raising animals. But it always bothered me that injustice was happening inside our beloved kibbutz."

"Injustice?!" Rebecca interjected. "We gave them work. The Arabs would kill us Jews if it were the other way around. The kibbutz life was hard, and we were nicer to our Arabs than other Arabs would have been. You can't imagine the stress of living with the fear that the Arabs would gas us or infiltrate our kibbutz and stab us if they had the chance!"

"Did they ever try to attack?" Murray asked, raising his bushy eyebrows. He hadn't realized how dangerous a kibbutz could be.

"Not within the kibbutz, at least while I lived there," Rebecca replied, "but I couldn't live with the fear of an attack anymore. So, when Matt left the kibbutz to return to California for seminary, I gladly followed. We were married before he finished his rabbinical training. Fortunately, he quickly received his appointment as head rabbi at Temple Shalom in Winston-Salem."

"And I'm so blessed," her husband said, looking at Rebecca, Murray, and the children. "In all ways."

"He got right to work," Rebecca said, "leading the temple membership into a more energized and socially committed community culture."

Murray had never seen the rabbi blush. "What a nice story."

"It wasn't just my work that changed things at the temple," Matt said. "Rebecca and I were—and still are—a good team. The community welcomed us and really responded to Rebecca's energy. She has a way of inspiring and motivating people."

"I've noticed," Murray said with a smile.

Rebecca laughed. "We did fall into a rhythm right away, didn't we?"

"She's always behind the scenes," Matt replied. "When I perform a *brit milah*, the circumcision ceremony, or officiate at a funeral, it's Rebecca who makes all the arrangements. She also helps arrange activities for the temple's youth group. I couldn't do it without her."

Rebecca smiled. "I enjoy it all. I enjoy motivating people, and I especially connect with the older people and try to include them. Of course, the young people fill all of us with their exuberance. They're our future, but we must always remember our forebears. We've poured our lives into Temple Shalom and made so many wonderful friends who are like family to us."

Before Murray could respond, a small voice broke through at his side. "Hi, Mr. Schwartzman," Asher said, smiling and looking up from his book.

"Hello, Asher," Murray said, handing him one of the candies from his pocket. "What are you reading?"

"It's a book I found in the school library. It's *The Structure of Scientific Revolutions*. It's a complicated book about science. I thought scientists' findings shaped their beliefs. This book says scientists' beliefs shape the conclusions they draw from their experiments. It says that science doesn't move slowly forward in small steps. Instead, people make sudden leaps in understanding when enough new discoveries force people to see things differently."

"That sounds like a grownup book," Schwartzman said. "Are you old enough to be reading this?" Schwartzman asked in a voice that illustrated his pride in the boy.

"It's kind of like when Einstein came out with his formula E equals mc squared, and people suddenly saw the world differently than they used to. Scientists before him kept trying to force the results of their experiments to fit an old way of how they thought physics worked."

"You can't fit a square peg in a round hole." Murray chuckled.

"Einstein" was a name that would resonate proudly with Schwartzman even though he hadn't studied physics because Einstein was Jewish, but Rabbi Matt interrupted the spontaneous lesson. "Kids, what do you think of going out to dinner with Mr. Schwartzman tonight?"

Rebecca shot him a grateful glance. She had enough to do thinking about preparing the Seder, and school was still going on, no holiday yet.

Miri popped up next to Matt. "That sounds good to me, Dad," she said.

"I'm in," said Asher. "Can we go to Sonny's?"

Their favorite restaurant, Sonny's, specialized in Mediterranean and Lebanese cuisine. Asher and Miri loved Sonny's falafel, pita, and hummus.

"That would be great," Rebecca said. "I've had a busy day. It's not as good as the falafel I grew up with, but it will do."

"You are a fan of the falafel?" Murray asked the rabbi in a jovial tone he rarely used.

The rabbi laughed. "There are some things that bring Jews and non-Jews together. A good falafel is one of them."

5

Outside the Kibbutz

Rebbetzin Rebecca

Rabbi Matt's next day was full. He wrote some notes for his response to Dr. Friedman, but he didn't have time to draft it. His door swung open and closed all day with people coming in with complaints about the letter, asking him what he was going to do about this "racist," the "Jew-hater," this "betrayer to the Jewish faith." They didn't seem to know what to do themselves. The rabbi settled each one down, but each one left his stomach tighter. He had to get that letter done, and soon.

The Seder meal was tomorrow, and there was much to accomplish at the temple, but he wanted to share dinner with Rebecca. She had seemed upset since the letter came out, and that was not a usual response for his calm, orderly wife. When Rabbi Matt got home, the kids were at a friend's house. He was ready to roll up his sleeves and start helping his wife prepare for their family's Passover meal. But when he walked in, the room was dim. The last rays of dusky sun peeked through the curtains, which were already closed to the world. Again, not the norm in his home, always brightly lit and open to the community, welcoming them in.

Rebecca was sitting on the moss-green couch, tears streaming down her face. He'd only seen Rebecca cry twice before, once when they'd lost their first baby and the other when her father was in the hospital.

He rushed over and held her. "What's wrong?" he asked. He could hear the concern in his voice.

When she didn't answer, he became more agitated still.

"Rebecca, is everyone okay?"

She nodded her head and wiped her tears away with a tissue. "I love Israel," she began.

"You know I do, too. Has another bomb exploded?" He moved toward the television to check for himself.

"No. No. Not today, anyway. It's just that all this Dr. Friedman... propaganda... has brought back memories. He's wrong. Dead wrong."

"I know," he patted her on her back and wiped away a stray tear. The tension seeped into his body again, intensifying. Perhaps he should go write the letter right this minute. "I'm doing everything I can to prove that to the paper, and to the community."

Something in her eyes made him think there was more to it than the letter to the editor.

"Are you worried about going to Israel?"

"No, I'm looking forward to it, looking forward to seeing my parents, hoping to catch up with some old friends I haven't seen since I left... it's just that..."

"Tell me," he said. "You can tell me."

The tears began falling again. "When I was young, I decided to sneak out of the kibbutz one night, just at dusk. I wanted to see the sunset outside the gates of the kibbutz, which obscured it as it sank deep into the horizon."

"Well, what's wrong with that?"

"I was just feeling so... so... confined."

"You were a child. That's a normal feeling around that age." He wondered why she was talking about her childhood, though.

"Yes, and a little rebellious. I didn't see what all the hullabaloo about Arabs was. They came and went from our camp every day. They looked completely human to me, like normal people."

She took in a deep breath of air.

"But they weren't. They weren't normal. My plan was to run around the camp's perimeter, get a good jog, and return—and no one would even have time to miss me."

"What happened to you, Rebecca?" His grip on her forearm tightened. He could feel the shock coursing through his body, even though this event happened to his wife long before he knew her. Whatever had happened. "Did someone hurt you?"

"They would have, I believe," she said, her large brown eyes looking up into his, as if searching for strength to finish her story. "Three Palestinians sat by the road, all men. I guess they were waiting for the bus. Or a ride. They began catcalling, first just *Habibi, hey ya Habibi,* but then switching to profane things, just awful things. About Jews. About my body."

"Oh no! Why have you never shared this with me?"

She didn't answer him but continued. "One of them had pulled out a knife, one they used to cut vegetables with. I can still see the blade glinting as the sun set." She paused. "I turned to run. I wasn't even that far out of the gates. And..."

Rebecca took a moment to catch her breath. "How are you even alive to tell me about this, Rebecca?" Matt asked.

"Luckily, my father had seen me leave and followed me. That awful Palestinian man saw him, that... that Palestinian... and he put the knife back in his pocket and looked at the ground. I thought my father might hit him for a moment, but instead, he said, 'How could you? She is only a girl. She is only a child.' And he put his arm around me and led me back to the kibbutz." She dissolved into weeping.

He wiped her tears and resolved he wouldn't let another day pass before he dealt with Friedman. Then they took some deep breaths and began to prepare for Passover here in this beautiful country, where Jews, at least for now, did not have to wall themselves off from others, where Jews, for now, were safe.

6

The Whole Torah

Murray Schwartzman

Murray Schwartzman parked his beige Oldsmobile in the large parking lot behind the synagogue. Two weeks had passed since Passover, and the neighborhood was filled with trees ready to explode with new foliage, and the azaleas were blossoming in a sea of colors. The sun, only just up, cast long morning shadows over the macadam. No time for shadows today. He had a job waiting for him.

Parents mingled beside a large bus in the synagogue parking lot, nervously reviewing their "What To Bring" checklists, preparing to send their soon-to-be Bar and Bat Mitzvah'ed children on their trip to Washington. The children were bleary-eyed and yawning.

"Good morning, Rabbi," Murray said.

"Good morning to you, Mr. Schwartzman. I'm so glad you are coming with us. The children are eager to hear what you have to say."

Murray nodded, not sure what to make of that. He didn't have any grand speeches planned because speaking wasn't something he enjoyed. To make it more difficult, he didn't often speak of his Holocaust experiences, either. He hadn't shared all of it with Miriam and had not shared the story with anyone since she passed. How she would have loved to have accompanied him on this day, would have listened to him, her right ear turned to him so she could hear him better, her big bright smile sending him confidence, confidence that was hard found without her by his side. Thinking of her was painful enough; the idea of speaking of his time in Poland, his agony in the camps, openly, to revisit what it was like out loud, seemed like torture.

"Anything new with Dr. Friedman?" Murray asked, curiosity getting the better of him.

Rabbi Matt sighed and shook his head.

"No, I'm still waiting to hear back from my contacts. I'm hoping to know something by the end of today. Since I haven't heard from Dr. Friedman yet, I'm afraid I'll have to send a response to the newspaper today." He shook his head and glanced over at Rebecca. He wanted to look this guy who had brought his wife to tears in the face. "But I'd rather speak with him first and allow him to retract what he wrote."

Murray wasn't sure about the rabbi's cautious approach. He thought these things needed to be nipped in the bud.

"In the meantime," the rabbi continued, "we seem to have a mob forming, ready to find this Joseph Friedman and take him to task. I've been tempted to join them, but I have held myself back from expressing my wrath at such an act." He motioned toward his wife Rebecca, who was standing with Miri and several of the mothers, reassuring them that the trip would go fine and that the city of Winston-Salem had not suddenly become a hotbed of anti-Semitism. "I am a rabbi. I have to think about my congregation. My actions need to be strategized, my thoughts organized."

"Something has to be done," Murray said, unable to stay silent, then resolving not to speak about it anymore.

Several older students arrived precisely on time. They had been on this trip some four or five years ago and were keen to accompany the younger kids a second time on what they already knew would be a very moving experience. This year, Rabbi Matt had also invited Pastor Gerald Johnston from the Methodist church next to the temple. Pastor Johnston was older than Rabbi Matt, yet the two had grown closer than brothers, sharing a similar temperament and devotion to improving the world. Pastor Johnston began to lead the teens in songs and cheers.

"The pastor seems excited to share this trip experience," Murray noted.

Rabbi Matt smiled. "He asked if he could bring some of the teens from his church, too. I was glad to have them. Many of the teenagers already know one another from school and social justice outings. I've enjoyed working with Gerald, whether it was building a Habitat for Humanity house or cleaning the city dog park."

Matt told Murray how he often aired his frustrations with Gerald about the conservative Christian pastors he had met who weren't supporting the LGBTQ movement and weren't working to remove the town's Confederate statue from the former courthouse square.

"I find myself wondering with amazement how otherwise good, moral people could be so blind to their own prejudices. Gerald always puts me right. He pointed out that he, like the other pastors, had been brought up in an earlier time and had grown up holding the same ideas that the conservative pastors in the town still held."

"But we should be optimistic," Matt added. "Change is slow, but change does happen. The pastor is a great example."

"Gerald," said Rabbi Matt, greeting the pastor affectionately, "You remember my friend, Murray Schwartzman?"

"Oh, yes," Pastor Johnston said. "You've come to some social justice activities we've done together. It's a pleasure—and an honor, really—to see you again."

Rebecca came over and suggested they board the bus and get the trip underway. After the hugs and goodbyes between the young people and their parents, the students clambered onto the bus, leaving their bags in the bus storage bins below. Asher sat with the other younger temple and church teens toward the back of the bus while Rabbi Matt, Pastor Gerald, and Mr. Schwartzman sat up front, along with college students Jeremy and Adina.

Murray normally despised travel, but he enjoyed listening to the chatter in the back, and he liked being around these Jewish children with their energy and innocence. Seeing this next generation take their place in the world warmed his heart. How different this trip was from the one he'd endured when he was only nine years old, packed into a cattle car with other Jews, not knowing where he was going, and unable to watch the countryside go by. Only the light and dark seeping through that tiny iron-barred grate high to the left of the car, sometimes barely visible, other times forming a design reminding him that he, like cattle to the slaughter, was imprisoned. He quickly blinked the memories away.

The students sang and talked and napped. Jeremy and Adina shared their plans for after college, including Jeremy's upcoming Birthright trip to Israel this summer.

Pastor Johnston, who had never been to Israel, expressed his excitement for Jeremy. "That sounds incredible. I hear the experience is amazing–it is a special place indeed. Mr. Schwartzman, have you been to Israel?"

"No," Schwartzman said, "but I would like to go there someday."

Just saying the words made him wish for it even more. To walk the land of his ancestors, to see the land that all Jewish people had dreamed of for centuries, was an experience he desperately hoped would happen before he died.

The bus reached the Washington, DC Beltway and ground to a slow crawl, leaving everyone more than a bit restless, and the excitement heightened when the bus wheezed to a stop in the middle of the city. They toured the Capitol Rotunda and stopped in the Gallery of the House of Representatives chamber. Murray looked around, amazed at the architecture and history.

The chamber was almost empty, except for a few representatives there to make brief speeches that could be seen on C-Span.

Representative Jones also welcomed the group to her D.C. office, and when she saw Murray, her eyes lit up. "Mr. Schwartzman, thank you so much for coming here with these beautiful children. We are honored to have you and all that you represent, here in the capital of the United States."

They shook hands, and Murray found himself speechless. He hadn't been expecting her to remember him, much less with such warmth and kindness.

North Carolina Senator Burt was there, too, and he suggested they take a group picture on the Capitol steps. Murray gazed out over the Mall, the reflecting pool, the towering Washington Monument, a testimony to freedom.

The kids peppered the legislators with questions.

"What is your typical day like?"

"Lots of meetings and reading, for the most part." Senator Burt chuckled. "I live for these days when I can meet my constituents. You're why I'm here."

"Do you have children?"

"Oh yes," both Sen. Burt and Rep. Jones answered together.

"We each have three children," Ms. Jones added. "I have two boys and a girl."

"My kids are all grown," Sen. Burt chimed in.

"Do you have pets?"

"I have a dog, Maggie," Sen Burt said, leading them back inside.

"I'd like to be a senator one day," said a young teen.

"We need young people here like you," Rep. Jones said.

Murray lingered and looked out over the Mall toward the Washington Monument. How tenuous freedom was. How many times had this building, the city, been breached by those who wished to bring the government down? As soon as it was built, and then again, quite recently. He shivered. "Never again," he murmured to himself, looking up to the sky and thanking his forebears in Poland and those here, an ocean away, who crossed that ocean and fought for his release, who made his freedom possible.

As he rejoined the group, now headed toward the White House, one student remarked on how she thought it would be different. "It's not like TV at all," she said.

"Yeah," Alina answered brightly. "They're real people. Like us.

Humans with lives and hobbies and families. And so friendly and committed to American ideals!"

Murray caught up with Rabbi Matt. "I feel like we're accomplishing our goals," the rabbi said. "The children are learning; their perspectives are broadening. But we're also making a good impression on the legislators. They are learning to see Jews and Israel in an even better light. This might even add to Congressional support for new initiatives. Don't you think so, Mr. Schwartzman?" the rabbi asked Murray as they navigated through the maze of streets surrounding the White House.

Murray shrugged, and the rabbi moved past him to speak with the Methodist minister.

Murray wasn't particularly interested in the White House architecture, although the history contained within did catch him off guard. He hadn't expected so many detailed stories steeped in each room. There seemed to be a piece of trivia about nearly every president, but the one that stuck out was about President Obama.

"Only a century and a half ago," the tour guide informed the group, "a Black man would have been considered property. That might seem like eons ago to you kids, but it isn't. Our country was born less than 250 years ago. Now, an African American can serve in the highest office in the country. Because of American voters, like you'll be."

"And what happens in the West Wing?" Rabbi Matt asked once everyone realized they would only be allowed to walk in the East Wing. Murray was curious, too, about what happened on the other side of the wall.

"Yes, are they as friendly as you?" Pastor Gerald asked with a smile.

"No, they're not," the tour guide said with a grin. "They're too busy and focused."

"So you've worked there as well?" Murray asked, assuming that must be true if the tour guide knew what it was like.

"Ha!" the tour guide said, laughing. "No, I haven't met them. But they're not like us. You don't have to meet people to know they are different from you."

Is that true? If we don't meet them, how do we know? Murray thought. A siren screamed past, and his fleeting thought was gone.

After lunch, Murray looked up in sheer wonder at the size of the Lincoln statue at the Memorial dedicated to him. The resolute gaze on the statue's face showed Lincoln knew about freedom and its price. He wondered why he'd never taken a tourist's approach to the city he'd visited a few times before. It was always to meet a business associate, to negotiate a deal, and to get out again, never to wander with total abandon.

"America is a great country," Rabbi Matt explained to the students, "but reaching the heights of its greatness took time. We have a history of freedom, yes, yet our nation was built in part on slavery and the dispossession of native people. We got past that. It took time. President Lincoln, here," Rabbi Matt said, looking up and pointing at Lincoln's statue, "took us forward, but not all the way. Ending the mistreatment of Blacks in America couldn't be done in one day. Or one lifetime. The Reverend Martin Luther King, Jr. led us even further down the path of justice. We Jews were on the front lines with him."

Standing underneath Lincoln's statue, the rabbi directed the group to the National Mall, the grassy area between the Lincoln Memorial and the Capitol building. And then, using his iPad, he showed them a video of Rev. Martin Luther King, Jr., giving his "I Have a Dream" speech to a mall full of people, White and Black, attending the 1963 March on Washington for Jobs and Freedom.

When the video ended, Murray felt chills race down his body as he imagined Martin Luther King, Jr., delivering these words from this very spot, speaking out over an immense crowd of people.

"Do any of you know what is written right in the very middle of the Torah?" Rabbi Matt asked them. No one said anything. "Right in the middle of the Torah, in Leviticus, section 19, passage 18, it says, '*Love thy neighbor as thyself.*' This is the central message of the Torah."

Rabbi Matt went on to tell them the story of Rabbi Hillel, who was asked to explain the whole Torah while standing on one foot. Hillel gladly obliged, saying, "*What is hateful to you, do not do to your neighbor.*

That is the whole Torah. The rest is commentary." Murray remembered that was the same story Friedman, the letter writer, had used so inappropriately as his punchline.

Rabbi Matt explained how these Jewish values were also American values, codified in the American Constitution; he also explained that Rev. King's work was not yet complete. "You will be the ones to spread King's message. You'll be the ones who complete his journey. Rev. King said that the arc of history is long but eventually bends toward justice, and I believe that," Rabbi Matt told the kids. "The world isn't perfect, but it is headed in the right direction, perhaps in fits and starts. It will be better for you and for your children. You can make it that way."

They'd listened to the words of Martin Luther King in complete silence, but now applause and cheers rippled through the group. Murray looked out over the expansive lawn again with a new awe. He didn't want to leave, but it was time to go. And the next stop was special.

The cheers faded as they arrived at the nation's Holocaust Memorial Museum. No one said a word on the way there.

7

Then They Came for Me

Murray Schwartzman

A line of solemn people wound halfway around the Holocaust Memorial Museum, waiting for their turn to enter. Murray wondered if some of the elderly had similar childhoods to him. Could there ever be an accurate reckoning of all the Jewish people endured during the Holocaust? He knew the answer before the question had even formed in his mind. No, never. They could not. But perhaps a place like this could help keep the memories alive. Help people to never forget.

Could a place like this stop something like the Holocaust from ever happening again? He wasn't convinced. It was happening in other places now. War. Genocide. But he hoped this museum and other places like it would keep his people safer in the future.

Rebecca had prearranged tickets for the group, so they entered directly, stopping briefly to read a sign at the entrance, a memorial to Museum Special Police Officer Stephen Tyrone Johns, who was killed by an anti-Semitic white supremacist while protecting people at the museum in 2009. "The memory of Officer Johns' outgoing personality, affection for people, and irrepressible optimism continues to inspire us to counter hate."

They saw the exhibits on the valiant Jewish partisans who fought to protect the Jewish community in Warsaw, Poland, as best they could. In contrast, they learned how other countries sent people trying to escape Europe back to their deaths. They saw the clothes, the shoes, the dignity taken from the Jews before they were gassed. They saw the teeth that were collected. The Holocaust Museum did the impossible, to take a cold statistic— 6,000,000 Jews killed—and create a moving experience that left no visitor untouched.

On the wall above them, there was a poem:
First, they came for the Socialists, and I did not speak out—
Because I was not a Socialist.
Then they came for the Trade Unionists, and I did not speak out—
Because I was not a Trade Unionist.
Then they came for the Jews, and I did not speak out—
Because I was not a Jew.
Then they came for me—
and there was no one left to speak for me.

Rabbi Matt broke the silence. "This is a good time to talk about Birthright. Israel was forged out of the flames of the Holocaust. A Jewish state guarantees that there will be a safe place for Jews in our own homeland. Some of you may make Aliyah someday and settle in Israel. As Jews, you have that right. In the Birthright experience, you can visit Israel for free, learn about the country, and see if it is right for you. If this interests you, have your parents speak to Rebbetzin Rebecca about it."

Rabbi Matt continued, "This poem is by Martin Niemöller, a German pastor who initially supported Hitler in his rise to power. Niemöller came to regret that and eventually spoke out against the Nazi regime. He spoke out against 'Aryan paragraphs,' clauses in legal documents that would reserve organizational memberships and land ownership for Aryans, excluding such rights from Jews. Niemöller was put in a concentration camp. He survived and became a vocal pacifist."

"Just for Jewish people?" a student asked.

"No, for all of us, Max," the rabbi answered. "That's what his poem is all about. For example, Niemöller didn't mention homosexuals in his poem, but you should know the Nazis came for them before they came for us Jews."

Jeremy turned toward Murray and asked respectfully, "Mr. Schwartzman, do you think there will be another Hitler?"

"Do not forget that this happened." Schwartzman could hear his voice shaking, but he forged on. "This could happen to us Jews again. Take the words of Niemöller to heart. Be against all injustice."

Schwartzman swallowed hard.

"Hitler was evil, but he did not kill all the Jews. Not by himself. Hitler did not round up Jewish families from our homes in the villages of Poland. He didn't stuff Jewish families on cattle cars. And he didn't put Jewish families in the ovens of Auschwitz or Treblinka. You saw the exhibits. German people—a host of human beings did this to us. Anti-Semitism and other forms of tribalism still abound. It seems, sadly, to be a part of human nature. We must be vigilant. We have to fight against discrimination all the time."

"Rabbi Jonathan Sacks, a chief rabbi of Britain, described a concept he called 'altruistic evil,' in which otherwise good people commit murder in the name of religion or go to war in the name of God," Rabbi Matt added. "He taught that this is rooted in a human 'us versus them' mentality. Hitler cultivated this tendency, scapegoated the Jews, and told Germans in a very upbeat way that Aryans were a superior race that needed more land to flourish. Hitler convinced Germans—the world's most cultured people: poets, philosophers, composers—that the monstrous things they did were in the name of the good. Rabbi Sacks taught that we must love not just our neighbor, but also the stranger. Whether it is people of another race, religion, or sexual orientation, we should stand with them against oppression."

Schwartzman gave Rabbi Matt a tiny nod of approval. He appreciated the rabbi's tenacity and determination to get him into the community. If he was being honest with himself, he was enjoying the experience.

Rabbi Matt beamed back and said, 'We are the ones who must stand with the oppressed against the oppressor. Always. Never again. Mr. Schwartzman," the rabbi said in a quiet voice. "Would you mind sharing with us just a little bit of what you went through?"

Murray felt something like a stone rise in his throat, making him feel like he might choke. Share his Holocaust experience? He had never done that before, never offering more than sentence fragments here and there, in answer to questions, brief adjectives that could never convey the reality of his experience. He looked at Rabbi Matt, quite prepared to turn him down—not in a mean way, but simply by shaking his head.

Rabbi Matt's expression changed his mind. The rabbi looked at him with such intensity, such earnestness. And, when Murray glanced quickly at the children to see if they had already lost interest at the thought of an old man telling stories, he found something he didn't expect. They were eager, leaning forward. Even those who had been whispering to each other now stared at him without blinking.

He took a deep breath. He nodded at the rabbi, a kind of reverential nod, took a deep breath, and exhaled.

"Very well," he said, trying to think back, trying to figure out where to begin. "I will tell you a little bit of what I have seen." He stared out into the small crowd of children. "I will tell you, but only if you promise you will never let this happen again, to anyone."

A host of solemn faces nodded.

8

The Horror of Which Humans Are Capable

Murray Schwartzman

Murray told the children what it was like to run out of his city as the bombs fell behind him, as buildings collapsed, people screamed, and children cried. The sounds reverberated in his ears and faded into a ringing that would not stop, and in the middle of this near deafness, he could see more clearly: a mother sat in the middle of the street beside her dying child, hands over her ears, screaming; a man wandered along the sidewalk, holding the outside of his arm where a red stain bloomed; human limbs peeked out from piles of rubble, motionless.

Then, Murray stopped talking for a moment. He knew that if the children were to understand what he had gone through, he would have to start at the beginning.

"When I was nine years old, I learned how to make myself invisible," he said. "Not literally invisible, but I had a way of not being seen.

"It was a rather handy talent to have, especially when I played hide-and-seek with my friends in the outskirts of Kutno, out beyond the houses, out where I could hear the river Bzura churning from here to there."

Then the memories took hold, and the words flowed like he was there, standing by that very river.

He slipped down along the banks where the river was narrow, lying in a straight line in the shadow of a summer tree, and he held as still as he could. No matter how many times his friends walked by, no matter how many times they called his name or pleaded with him to come home, he didn't move. He closed his eyes and felt the warm light on his eyelids and smiled because even though he didn't know how he had done it, he knew he was invisible, and this was something to be pleased about.

Being invisible also had other benefits, such as when his father, Ehud Schwartzman, came home in the early morning hours, depressed because his bakery was not doing well or drunk from sharing a bottle with his friend Zelig or, worst of all, depressed and drunk—and looking for someone to spend his anger on. With every call of his name, Murray slipped further, with careful movements, under the basement steps. He blended into the shadow with his eyes closed, and while he did not smile, as he often did when hiding on the riverbank, he was still pleased with his ability to disappear, even as he pretended not to hear the cries of his older brothers or the pleading of his mother. Because when he disappeared, he could also mute the sounds around him—another handy skill.

That morning, he disappeared again. It was September 1939, and he could hear the two-step march of the Germans advancing to his beloved Polish village. At first distant, but as the army drew near, Murray disappeared into the ether. He could come and go at will, almost like he was flipping a switch. No one noticed he was there, not the Germans, not his neighbors. They were busy wringing their hands in dread. He could slip through the town completely unseen, gathering news and perhaps a treat as well.

"The Germans are nearly here," some said, panting in fear.

"Our army is defeating them," other voices proclaimed, never imagining their own army could be defeated.

Everywhere, people talked about how to prepare, to protect their community, their children, and themselves.

And then the bombs began to fall. Like whistling dervishes flying faster than light through the sky, then landing with a huge thud, then splintering in light, sound, debris, and blood. Raining down and destroying them before they had a chance to react. One day, soon after, a German dressed in all white lay in the middle of the street and served as a target for their bombers, so it was said. Some voices whispered, afraid of a race willing to make such sacrifices. If they were willing to give their lives, without any fight at all, everyone in their town was doomed to death as well.

"We are nearly defeated."

And he, during the marches and the boarding of windows and the bombs and the whispers of gossip in the streets—he saw himself as the child he was, running so fast no one could see him, not even his shadow. Yes, he, little Murray Schwartzman, would run as fast as his legs would carry him, all the way to his home outside of town, carrying the news to his older brothers, his mother, and his father. His father now spent most of the day passed out on the stoop, drunk with fear.

One day, the town grew silent, and then, far away, Murray could hear the grueling whine of heavy equipment and the rhythmic cadence of marching soldiers. He ran through the empty streets of the town until he saw the soldiers, and then he ran home again through alleyways and past bombed-out houses and piles of rubble. Arriving home, amazed to see it standing with smoke coming from its chimney, he stood by the fire for a few precious minutes, warming his frozen fingers. He warned his mother and father and brothers about what was coming, even though he could only imagine what would happen next, after the machines arrived, even though he could barely breathe. And his mother did not cry even once but packed as many things as she could, putting the packs on the backs of the boys and telling them to run. He argued, saying she needed him to gather and report news back to them. She should go. She should hide in the woods with the boys, and he would remain. No one could see him anyway.

She tousled his hair and kissed him on the crown of his head, a bemused look in her eyes. "I am proud of you, my son, my little Moses. And I thank you, and I love you. But I will be fine. Don't you worry. You need to take care of your brothers."

And he had answered, "Because they do not have my invisibility!" He'd said it loud and true. And he'd taken their hands and run off with them. Only looking back once at his mother, standing there in her apron and knit cap, leaning against the door jamb, watching them go.

They ran to the river, and they hid along the shallow banks. While they hid there, Murray saw the remains of the Polish army floating past, wagons and crates and eventually even the bodies of soldiers, drifting from here to there, bloody, eyes opened, swollen to bursting, and he tried to close his eyes, but he could not look away. None of the boys said a word.

But he knew he needed to warn his mother.

The next day, he left his brothers, where they slept under a muddy overhang along the bank, and hiked further along the river, wanting to see what remained of the great Polish army in which everyone had placed their hope. Surely, some were left to fight. But he found it all, everything, everyone, there in the river: artillery equipment mired in the mud, the great guns pointing at the sky. Bloated horses lying on the bank, as if they were sleeping. A great tank somehow submerged in the middle of the water, only its turret visible above the gentle current.

The dead horses that looked like they were sleeping reminded him of his brothers, and he ran back to find them. They still slept, unaware of his coming and going.

And then he went to find his mother. He watched her through the window, then crept in to warn her. She sent him back to his brothers. Scolded him for coming. Even though Murray was the youngest, he willingly crept back to their house each night. She knew it and told him never, ever to return. She made him cry.

But he returned anyway. And one night, his parents were gone. They had evaporated into the air. He called to them but received no answer. Perhaps they'd become invisible, too. Still, he returned, hoping they would somehow make it back to him, but no one was there anymore.

On later nights, he crept even closer to the center of town. He took any food he could find—a molded sausage, a dry crust of bread, a cracked jar of pickles—and went back to the river. "The Polish Army is dead," he told his brothers.

They shook their heads in disbelief. So he continued to tell them about all he had seen and heard, there in the darkness where no one could see him, but he could see it all.

"The Germans have taken all the Jews and keep them in a part of town that they have separated from everything else with a wall of menacing barbed wire. The Polish people who are left are afraid to leave their homes. I asked what the Germans were planning next, but no one knew."

He didn't tell his brothers about how he had seen Germans beating Jews in the street or how some Polish people had tried to start a resistance and had been shot—men, women, and children, all standing in a row. When night fell, he made himself invisible again, each night, every night, and searched the edges of the Jewish ghetto, always looking for his mother, never seeing her.

But it turned out a young boy's powers of invisibility would cheat him at the most inopportune of times.

Murray and his brothers were growing hungrier by the day. Months had passed, and the days grew shorter, until night overtook the dark in winter. A new year must be upon them, but the boys had stopped counting days. He didn't know how they had managed to stay alive after so much time. All the flowers and the roots now slept below the ground, what they hadn't already devoured. Food was hard to come by, and they were afraid to drink from the river, though they all grew so desperate that they sneaked sips from the frigid gray water when the others weren't looking. One night, his eldest brother fell ill. Murray promised to return with food, and he walked quietly through the town, so desperate he even knocked hesitantly on strange Polish doors, hoping to beg for a loaf of bread or a cup of water. But no one opened their doors to a strange child. He stopped by the doctor's home and the pharmacist's home, but they were dark. Even candlelight was snuffed upon his knock.

Everyone was too afraid. They had good reason to be. Even a German who helped a Jew would be considered a "traitor to the Aryan people" and could be killed.

Then, Murray heard a sound he hadn't heard since the Germans arrived—the loud, distant churning of the trains, a strange sound after the silence that had ruled the city for so long. He ran through the streets to the massive railroad in the center of town, where the train tracks went out in different directions like the spokes of a great wagon wheel. There, he saw crowds of Jews lined up in the streets, flanked by young German soldiers holding imposing guns. The Jews, Murray's people, his neighbors and friends— and so many he did not know, moved slowly, like leaves drifting from the trees.

"This is when my powers of invisibility failed me," Murray told the children and the other museum visitors, gathering around, listening to his story. "A soldier wandering the back alleys spotted me and shouted, and I ran this way and that, always led by the twists and turns of fate, a little closer to the parade of Jewish people."

Soon, Little Murray had only two choices: stop and let the soldier catch him or vanish again, this time into the slowly moving river of Jewish prisoners being led to the filling train cars. He slipped in between the soldiers and joined his people, his neighbors, and somewhere in the midst of it all, he hoped, his mother and father.

Once in that long, slow-moving crowd of people, Murray couldn't see anything apart from the elbows, backs, and shoulders of those around him. He saw very few children, and those he did see were hidden among the crowd, like children playing hide-and-seek in a forest. Parents kept their children close, as if they were satchels filled with secret caches of gold.

"Are you lost?" a kind voice whispered to Murray, and he turned and looked up into the face of an old Jewish man with graying hair and haunted, deep-set eyes.

"Yes, Uncle," Murray whispered back, unsure why he had called the man *Uncle*, but the man seemed to like the title.

"Ah, yes, Uncle," the old man whispered. "And what is your name?"

"Murray. Murray Schwartzman." The people closest to the pair glared at them, not wanting to receive unwelcome attention from the soldiers lining the streets, the soldiers with hard eyes and their fingers on triggers.

"Well, young Schwartzman," the man whispered. "It would appear that we are about to embark on a luxurious train ride."

Murray smiled. It felt good to smile.

"Yes, Uncle," he whispered. The man was bent but nearly as tall as a fruit tree in Spring. And the man smiled back, his eyes twinkling.

"You stick with me," the old man said, his voice hoarse. "Yes, you stick with me, young Schwartzman." His eyes grew sad, and he placed a gnarled hand on Murray's shoulder. Something about the man's touch drew tears into Murray's eyes from some deep place. Murray suddenly realized how tired he was, how hungry he was. And just in that moment, he gave up; he gave in. He felt his body sag forward, but the man's old, wizened hands caught him, holding him up. Just as he did the rest of their time together.

And the journey had not even begun.

It took hours for them to make their way to where the train cars sat in the railroad yard. The doors to the empty cars yawned before them like great, dark, toothless maws while soldiers stood on each side.

"Up you go," one of the soldiers said to a young woman Murray knew, hoisting her up. She wasn't heavy, mostly just bones with skin. And Murray looked at the man and saw that he was a normal man. Murray was shocked that a normal man—not a monster could wear that uniform—that a normal man and not a machine could usher them into those cars in a normal tone of voice. The old man reached and gently turned Murray's gaze away from the soldier.

"Do not look at them," he whispered. "It is best not to look at them."

"But he's a man just like you, Uncle," Murray whispered, the surprise evident in his voice.

The old man looked at Murray with something like astonishment, and he glanced quickly at the soldier, then quickly away. He did it again—looked quickly at the soldier and quickly away.

"So he is," the old man whispered. "So he is."

For a long time after Murray looked away, he could not push down the surprise at what he had seen in that uniform: a man, a flesh-and-blood human, someone just like him, or his father, or this old man beside him.

The old man needed help getting into the car, and then he turned and helped Murray in. They were pressed together more tightly as people squeezed into the box car. It was a relief, at first, being hidden away like that, away from the watchful gaze of the Nazis. He and Uncle were nearly separated many times, but the old man always pulled Murray close or sometimes squeezed his own body through tiny gaps so that they remained together.

"That's when I realized we were in a cattle car," Murray told the audience, now fully surrounding him. "That we were as good as farm animals to them."

There were narrow slats along the cattle car's top, middle, and bottom, but when the great doors were slammed shut and latched, Murray could barely breathe. He closed his eyes and pretended to disappear, but the old man could still see him.

"Here we go on our great adventure," Uncle said, and Murray could see the smile in the man's voice, even in the dark, even with his eyes closed.

When the great car shifted into motion, everyone leaned closer together one way, then the other. They were packed so tight it was impossible to sit, and it was nearly impossible to turn around. Murray could do it only because he was small. And, amid all those bodies, he could not see another child.

Night came, and Murray slept standing up, held by the man so he would not collapse beneath all those unknowing feet and be trampled.

And then the old man fell asleep, and the night passed in this way, the two of them holding each other up. Every time he woke, it was pitch dark.

The sun rose and set and rose again, and that is when the shadows began playing between the bars high above. Often, he would lose sight of it, but then, there it would come again, reminding him that day did exist outside this dark cavern of a train car full of the stench of sweat and urine and feces, and then soon, a new smell, like rotten meat. Still, Murray did not move from where he stood with the old man. The stink was unbearable, and the heat swelled during the day, but the cars were mostly quiet, except for whispered questions as they slipped in and out among the people.

"Where are we going?"

"How long must it be like this?"

"Is there no water?"

A low moan.

A woman weeping.

Sometime during the second night, a woman's voice cried out, muffled by those packed in around her.

"He's dead! My father, he is dead!"

And her voice broke. Everyone else was far too tired to cry, move, or ask any questions. After that, the night passed in silence.

The next day, the train stopped. It had slowed before but had never come to a complete stop, and hope found its way back in among them. Maybe this was the end of their travel. Maybe now they could have some water, eat some food, find loved ones who had been separated from them. Perhaps he might find his mother in one of the other train cars. He had been building up this possibility in his mind during the entire trip, imagining reuniting with her, the softness of her dress, how wet her cheeks would be with tears of joy after seeing him! How they would embrace and look around and find the rest of their family or slip away and return to Kutno to find his brothers waiting for them along the Bzura. And when they did, all the signs of war would be washed from the water, washed away by the water.

But even though the train stopped, the doors did not open. They stood there, all on the edge of consciousness, surrounded by the dead and dying. For a long time, they remained in that static place; how many hours he did not know because he had lost track of time long before. Had they been in the train—two nights or three? Or four?

"I am so thirsty," he whispered.

"Nearly there," the old man said, and while he tried to feign cheerfulness, Murray could sense the weakness in his spirit. "I hope you have been enjoying our luxurious journey."

"This is not luxurious," Murray said.

"Ah, but you only say that because you cannot see the sun shining on the beach just outside the train. You cannot see the feast set at the table. You cannot see the people waiting for you."

"That's enough talk of a feast," a bitter voice mumbled from the throng.

"Oh, but it's true, Young Murray. Do not give up hope."

Murray would have argued if he'd had the energy, but he didn't.

***

When the train doors did slide open, the light blinded Murray. The old man didn't have to tell him to look away. He shut his eyes tight against the bright sun, fearing it might take away his sight. Those closest to the door tumbled out, falling four or five feet to the ground. This set off a domino-effect of collapsing legs, some of which belonged to those too exhausted to stand without support, some of which belonged to those who were unconscious with hunger and thirst, and some of which belonged to those who had died on the journey.

Those still living in this pile of humanity climbed slowly over each other toward the bright light of the opening. They helped each other to the ground and looked around, afraid that some fresh hell awaited them. Those whose loved ones had died did not know what to do, did not want to leave them, so they sat in the cars for as long as they could, weeping, until the soldiers came and dragged them out.

"I don't see a beach," Murray said to the old man. "And I don't see a feast."

"Ah," the old man said, "but don't you see how they are lining us up? How are they taking us into that building? Surely, that is where the feast is waiting. And you see these tall walls? The beach must be on the other side."

Murray looked around. "Do you see my mother, Uncle? She is beautiful, with black hair and dark eyes."

"I'm afraid I don't know what to look for," the old man said, and the two stood there watching as more cars were unloaded of their human contents. Men and women and a few children crawled from the cars, more than you ever thought could fit inside, and they stumbled in the direction they were led: to a small gate and a space between two buildings, encircled by a fence.

Murray hesitated before saying what he said next, then thought he had to trust someone, and this man was all he had left. "I should warn you, Uncle."

"Yes?"

Murray tried to lick his lips, but all was dry and parched.

"I can make myself disappear." He whispered this, looking around to ensure no one else heard him.

"Well, that is a useful skill," the man said, raising his eyebrows.

"Yes, and I'm going to do it now so these men don't see me. I don't know. You might not even be able to see me, but I will stay close to you."

The old man nodded. "That is fair. Thank you for the warning."

Murray closed his eyes. The old man reached down and held his arm, and the two of them moved forward with the crowd.

A guard approached them.

"Move," he said quietly, pulling on the old man's shoulder. Murray looked up into the soldier's face and saw it there again–this man, like the other guard he had seen, was human. This man was a father, or a husband, or a son, or a friend.

"This man is human, too," he hissed at the older man, but Uncle only covered Murray's mouth and whispered the same reply.

"Do not look at their faces. Look down. Always look down."

"So, my invisibility saved me, not only that day, but the next and the next. It did not save anyone else." Murray looked down into the children's faces, their wide eyes, their furrowed brows. "And that, my friends, is enough for today."

He glanced apologetically at Rabbi Matt and thought, *Why would God have allowed the pure at heart to experience such evil? For what purpose?*

The room erupted into applause, but Murray brushed it away, his hands waving in front of him. He didn't deserve applause. All he had done was live. So many had not been able to disappear when he could. He was lucky, that's all. He gazed at the hard stone floor and tried to ground himself, to keep the tears at bay. No hero would weep, but he was no hero.

9

The Rabbi Is Ready to See You

Dr. Friedman

Dr. Friedman stared out the window, trying to determine the diagnosis of his last patient, one who had presented him with a particularly difficult set of symptoms. His assistant dinged in and connected him with a woman from Temple Shalom.

"I'm Sarah," she introduced herself. "Our rabbi would like to meet with you."

"That would be wonderful!" Dr. Friedman replied. He had heard a lot about Rabbi Matt. "Can we do it today or tomorrow? I would be more than happy to come to his office."

"The rabbi is out of town today, but he returns Thursday. Would Friday morning work for you? Perhaps at 9 or 10 am?"

"Nine a.m. Friday is perfect," Dr. Friedman said.

"Do you need directions?"

"No, no," said Dr. Friedman. "I'm only a few blocks away. I'll see you Friday."

***

A few days later, Dr. Friedman drove to the temple, nearly certain that the rabbi's call for a meeting must be related to Friedman's published letter. *The rabbi probably has been moved by my words*, Friedman thought. Rabbi Matt was all about justice for all people. Maybe he wanted to join Friedman in speaking out in support of Palestinians, too.

The "We Stand with Israel" banner in front of the building dimmed Friedman's hope. He found himself clenching his jaw. He wondered if it were possible that the rabbi could be so supportive of human rights locally but unaware of human rights abuse in Israel.

He approached the secure glass doors and pressed the call button, taking in his reflection. It was a perfect mix of Woody Allen and Doc Brown. He tried to smooth his disheveled gray hair and adjusted his round glasses. There, that was better.

"Dr. Friedman here to see the rabbi."

The door made a loud buzzing sound as it unlocked, and Dr. Friedman made his way inside.

"Please, have a seat in here," the receptionist called to him, motioning toward three chairs sitting side by side in the small foyer once he peeked into her office. "He should be with you in a moment."

He couldn't be sure, but the receptionist's voice seemed rather cold and curt. The building gave him the feel of an old elementary school with faux stone floors and beige polished block walls. He remembered what it was like to be called to the principal's office, which made him smile. The bright student artwork lining the walls made his smile broader. This was a happy, nurturing place.

"The rabbi is ready to see you." The receptionist led him into the adjoining office.

The office was empty.

"The rabbi will be with you momentarily," the receptionist said. "You can have a seat."

Dr. Friedman sat down, taking in the rabbi's office. He looked over his shoulder and couldn't take his eyes off the beautiful calligraphy above the door with words that raised his expectations:

"All human beings are created in God's image.

Tikun Olam – repairing the world – is a hallmark of Judaism, and we strive to bring peace and justice to all people."

When the rabbi entered, Dr. Friedman stood and gave the rabbi a big, enthusiastic smile. "Hi, Rabbi. I'm Joe Friedman. Thanks for taking the time to meet with me."

The rabbi acknowledged Dr. Friedman respectfully, walked past him, and sat in his desk chair.

"Dr. Friedman, you probably know why I asked to see you," Rabbi Matt said flatly.

"Your assistant said you've been traveling?" Dr. Friedman asked.

"Yes, we took a group of our young people to Washington, D.C. We met with some of our representatives in Congress, and we visited the Holocaust Museum." Rabbi Matt's voice emphasized *Holocaust Museum.*

Something was simmering to a slow boil somewhere beneath the surface of the rabbi's words, but Dr. Friedman wasn't sure what.

"We learned how important it is to make a stand against the anti-Semitism that is still so prevalent in the world today," the rabbi continued. "Never again."

"Yes, never again," Dr. Friedman repeated. "Not to anyone. I'm glad you wanted to meet." The doctor glanced around the room, feeling more confused.

The tone didn't match his surroundings. Photos lined the walls and bookshelves: In one picture, Rabbi Abraham Heschel, a prominent rabbi who'd escaped Germany and championed social action, walked hand-in-hand with Martin Luther King, Jr. across the bridge in Selma. By its side, another picture showed Rabbi Matt in an Israeli park surrounded by smiling young children in a playground, with old tanks painted in a rainbow of bright colors in the background.

"Is that photo from your recent trip?" he asked, pointing at the tanks.

"No."

Not waiting for the rabbi, Friedman got straight to the point. "We need to do something to stop Israel's mistreatment of Palestinian families," he said. "Did you know that we continue to expel many peaceful families from their homes? I brought some of the documentation I found. All of these are from Israeli-Jewish sources."

"Joseph," the rabbi said in a suddenly tight and angry voice, "the letter you wrote in the newspaper was unbalanced and harmful."

Friedman was taken aback. He shuffled in his seat, sat up straighter. "Rabbi, we expelled entire villages of peaceful families from their homes. Here, look. Doing that is completely inconsistent with our Jewish values." How could the rabbi be okay with such terrible actions?

"It was a war," the rabbi replied, his voice dripping with rage. "It *is* a war. Jewish people were, and are, under attack. They have every right to defend themselves."

"We have a right to defend ourselves, but Palestinians don't?" Friedman asked, his voice getting louder. "Rabbi, we turned Palestinians into refugees, and now we're slaughtering them." He wasn't doing a good job of keeping his voice light and calm. What kind of rabbi would be okay with slaughtering peaceful individuals? This felt like insanity. Was he in the middle of a bad dream?

"It's much more complicated than that," the rabbi scoffed. "Surely, you can see that Israel must defend itself from terrorists. Israel does everything possible to protect civilians, even Arab ones, while Palestinian terrorists target Jewish children!"

"Actually, it's not that complicated. We made them refugees. We don't have a moral high ground for the killing we commit. It's apartheid. You don't support apartheid, do you?"

"Are you insane, Joseph?" the rabbi replied, his face growing redder and more animated. "Israel made the land bloom! Israel brought life to the desert! We contribute to medical breakthroughs and scientific discoveries. Our hospitals take care of Arabs, just as they do Jews. It's not apartheid at all—Arabs have rights in Israel. They're better off in Israel than in their own countries!"

"Own countries? Rabbi, with all due respect, Israel is all Palestinians know. It is their country, too. It was their forebears' country when Israel was formed. Rabbi, take a look at the sources of these reports I've brought you," Friedman continued. "We expelled entire villages of peaceful Palestinian families. We mined the villages so they couldn't come back. We were taught that we were the good guys, but does it make any sense to try to create a state run by and for a Jewish minority in a land where non-Jewish people used to be the majority?"

"We created a democracy, Joseph, the only one in the region. If Arabs hadn't attacked Jews, we could have lived together peacefully. We begged them to stay, and they left to further the killing of Jews."

"We were taught that, yes, but none of it is true, Rabbi." Friedman thought he'd best leave before he said something he'd regret. "Here, I'll leave you the documents. You'll see. I know in your heart that you cannot support evil. You have a picture of Rabbi Heschel there, marching with Martin Luther King, Jr.! We must stand against discrimination, not just against discrimination aimed at Jews, but against all discrimination. How can you support gay marriage but not other oppressed peoples?"

Joseph was not only sure his reasoning was right; he was certain that Rabbi Matt would eventually see things his way.

"Joseph," Rabbi Matt said in a stern voice. "Don't write any more letters like this. It's not helpful to the Jewish community. Anti-Semitism is growing, and you are feeding it! In Pittsburgh, in the heartland of America, innocent Jews were killed, eleven people at The Tree of Life. For what? For being Jewish. For standing for Jewish values by working to protect innocent immigrants! That's just one recent example of the threat we're all under right now. A Holocaust survivor who attends Temple Shalom was horrified by what you wrote. That, at least, should make you stop and think about the trouble you are causing."

"Rabbi," Dr. Friedman said sincerely, "Let me speak to your congregation. If they hear the evidence, they, including the Holocaust survivor, will come to see that Palestinians need their freedoms returned. Their homes returned."

Adrenaline coursed through Matt's veins. All the more inflamed, he might have slapped Friedman, had the desk not separated them. "Are you insane?!" Matt replied before the words had barely left Friedman's mouth. "I'll not support you to defame Israel! In my synagogue, no less?!" he shouted, motioning for Friedman to leave.

"I can promise you that I won't do anything that isn't rooted in a desire for peace and justice for all people. I'm sure you feel the same," Friedman said as he stood. "Be well," he added as he left the rabbi's office.

The rabbi waved Friedman off without any more words, sat back down, and, seething, brushed the papers Friedman had brought him to the floor. *Speak to my congregation!?* Rabbi Matt thought. *What chutzpah.*

10

The Diagnosis

Dr. Friedman

Friedman returned to work right after his disappointing meeting and, between caring for patients and teaching students, quickly put his frustration with Rabbi Matt behind him. Friedman enjoyed practicing dermatology and took special pleasure in teaching students lessons about being a better physician. This afternoon, he had three medical students working with him, and it was their first day on the dermatology rotation at Methodist Hospital.

Two of them, Tim and Dan, were visiting Methodist from other medical schools, Tim from Chicago and Dan from Texas. They could have been twins, though Dan had a darker complexion.

The third, Katie Summers, was a Methodist Hospital medical student, cheery but introverted, redheaded, who took notes with immaculate handwriting. Sometimes, his rounds seemed like a clown car, with all of them crowded around a patient in one of the modest examination rooms. Most of the other dermatology faculty allowed only one student with them at a time. But, as far as Dr. Friedman was concerned, the bigger the entourage, the better.

He thought patients were getting top-notch care from the care team. He didn't sense his patients' need for privacy. But maybe that was because he was on the autism spectrum.

His first patient was a seven-year-old boy with eczema, referred by his family physician. The disease wasn't getting better with standard treatment.

But Tim and Dan were both a bit perplexed as to what should be done next. The doctor who had cared for these children before seemed to have done everything right.

Friedman nodded thoughtfully after hearing Tim and Dan describe the situation. Then, he turned rather suddenly toward Katie. "What do you think about all of this?" he asked.

Katie looked like she had been caught off guard. "Perhaps the diagnosis was wrong," she said, fidgeting with the cross on her necklace.

Friedman's eyes widened. It was the answer he had been expecting, but he liked to dramatize the dialogue a little—he had been having this conversation with students for years.

"That is a very good thought," he said, furrowing his brow. "You're planning to become a family doctor, isn't that right, Katie? Of the thousands of patients that family doctors have sent here, I've seen so many where they got the diagnosis wrong or prescribed the wrong treatment. Many times, the treatment the family doctor prescribed made things worse! I think I can still count on just one hand the number of patients I've seen for a skin disease that was cured by those jokers in family medicine. Do you know why that is? What do you think, Katie?"

Katie replied timidly, trying to defend her chosen profession. "Well, I've worked with family medicine practitioners, and I know they care. Maybe they aren't well-trained in dermatology."

"Katie, let me explain," Dr. Friedman said with a good-natured smile. Now, it was time to let her in on the secret. "Of course, they care about their patients. I have no doubt they are well-trained physicians. In fact, they may do a better job caring for skin rash patients than I do. Isn't that interesting? They may get it right 90 or 95 percent of the time. But when they *do* get it right, and the patients get well, they don't send me the patient."

Dr. Friedman paused for dramatic effect and looked around the room.

"I only see their failures. You are going into family medicine. You need to know that, based on their experiences, doctors in other specialties will only see your failures and will have a very warped perception of the quality of care you offer. That's why dermatologists, in general, believe that family doctors don't know what the hell they are doing. It's why surgeons think you would be crazy to have a skin cancer removal operation performed by a dermatologist. They only see our failures."

Friedman went on. "This is a general principle that often causes conflicts, not only between doctors, but also between people in different groups worldwide. When you see something coming from another group, you must always ask yourself what you *don't* see. Observations can be very misleading if they aren't representative of what usually happens."

Dr. Friedman paused again. He could see that the students weren't quite getting it.

"Think about what people know about doctors. There are *millions* of visits to doctors every day. And, unless something terrible happens at one of those visits, those visits don't make newspaper headlines."

He paused, thinking up other examples.

"Hey, I'm Jewish. I don't know many Catholic priests personally, but I've read about a few on the newspaper's front page. Do you know why they made front page news?"

Tim said, "Because they're pedophiles."

"Exactly!" Friedman exclaimed. "Now, I know that all Catholic priests aren't child molesters, but you can see how someone who isn't Catholic could get the idea that it's a common occurrence." Friedman was reminded of his visit with Rabbi Matt. "Or consider what people here in Winston-Salem know about Muslims." Friedman turned to Dan, "If you see the word 'Muslim' on the front page of our local paper, what is the next word?"

Dan didn't take long to say, "Terrorist."

"That's right," said Friedman. "There are over a billion Muslims on the planet. They go to the mosque and pray for peace five times a day. Does that make the news?"

The students shook their heads.

"If any one of those billion-odd Muslims on a particular day commits an act of violence against Americans, does that make the news? You bet it does. This form of selection bias is one of three principles about conflict between people in different groups that I want to share with you today.

"But here is an important conclusion: I'm quite sure the doctor didn't miss the diagnosis of eczema, and Tim and Dan wouldn't miss it, either," Friedman added.

"If the diagnosis *is* eczema, why didn't the eczema clear up with the topical cortisone medicine? Even the strong ones didn't work," Tim said.

Friedman smiled. "Because the patient isn't using the medicine," he explained. "The low-strength steroid didn't work because the mom was afraid to use it. Do you think you can get a mom afraid of putting low-strength steroids on her child to apply the medicine if she hears you say, 'We're going to have to switch to a *super-strong steroid* instead'?"

The students were nodding, clearly caught up in the lesson.

"Always remember, don't trust what other people, even experts, tell you. When experts draw their conclusions with distance from the people they are talking about, when they don't have firsthand experience of people in another group, they are often sorely mistaken. Principle number 1: We must make direct observations. And as we saw with dermatologists' experience of family doctors, principle number 2, we must ensure those observations are representative, not just outliers. These principles work across the board—from medicine to parenting to global affairs."

Katie was looking down at her feet. Maybe she was uncomfortable hearing him blame the patient's parents for not getting well.

"Eczema is a terrible condition, right Katie? The children are suffering. The parents, who love their children more than anything, are also suffering. So they'll use the medicine, right?"

Katie nodded.

"No!" exclaimed Friedman, startling her. The other students chuckled. "Parents *do* love their children. That part is true. In the Jewish circles I grew up in, we were told Palestinian mothers don't love their children as much as they hate Jews. That's a ridiculous, racist notion. Mothers everywhere love their children. But that doesn't mean they treat their children's eczema. Getting medicine on a kid isn't easy. Plus, moms may be afraid of putting steroids on their child. They may not trust the doctor's advice. Part of our job is to *make* them use the medication."

Friedman knew this would not sound ethical to Katie, but he wanted to drive home the point. "There's a lovely nugget of wisdom from Thích Nhất Hạnh, a Vietnamese Buddhist. I think it goes something like, 'When you plant lettuce, if it does not grow well, you don't blame the lettuce. You look for reasons it is not doing well.' Katie, I'm not blaming the patient or the family. We doctors have to take responsibility when our patients aren't doing well, even if it's because the medication wasn't used.

"Let's move on and put all this into practice," he said. "We've kept the patients waiting long enough."

Friedman's students followed him to the next exam room, where he stopped to knock on the door and then slowly opened it.

"Hi, I'm Joe Friedman," he said as he entered. The patient, John Dalton, sat on the exam table with his mother, Sally, in a chair beside him. "Tim has told me all about the eczema. Eczema can be so frustrating," Friedman said.

Sally responded that it was.

"We can clear it up quickly," Friedman said. "We'll have you apply some triamcinolone ointment six times a day. No, wait, that's too much. Let's just do it twice a day. I know it won't be easy, but it's just for a few days. The eczema should be gone by this weekend."

"That would be wonderful!" Sally said. "John's been suffering with this for a couple of years now. We've seen several dermatologists, and nothing they've prescribed worked. It's hard to believe anything could work that quickly. This medicine you are prescribing, I think we've tried it before. Is it a steroid? One of the other dermatologists wanted us to use a steroid."

"Great questions!" Friedman said. "Trust me; this medicine will work —and work fast. It's an all-natural, organic, topical anti-inflammatory. I like to use it because it will complement John's natural healing mechanisms, bringing his skin's immune system back into balance. I like to take a holistic approach."

As he spoke, Friedman could see Katie squirm. She was uncomfortable with his wording. He wasn't lying. Steroids *were* all natural. Triamcinolone is a steroid, *and* it was natural.

"That sounds great," Sally said. "Are there any side effects I should look for?"

"No," Dr. Friedman said. "This medication is very safe. It would be best to call me Sunday night to report the progress."

"Sunday night!?" Sally exclaimed. "I don't want to bother you on a Sunday."

"It's no bother," Dr. Friedman said. "I'm so busy during the week. Calling me in the evening or on the weekend is best. The rash may clear up even before the weekend. I love hearing from patients who are doing well."

***

They continued their rounds, treating an array of patients with acne, warts, and skin cancers. The last patient they saw that morning was another child with eczema. At the end of this last visit, Friedman asked the mom if her children would like to see a magic trick. Her eyes brightened, as did those of the children.

Friedman pulled out his "magic tongue depressor," a small, plain, flat, wooden stick. He had the patient put his small hand on the stick; when he pulled the hand away, three happy-face stickers appeared on the end. Friedman made the stickers appear and disappear at will. Then he pulled out another plain wooden stick, and magically, the happy faces jumped from one stick to the other as the children giggled with delight. Eventually, the happy faces appeared on both sides of both sticks.

After the visit, Friedman explained to the students the underlying principle of the trick—that the human mind sees things in context, not in absolute realities. "People see things depending on what they bring to it," he said.

Dan asked, "Yeah, but exactly how does the trick work? You've got me stumped!"

Friedman smiled. "That's principle number three. Sometimes, like with these sticks, people don't see what is right before them. Then again, sometimes when I show this trick to a child who has autistic tendencies, they see right through it."

Dan still wasn't satisfied with the answer.

"I apologize for being pedantic," Friedman said. "The magic tongue depressor is a particularly powerful form of magic that works based on an understanding of neuropsychology, and it's a nice illustration of this third principle I wanted to leave you with," Friedman added. "Our brains perceive things based on the context in which we see them. Take the blue vein on your wrist, for example. Katie, do you know what makes it blue?"

"It's the deoxygenated hemoglobin," Katie said with confidence.

"Yes, and that's exactly what we were taught," Friedman said. "But the weird thing is I give blood at the Red Cross every two months. And every time they stick a needle in my arm, red stuff comes out. I look around the room, and there's red stuff coming out of everyone's arms. Katie, you've taken blood from people's veins. What color was it?"

"You're right," Katie said. "It's always red and never blue."

"Veins are just a bluer shade of pink than the surrounding skin. Our eyes evolved to see a brown lion hiding in the brown grass. Our minds heightened the contrast so that we wouldn't get eaten. Our brain sees that the vein is bluer than the surrounding skin, and consciously, we perceive the vein to be blue. Now you know there's nothing blue there. You know the vein cannot be blue. You understand it to be an optical illusion. Look at your vein, Katie. What color do you see now?"

Katie studied it for a moment. "It still looks blue," she said.

"Exactly," Friedman said, rather pleased with himself. "You cannot control what your mind sees. We prescribe isotretinoin, a drug that can cause birth defects to patients with horrible scarring acne, and we improve their lives. We want this drug on the market. Pediatric birth defect specialists look at the same drug and data, saying the drug should be taken *off* the market. How we and *they* see the drug is completely different, even though we look at the same statistics. If you see a fetus as a baby, you perceive that abortion is murder, and if you see the pre-born baby as a fetus, you probably see abortion as a mother's right to control her own body. Good luck convincing people who see it one way to consider how someone else views it, even for one moment!

"There's a lovely quotation, 'We do not see things as they are, we see them as we are,' that may have its origins in the Jewish Talmud. How our background affects our perceptions and thinking may be the most important thing I teach you. When someone kills an American, we see terrorism. When we Americans kill tens, hundreds, even thousands of people in some other country, we think we're doing it for the cause of peace and justice. But imagine how the families of those we killed view us. They see us as terrorists. All the killing—whether they do it to us or we do it to them—is horrible. But it isn't easy to see that. The vein still looks blue."

11

A Confrontation

Rabbi Matt

Rabbi Matt felt anxious and shaken in the days following his meeting with Dr. Friedman. These were rare emotions for him. While he often lived in the crosshairs of conflict, speaking on behalf of marginalized people, he was usually surrounded by like-minded friends and family who supported him. Whenever he thought of Friedman, he thought of Rebecca, which made his blood boil. He couldn't understand what made Friedman tick, what made him accuse innocent people of his heritage of the things he said.

He was confounded with this Dr. Friedman, but mulling it over didn't result in anything but higher blood pressure. Not only was the man well-educated, but he was also Jewish! And he was liberal—the kind of a person Rabbi Matt normally agreed with. He was so frustrated with the strangeness of the situation—and the vehemence with which Dr. Friedman had defended Palestinians. *The Palestinians? He's Jewish, and he's defending them? He* stomped his foot to release some building anger, then rubbed his toes to soothe them. Anger solved nothing.

Thank God Murray wasn't here for that, he thought, picturing the older man lumbering up from his chair and physically threatening the doctor.

Rabbi Matt took out the current draft letter—the one that pegged Dr. Friedman's comments as fringe, exposing them for the dangerous, anti-Semitic propaganda that they were. He shook his head in disgust and re-read his words one last time:

Hamas has launched 2,000 rockets into Israel, over 10,000 since 2006. They intend to murder, and it does not matter who they kill as long as they kill Israel. Hamas wants to kill Israel. That's its only goal.

Hamas is evil in ways civilized people like us cannot understand. They are terrorists and fascists. They use children to build tunnels of death, caring neither for the Arab children who die in those tunnels nor for the Israeli children those tunnels will be used to kill.

In contrast, Israel does everything it possibly can to avoid civilian casualties, even at the cost of the lives of Israeli soldiers. As Israeli Prime Minister Netanyahu said, "We are using missile defense to protect our civilians, and they're using their civilians to protect their missiles."

Israel peacefully withdrew from Gaza and got only violence in return. The international community tried to help rebuild Gaza, and Hamas used the financial assistance they received to dig tunnels to raid and murder Israelis.

The situation in Gaza should horrify anyone. People there are suffering. It doesn't have to be that way. Gaza could be beautiful, lying on a stretch of Mediterranean coastline with tremendous potential. Like Israel, it could be full of modern cities, farms, and happiness. But rather than building Gaza, Hamas focuses on spreading rage, fear, and destruction. If, as Golda Meir said, Palestinian mothers loved their children more than they hated Jews, there would be peace.

Israel wants peace. Israel has wanted peace for three score years now! Israel is the only democracy in the Middle East, a place where Jews and Arabs are treated equally. Yet, Hamas doesn't want peace. They want to oppress women, to kill gay people, and to teach their children to hate. Israel is not only fighting for survival; Israel is fighting for the democratic values and human rights for which we all stand. Let us pray for peace, but let us not back down from the fight against terror.

In a few days, his editorial appeared prominently on the Sunday editorial page. He was sure Schwartzman saw it there and would be pleased, as would Jon Lerner and Sam Weisblatt. He handed the paper to Rebecca at breakfast.

"That should do it," he said.

Rebecca didn't look so sure. "It's tough to stop a man who hates his own people, who wants to bring down their only safe harbor," she said as she went to get the kids ready for sports practice. Rebecca would come around, though, when she saw this silenced Friedman. Rabbi Matt couldn't help but be pleased with himself. This letter would be seen by almost everyone in the community. They would be reminded that Israel is America's ally, that the Jewish state is a beacon of light to all nations.

Rabbi Matt immediately received calls, texts, and emails thanking him for his unflinching support of the Jewish people and the Israeli state. He wondered if Dr. Friedman had read his article. He wondered if Friedman would respond. He didn't have to wonder for very long.

The next morning, Rabbi Matt received a call from Sam.

"Have you seen the doctor's reply to your article?" he asked the rabbi.

"No, I haven't seen today's paper yet," Rabbi Matt replied, taken aback. "How did he have a rebuttal published so quickly?"

"He added a comment to the online version. You should probably take a look at it. I think a response is necessary."

Rabbi Matt hung up, sighed heavily, and opened the online version of the Winston-Salem paper. The very first comment under his letter was a reply from Dr. Friedman.

You are probably well-meaning but, unfortunately, clueless about Israel and the reality of what is happening in that part of the world. For example, the Hamas Charter specifically calls for Jews, Christians, and Muslims to live in peace together, yet you call for a separate and unequal solution! You also claim that Israel is a democracy where people are treated equally, yet over 50 Israeli laws discriminate against non-Jewish Israelis! There is clearly no basis for your views other than racism against Palestinians and an inability to see the wrongs our own people are committing.

His pulse quickened. Only recently, he had counseled Asher not to engage in Facebook arguments, especially with those who only engaged for the sake of an argument. His exact words were that arguing with such people was "unproductive and a poor use of time." But if he didn't reply, wasn't he admitting to the world that he had no response for Dr. Friedman's accusations? Why should he sit back and let Dr. Friedman call him a racist?

You may think I am clueless, but my life experience says otherwise. I lived in Israel for years and saw firsthand the terrorist acts of the Palestinians. Besides, there is no such thing as a Palestinian—the term is a made-up word meant to give people claim to a land over which they have none. And while you mistakenly refer to me as racist, it is obvious that when you single out and condemn Israel without mentioning the far-worse things done by others against them, you are revealing your own anti-Semitism.

Friedman replied within minutes. *Does this man ever get off his computer?* he wondered.

It's absurd to support Israel by claiming there is no such thing as a Palestinian—no matter what you call the peaceful, non-Jewish families who live in the land called Palestine, it is wrong to colonize them. And you're the one singling out Israel, the only country on the planet whose misdeeds you would defend.

Rabbi Matt was furious now.

Colonize? We didn't colonize them. Israel is the land of the Jewish people. We were there 2,000 years ago, and we Jews are simply returning to our homes and the land that was taken from us.

A few minutes later, photos appeared as a reply to his comment—

pictures of 1930 certificates from the Jewish Colonization Trust and the Palestine Jewish Colonization Association, along with a caption by Dr. Friedman:

The Jews who did the colonizing even called what they were doing "colonizing." How can you say that's not what is happening when the Jews who did the colonizing called it that? It's wrong to expel Palestinian families from their homes, wrong to make them into refugees and give them no tools to shed their displacement and isolation. And it's ridiculous of you to claim that we Jews had a right to go to Israel after 2,000 years while denying Palestinian families the right to return to their homes after just one generation. Your separate standards for Jews and non-Jews are just more evidence of your racist thinking.

And so it continued. Rabbi Matt would have turned off his computer and tried to forget about the whole thing were it not for emails coming from Sam and Jon, further egging him on.

Rebecca came and looked over his shoulder, her grip tensing on the kitchen stool as she did. "That prick!" she yelled. "Screw him. I have to take the kids to practice." She stormed away. As the door closed behind them, he began to worry about her driving. He'd never seen her anger this white-hot.

And his thoughts of Rebecca and what she'd endured spurred him on to another reply.

Israel does not force the Palestinians to remain as refugees—that responsibility falls to other Arab nations. In fact, if Arabs cared as much about human life as Jews do, they would have taken the Palestinians in and given them their own homes. Israel has often tried giving Palestinians more land, withdrawing settlements from Gaza, but what do they get in return? Nothing but more rockets, more bloodshed.

Again, Friedman wasted no time in replying.

Blaming other Arab countries for Palestinians being refugees is like blaming

African countries for not taking South African Blacks in during apartheid.
We Jews expelled these families from their homes and made them refugees. We
made Gaza an open-air prison, and we didn't allow the refugees living there
to return to their homes. We are the only ones keeping them from returning
to their homes; no Arab country is keeping them from returning. You, Rabbi
Rabinowitz, are being ridiculous yet again. It's appalling that a Jewish temple
would have a racist for a rabbi who speaks out for security for Jews, but not
for all people in the Holy Land.

The rabbi was apoplectic.

Oh, that's interesting, calling me a racist when you don't know me at all.

This time, Friedman laid down a challenge that left the rabbi's
heart racing.

Oh, but I do know you. You are just like the worst of the southern white
racist preachers who were here only a generation ago. Just as they were good,
warm, caring Christians in other areas of their lives, they were horrific racists
regarding Blacks, just as you are regarding Palestinians. Big problems in our
world aren't because of bad guys. Problems come because of nice guys like you,
full of righteous indignation and advocating violence toward others in the
name of peace, even when you should know better. Well-meaning people like
you are all too convincing.
If you aren't a racist and genuinely believe in what you are saying, why
don't you join me in an open, public debate where the two of us can present
our views to the public?

The rabbi immediately accepted. He couldn't back down now,
not with the entire community watching. Friedman added another
comment.

While I don't fully expect you to show up—your arguments have no real leg to stand on—I have reserved the new auditorium in the public library in downtown Winston-Salem for our debate. Next week, Wednesday, at 7 p.m.

I look forward to it.

He allowed Dr. Friedman the last word in the comment thread. The event was a good idea. Israel was still at war in Gaza. Rabbi Matt would be well-prepared, and who better than he to debate Friedman? He could snuff out any pro-Palestinian movement in Winston-Salem before it even began.

He closed his computer and went on with his day. But it took a long time for his heartbeat to normalize.

As the days passed, temple members encouraged him, coming up and putting their arms around his shoulders or shaking his hand and wishing him luck. They promised to come out in large numbers and support him. Mr. Schwartzman emphasized the importance of the debate in securing support for Israel in the community. Several of the temple youth had shown him the online exchange, allowing Mr. Schwartzman to borrow their phones and scroll down through the comments. Everyone seemed excited to see Rabbi Matt destroy Dr. Friedman in public. Rebecca was gathering people together to attend live.

But there was one lone voice among the temple members who wasn't so sure.

"You've been very quiet during this meeting," the rabbi said to Jon Lerner one afternoon during the buildup to the debate. They were discussing a few different fundraising options, and Jon had, quite uncharacteristically, withdrawn toward the end of the meeting.

"I'm sure it's nothing," Jon said quietly.

"Go on," the rabbi encouraged him. "What's on your mind?"

Jon waited a moment, but his words rushed out as if he'd decided to say what he had to say. "You should withdraw from this debate, Rabbi," he said.

"What? Everyone is looking forward to it! This is our chance to publicly dispute Friedman's false claims. Other people may be out there thinking the same thing he's thinking. This debate will open everyone's eyes!"

"I know. I know," Jon said, shaking his head. "That's how I felt, too, until I spoke recently with my contacts at the national AIPAC fundraising team. I told them you were taking on an anti-Semite in a debate open to the community, but instead of being excited, they were quite concerned. They've been calling me every day! I even heard from the Israeli embassy in Washington!"

"What are their concerns?" the rabbi asked, caught completely off guard.

"They say it will only give greater exposure to his anti-Semitic rants —that he could never draw a crowd as big as you will draw—and that by standing on the same stage as him, you are indirectly validating his side of the argument."

Rabbi Matt was taken aback. He couldn't have imagined that any Jewish person would think this debate was a bad idea, but Jon's points were valid. He sat in silence for a moment, contemplating his options. Finally, he looked up at Jon. "There's no better disinfectant than oxygen," he said with determination. "These awful beliefs need to be brought out into the open. We must shine a light on the darkness. We need our children to see that we stand firmly with Israel."

"Then teach them that in the temple, and don't engage with this anti-Semite!" Jon said rather loudly.

"Jon, I understand your concerns. I do. But how will it look to the entire community if I back out now? Israel is a beacon of righteousness, and I need to show I stand behind it. What will people say if I don't? They'll assume that I realized my argument wasn't strong or that the doctor's point of view has merit. I can't back out now."

"Very well," Jon said. "I'm only passing on the concerns of the AIPAC leaders. I hope you know you have my full support."

They shook hands. "We will tear his argument to pieces, and it will be the end of anti-Semitism in Winston-Salem," the rabbi said solemnly.

12

The Debate Begins

Katie Summers

Katie took a seat off to the side, where she hoped she wouldn't be noticed. The new auditorium at the library was large and dark, and an excited hum began to build. Everybody in town had heard about the event.

Most of the people wore "We Stand with Israel" pins. Jewish youths took up the seats toward the front of the auditorium. A group of women came in together. Evangelicals, maybe. One wore a "Christians for Trump" button. Katie saw a stern elderly man walk in, and she almost offered to help him since he had a cane. But he rapidly sat down alone in the back corner.

Looking just like his newspaper photo, Rabbi Matt arrived with his wife and children, choosing seats in the front row. He didn't sit down—he warmly greeted practically everyone in the auditorium, appearing to know them all on a personal basis. The rabbi made his way through the crowd, shaking hands with a man only a few rows in front of Katie.

"Thank you for coming," Rabbi Matt said with a kind smile. The man stood, and Katie realized it was Dean Jacobs from the medical school she attended—and where Dr. Friedman worked.

"No, no, thank you," the dean said seriously. "Thank you for your determination, your steadfastness. I am sorry that one of my faculty is putting you in this difficult position."

The rabbi gave the dean a winning smile. "The truth always comes out. Isn't that so?"

The rabbi returned to the front. Katie smiled to herself. A few days ago, Dean Jacobs had called her to his office before her dermatology rotation and asked her to record and report on her impression of Dr. Friedman. She'd said she liked the doctor, had learned from him, but that he did seem a bit avant-garde. She still liked him even though she didn't agree with his arguments.

Dr. Friedman arrived, as disheveled as ever, and also took a seat in the front. She couldn't help but notice how the rabbi was surrounded by friends while Dr. Friedman sat alone; no one approached him to say hello. She wondered if she had more in common with her teacher than she had first believed. She was sitting alone, too. Then she saw someone approach Dr. Friedman—a tall, clean-cut, young man smartly dressed in slacks and a polo shirt. Friedman and the young man exchanged a brief greeting and polite smiles, and the young man took a seat beside the doctor.

Then, an older woman approached the doctor. "Remember what they did to Daniel Pearl!" the woman practically shouted, wagging her finger at Friedman and garnering some looks of curiosity from others in the auditorium. "Don't forget Daniel Pearl!"

Dr. Friedman seemed unfazed. He reached forward and took her hand as if addressing one of his patients. Katie leaned forward, trying to hear his response. "Oh, yes, Daniel Pearl. They killed him in Afghanistan. You are right. We cannot forget that! Never! I'll make sure to bring it up. Thanks so, so much for reminding me."

Seeing how Dr. Friedman's clinical demeanor played out in real life was fascinating. How he used "Yes, and..." to help transition people away from one idea to another.

"This is one of those times when someone is so focused on a single anecdote that they can't see the larger picture," he had said once in rounds. "There's no point in arguing with someone who is focused on a single anecdote. All the data in the world will not change their mind. In these cases, you must agree with the patient and move on. Anecdotes are powerful. One story can change how patients see things more than piles of data would."

The auditorium was almost full. A young man approached and sat down next to her. "Hi," he said in a nervous voice. "My name is Jeremy. Would you like to come and sit with our group?"

"Oh, thank you. That's very kind," Katie said. "But I'd rather sit here. I'm Katie. What group are you with?"

"We're all in the temple youth group, hoping to see our rabbi embarrass the anti-Semite who has been spewing lies in the local paper." Jeremy laughed.

Katie smiled politely. "Are you talking about Dr. Friedman?" she asked. "I've actually been working with him."

Jeremy blushed and crossed his arms. "Are you a medical student? What's Dr. Friedman like?"

"Funny you should ask! I think he likes to teach... even more than he likes caring for patients. And he's a magician. He isn't incredibly personable, but I can tell he cares about his patients. He's taught me so many things," Katie replied. "Some of them seemed crazy at first. That's why I came to hear him tonight. He looks at things a bit differently, and I find it refreshing. I thought it would be good to hear him speak."

"What kinds of things? Is he a racist?" Jeremy asked.

"Oh, no, just the opposite, in my experience," she said. "One time, I told him I was taught not to judge someone unless you walk a mile in their shoes. Then I asked him, 'But aren't there some people who are just plain bad? Take ISIS, for example.'

"He told me that my church values serve me well, and then he said ISIS *is* horrible. He said that what is happening in Syria is devastating. He asked if I had heard about when ISIS captured a Jordanian pilot? Did you hear about it? ISIS put that pilot in a cage, burned him to death, and released a shocking, absolutely shocking, video of it. My God! What could be more uncivilized?"

Katie had Jeremy's full attention.

"Then Dr. Friedman asked me if I knew what ISIS said when people accused them of being uncivilized. He told me they said it was retaliation for the thousands of Muslims we killed, burned alive, and buried under the debris of the bombs we dropped on them. 'Is our burning of so many of their brothers and sisters so much better?' he questioned. Then, he asked me to think of how each one we killed was someone's child, just like that pilot. Then he went on about Al-Qaeda and 9-11, too. Did you know that the sanctions we put on Iraq in the years *before* 9-11 reportedly caused the deaths of half a million Arab children? That's what Friedman told me.

"At first, I didn't think that was possible. Then he showed me a clip from *60 Minutes* where Clinton's Secretary of State Madeleine Albright was asked about it, and she said, 'I think this is a very hard choice, but we think the price is worth it.' Of course, Dr. Friedman didn't know if the sanctions really caused 500,000 deaths. Maybe it was only a tenth of that, he said. But he clearly didn't think terrorists hated us for our freedom. 'We don't have to worry as much about bad people as we do the good people who think that the solution is violence,' he said once with an unusual urgency.

"Dr. Friedman is somewhat unconventional, but much of what he said seems to make sense, and he always has facts to back them up. I came today to hear his take on Israel. I love Israel. Everyone in my church loves Israel."

"So how can you condone what he's saying in the paper then?" Jeremy frowned at her.

"Well, so much of what he told me fit with what Jesus said, 'First take the log out of your own eye, and then you will see clearly to take the speck out of your brother's eye.' When I told him that Jesus said that, he said that he'd never heard it before but thought it was very good wisdom."

Katie could tell she had Jeremy's full attention, but the lights dimmed, and someone rang a bell. The event was starting. Katie smiled at Jeremy, and they both turned their attention to the stage.

A man wearing a navy-blue suit with a red tie stood and walked onto the stage. "Good evening, everyone," he said in a smooth, reassuring baritone. "I'm Pastor Johnston from the Methodist church with the honor of neighboring Rabbi Matt's temple. Welcome to you all, and peace be upon you."

"And with you," a few audience members replied, drawing a good-natured laugh.

"We are here today," the pastor continued, "to hear in a spirit of open discussion two passionate people who will, we hope, enlighten us about an issue that is dear to our hearts. The strife in the Holy Land is distressing to everyone—Christians, Jews, Muslims—everyone. We desperately want to see peace reign, and our speakers, who have divergent views, to say the least, will give us their perspectives. Each will have the opportunity for a brief opening statement, and then they will answer questions. We will begin our program with words from someone I think almost all of you know or recognize, Rabbi Matt Rabinowitz from Temple Shalom."

Katie quickly realized that Rabbi Matt was in his element, comfortable, not at all nervous, and completely used to holding center stage in front of a large crowd. She took in the large number of people who had turned out for the event, and she caught a glance, again, of the older man sitting at the back. He wasn't exactly beaming, but he had an expression of pride and approval for Rabbi Matt.

"Welcome," said Rabbi Matt. "I'm so glad you are all here. Truly, thank you for taking the time to join me. In some ways, I'm sorry we must be here, but on the other hand, I'm awfully glad that we have this opportunity to set the record straight and to share what is really an incredibly special story—the story of the return of the Jewish people to Israel."

A smattering of applause sounded from the area where the Jewish youth were sitting, and Jeremy grinned at Katie.

"We Jews have had a continuous presence in the Holy Land for over 2,000 years," the rabbi continued. "After suffering in the Holocaust," he paused, looking at the back of the room where the old man was sitting and giving him the slightest of nods, "we returned to Israel, seeking only peace, to live alongside non-Jewish inhabitants as equals. Arabs, jealous of us, tried to throw the Jews into the sea, yet with the help of God, we prevailed against all odds and created a Jewish state, a democracy, a place where all people—Jewish and non-Jewish, men and women, people of all races—would be treated equally."

Again, the young people applauded. The rabbi gave them a smile but motioned for them to quiet down.

"In short, a country consistent with our Jewish and our American values. Whenever there is a natural disaster anywhere in the world, Israel volunteers to help. Yet, Israel is surrounded by Arabs bent on Israel's destruction, and we must not yield in our support of Israel."

Rabbi Matt started a video. Katie had seen this kind of travelogue footage: the vivid green landscape of farmland reclaimed from barren desert, pine groves, and rows of orange trees. Wetlands with flocks of large birds of every color. And sunshine. Always sunshine. Time-lapse video of wasteland turning into modern settlements with children playing in the Judean sun. The camera soared above the countryside, then panned along modern highways named for Israeli Prime Ministers Begin and Shamir, the hilltops drenched in the Judean sun.

The film then shifted its focus toward Tel Aviv, where a time-lapse video highlighted the vibrant movement of cars and people through the day, streaks of red and white lights at night. There were clips of bikini-clad Israeli women on the beach, of Israeli hospitals, and high technology centers. Finally, the film showed people in Jerusalem, people of many faiths, celebrating together. Jerusalem looked modern, with its growing suburbs reached by hypermodern rapid transit tram systems. Its bars, pizza parlors, and youthful nightlife paralleled ancient alleyways in which Jewish, Christian, and Muslim merchants sold all manner of Holy Land souvenirs in the market of the Old City. Jerusalem, with the temple's Western Wall, with throngs of people praying in ancient and modern ways, leaving their notes to God in its cracks.

Suddenly, the auditorium reverberated with the sound of an explosion. The audience was visibly startled. Stripped by sudden fear, Katie grabbed Jeremy by the wrist, then blushed and let go. Katie looked at Dr. Friedman, who seemed to shake his head. Sirens blared over the auditorium sound system, and the video shifted to a scene of people running to a shelter. Children wept in their mothers' arms. This was Sderot, the site of a Palestinian rocket attack. Most of the audience likely didn't recognize the location, but they could see the pure horror being inflicted. They could sense the terror those Israeli children felt.

The video ended with pictures of Israeli military forces restoring order and the friendly faces of the young Israeli soldiers, boys and girls in their late teens, carrying rifles and speaking of their commitment to defend their country.

The audience sniffled as the lights came back up. Katie felt strangely moved by the intensity of the last images. How could this kind of brutality happen in such a modern country? She had always pictured Israel as a kind of backward, desert country in the dust of the Middle East.

Rabbi Matt looked around the room, making eye contact with nearly everyone, and concluded emphatically, "This isn't complicated. Israel is a miracle. Israel must defend itself. We proudly support Israel!"

The crowd gave him a standing ovation. Jeremy was on his feet, hooting and hollering. While Katie gave the rabbi a round of applause, she couldn't help but feel that she had been given a surface-level view of something that contained much deeper truths. *First, take the log out of your own eye, and then you will see clearly to take the speck out of your brother's eye.* She wondered what she might be missing. She was anxious to hear what Dr. Friedman would say.

13

Friedman's Response

Katie Summers

Rabbi Matt made his way back to his seat. The applause subsided. Pastor Johnston walked onto the stage and motioned for Dr. Friedman to join him, saying, "Now I present to you, Dr. Joseph Friedman."

Dr. Friedman struggled to start his slide show. People began to fidget, and Katie felt embarrassed for him. Maybe he wasn't ready for this. How could he, someone who was relatively awkward around people anyway, hold his own after the moving presentation the rabbi had just given?

"As the honorable Rabbi Rabinowitz said, we Jews have been living in the Holy Land for over 2,000 years," Friedman began emphatically. "We never left, not completely. It has been in our DNA to return." He paused. "We returned in peace, and we are good people. You know that, right?" he asked, only to be answered with silence.

On the screen behind Friedman was a picture of a man, Northern European in appearance, with short hair combed tightly back, piercing eyes, a narrow nose and chin, and a precise bearing. He had all the hallmarks of a Hitler follower.

Friedman fumbled with his notes. "Does anyone know who this is?"

The crowd remained still, silent. It was as though the audience was waiting to see where Dr. Friedman was going.

Friedman seemed to revel in the moment. All eyes focused on the stage—the anticipation palpable. "This is Count Folke Bernadotte. A Swedish diplomat and nobleman. He saved Jews from the Holocaust. He saved tens of thousands of prisoners from German concentration camps. Have you not heard of him?" Friedman asked and then paused for effect.

"Bernadotte," Dr. Friedman continued, "was the United Nation's mediator, trying to bring peace to Palestine in the late forties. He was assassinated on Friday, September 17, 1948, by the Stern Gang, a Jewish terrorist group led by future Israeli Prime Minister Yitzhak Shamir."

Gasps and murmurs peppered the auditorium. Katie could tell that most people around her were uncomfortable with the term *Jewish terrorist group*.

Dr. Friedman looked directly at the temple youth group. "Did you know there were Jewish terrorist groups?" he asked rhetorically.

Beside Katie, Jeremy leaned forward, his hands balled into fists.

"But those were fringe groups," Dr. Friedman added with a trace of irony so slight it was almost impossible to recognize at first. "We Jews never robbed, looted, or raped when Israel was founded in 1948. Of course not! We were moral!" Friedman exclaimed, pausing, and then he spoke as if he was interrupting himself. "Well, there was one town, Deir Yassin, where our forces committed atrocities, killed civilians... men, women, and children. Have you heard of this place, Deir Yassin?"

Again, he looked around the room, and Katie let her eyes wander the crowd, too. She searched out the older man, now standing at the back of the room and leaning on his cane. His face had gone gaunt and long, and his mouth was slightly open. In amazement or horror, she couldn't tell.

"But this abomination was an aberration. This is not what we are like," Friedman spoke in an authoritative voice, but he paused again before continuing. "Well, there was another town, Safsaf, where the Jewish army massacred about sixty men and raped a few women, at least according to the Jewish Israelis who reported it. We're good people, you know? When we do something wrong, we report it."

Many in the crowd began shifting in their seats.

"But again, this terrible event was not indicative of who we are."

Jeremy muttered something under his breath, then louder. "Don't be so sure what he's saying is the truth." He looked at Katie as if he were going to say something more, but then he turned and looked forward again.

"I am no orator, as Rabbi Rabinowitz is. I have no glitzy, polished video to show you. But Israeli-Jewish historians have studied how, in 1948, a Jewish country was created in a land where most people were not Jewish," Dr. Friedman said.

Suddenly, he was interrupted by a member of the evangelicals. "There were no Palestinians!"

People turned to see who had shouted, and for a moment, the crowd seemed unsure what to do, as if their attention and allegiances were torn. Friedman didn't seem rattled. He seemed prepared for this, as if he had heard it said many times before.

He peered into the dark corners of the auditorium where the voice had come from. "That's right. Thank you for pointing that out. There were people, though, good people. Jewish and non-Jewish families living together peacefully in towns and villages in the land that was then called...." Friedman flashed a picture of an old map of Palestine on the screen as he emphasized the word "Palestine." Large text at the bottom of the map revealed it was made in 1750 and had come from the Library of Congress website.

Friedman continued. "Israeli-Jewish historians have documented—in addition to the rapes and massacres we committed—that the Jewish army expelled the entire population of over *four hundred* towns—the men, the women, and the children," he emphasized.

Behind Friedman, the screen scrolled through a list of those towns. Then, the screen displayed a book whose cover title was in Hebrew. Friedman held up a copy of the book in his hand.

"This," he said, "is the history of the Haganah, the history of the

Jewish army that created the State of Israel, and here is where the book describes the war plans of the Haganah, where it explicitly says to destroy Palestinian villages, burn them, blow them up, and plant mines in the debris."

Dr. Friedman looked at the section where the young people were sitting. "Did the honorable Rabbi Matt ever mention any of this to you? Or did he tell you that we Jews begged Palestinians to stay? Destroying their villages doesn't sound like we wanted them to stay. Planting mines in the debris doesn't sound like we wanted them to return. Oh, and those trees we've been planting in Israel for decades, did the honorable Rabbi Matt tell you that those forests you and I helped plant cover over the remains of the Palestinian villages we destroyed?"

"Lies!" screamed a voice from the back.

"Lies!" echoed several students in the youth group,

"Lies," Jeremy said in a lower yet just as firm tone.

But Dr. Friedman steeled himself and continued. "Here is a report from the Israeli Defense Force on how Palestinian families became refugees. This is not from a Palestinian source. This report is from the Israeli Defense Force, our own Jewish army. We can trust what the IDF says, right?"

Dr. Friedman held up a small pile of papers, and behind him, the text of those pages began to scroll on the screen.

"The IDF made this report in July 1948, when Palestinian families became refugees. The report explains why Palestinian families became refugees in order of importance: One, direct hostile Jewish operations against Arab settlements; Two, the effect of our hostile operations on nearby Arab settlements. Three, operations of Jewish terrorist organizations."

As Friedman read the reasons Palestinians fled, there was grumbling in the audience. Many groups in the room—the churchgoers, the husbands and wives, the teenagers —were all looking at the research material and back at each other.

"Lies!" came the cry again.

"That's not what happened!"

"Palestinians hid in wait for the Jews!"

"They want to throw Jews into the sea. Yesterday! Today! Tomorrow!"

A middle-aged man in front yelled, "You traitor! You defame Israel! You are worse than Hitler!"

Dr. Friedman always presented hard data to back up his points. Katie turned to Jeremy and whispered, "I told you he sees things differently."

She felt a small spark of concern for Dr. Friedman. This audience was disintegrating into chaos. Maybe he shouldn't keep going. Taking questions from the audience was going to be like rebuilding sandcastles against ocean waves.

Pastor Johnston stood up, but the crowd drowned out his voice. Friedman gauged the room; he likely had only a few moments left before all control was gone. He flipped to the next slide. It was hard to make out the text, but the newspaper headline was clear. "Israel Bars Rabin From Reporting 48 Evictions of Arabs."

Friedman locked his gaze on only one set of eyes now: Mr. Schwartzman, who was still standing in the back of the room.

"Israel Prime Minister Rabin wrote in detail about how he and his army expelled 50,000 Palestinian men, women, and *children* from the towns of Lydda and Ramle alone." Still looking at Schwartzman, he pointed at the young man sitting quietly, peacefully, in the front row. "This man's father was one of those refugees. He and his family lived through those expulsions. But the story of these expulsions didn't make it into Rabin's book. The Israelis censored him from publishing it. Did they not want you to know about it?" Friedman asked, his eyes still fixed on Mr. Schwartzman.

Jeremy noticed. "Katie, that's Mr. Schwartzman! He's a Holocaust survivor who goes to our temple."

Schwartzman was staring directly back at Friedman, never blinking, and his eyes were beginning to water.

Behind Friedman, the screen now showed ragged refugees on a dusty road, carrying what possessions they could, followed by pictures of a tent city of refugees. A caption said these were Palestinian families on the road out of Lydda.

"Those who could make it out of the country did," he said. "Fleeing to Jordan, Egypt, and Lebanon. But many fled to other locations, with most Arabs going to places like Gaza and Jaffa. And yes, Bethlehem. There they stayed, with no way to leave."

Finally, Friedman displayed a picture of a building, reduced to rubble, amid a modest Gaza neighborhood. Standing in the middle of the debris, a Palestinian man holding a small lifeless child in his arms, turned toward the blue sky, his face contorted in pain.

The audience's cries of "Lies!" grew stronger, but Dr. Friedman persisted.

"I gave Rabbi Matt a copy of this article and all these other sources. You can ask to see them up close, from him or me. Israel still rains down death and destruction on these same families. All with our support," Friedman concluded, showing a final image that superimposed a picture of the temple's "We Stand with Israel" sign into the corner of the picture of the Palestinian man and his dead child.

Sam Weisblatt stood. "This is ridiculous," he said in a firm voice. None of that ever happened. I don't believe a word of it. This is a bunch of anti-Semitic fabrications. You just want to destroy Israel. This is all just made up by a self-hating Jew!"

The crowd murmured their agreement.

"That's right! It doesn't matter what he stands up there and says. God gave Israel to the Jews! We support Israel!" a person with the evangelical group said.

Jeremy, still sitting with Katie, stood up, too. "Rabbi, tell him that none of this is true."

Rabbi Matt stood up confidently, apparently unmoved by anything Friedman had said. The debate format had clearly been abandoned, but the audience quieted for the rabbi.

Looking to the temple youth, Rabbi Matt began. "Look, it's complicated. It was war. Yes, some bad things were done. But it was war. It happened seventy years ago. The only thing that matters now is working for peace. Peace for everyone, Jews *and* non-Jews. We can't change the past. We have to have peace, we have to have security, and we have to defend Israel from Palestinian terrorists."

Mr. Schwartzman moved toward the stage. No one said a word. Halfway down the aisle, he pointed at the Rabbi. "Rabbi, is this true? Did you know about this terrible violence the doctor has described?"

Katie was surprised that someone as wizened as Mr. Schwartzman wasn't aware of the atrocities highlighted by the doctor. Then again, no one seemed to know about it. Was it true?

"Murray," Rabbi Matt replied, but that was all he said.

Schwartzman turned and walked out through the swinging double doors. Rage and confusion filled the room. Pastor Johnston said a few words in a futile attempt to regain control of the audience. The debate was over.

"That didn't go exactly as you expected, did it?" Katie asked Jeremy as they rose to leave.

"I—I need some time to process all this," Jeremy said. "Would you like to meet to talk about it later this week once I have time to do my own research?" He handed her his phone number.

Katie took his number. She didn't accept or decline the invitation, but she knew she needed someone to discuss it with other than Dr. Friedman.

The next day, there was an article about the event. Only a paragraph long, it was buried on page B6, alongside worship announcements. They used the word "rowdy" to describe the event.

14

The Truth Seeker

Murray Schwartzman

Murray returned home from the debate and sat in his well-worn plaid chair, setting his cane on the adjacent pile of newspaper. What he'd heard didn't make sense. He stood, shuffled over to a bookshelf, and pulled down several books, everything from *The Six Day War* to *A History of the Jews* to *Son of Hamas: A Tale of Terror*. To comfort himself, he decided to peruse them again. The books, including the one about Israel's miraculous re-founding, said nothing about expulsions. None of what that Friedman character said was there.

But he wasn't completely reassured. For the first time, he wondered how so many Palestinians had become refugees. Would the population of entire villages run away to make it easier to kill Jews? Murray had grown up in a small village. It would have been unthinkable for them to have all gotten up and just left. They didn't leave, even in the face of the approaching German army. Oh, how he wished they had. But there had been no place for most of them to go. And so the Germans rounded them up and "processed" them, sent them to the camps. Those who had survived the initial invasion, that is.

The dream returned that night and continued every night that week unabated. It was dusk, with the low clouds that blanketed the Polish sky in winter, hiding something evil above them. Then he heard the drone of a squadron heading his way. Warplanes overhead, hordes of them, in formation. He strained to see the insignia, but the clouds obscured them. The planes would dive below, release their deadly cargo, and soar back up above the dark, grey horizon.

Bombs exploded just in front of him as he raced back into the city to find his family, his mother. "Mama! Papa! Mama!" He shouted and called to them, the tracers lighting up the darkening sky, the sound of low engines whining through the air, the smell of burning flesh wafting toward him as he reached his town. Other screams met his, but he didn't recognize any of them. They were speaking another language entirely, but he knew they were injured. One of many, blood gushing from the back of his head, picked through what was left of his dwelling, searching in vain for his dead.

When he finally reached his home, it was gone. In its place, rubble, the remains of a modest dwelling in the Gaza Strip.

Every morning, he awoke with a start, on the verge of tears, unable to shake the vision. It was the building Dr. Friedman had shown them during the debate.

That Saturday, probably for the first time anyone could remember, Murray did not attend the temple for the morning service. The weeks passed, and Murray couldn't bring himself to return, no matter how often he imagined Rabbi Matt's disappointment, Rebecca's gentle concern, or the questions others might have, especially seeing that his absence began in the wake of the now infamous debate with Dr. Friedman. He awaited a call from the rabbi, but none came. The rabbi had watched Murray walk out of the debate. It was up to him to make the next move.

By the time three weeks had passed, the germ of an idea began swimming around in Murray's mind. At first, it seemed like the pointless ravings of an old man, but when the thought refused to leave him, he began considering it seriously, gnawing on it like a dog with a bone. Finally, he reached for a thin, spiral-bound book with a blue cover, the temple directory that listed members' names and contact information. In it, he found what he was looking for, picked up the phone, and called Jeremy, the young man he knew from the temple's youth program.

"Hello?"

"Jeremy?" Murray asked.

"Yes?"

"This is Murray. Murray Schwartzman."

"Mr. Schwartzman?"

"Yes. Yes, that Mr. Schwartzman. Can you come to my house to help me with something?"

"Of course, Mr. Schwartzman. When?"

"Oh, whenever. When can you come?"

"I could come tomorrow afternoon."

"Good. I'll see you then."

"What do you need help with, Mr. Schwartzman?"

"Just bring your computer," Murray said, hanging up the phone.

The next day, Jeremy pulled his car up in front of Murray's small brick bungalow and parked along the sidewalk. Murray watched him through the window. Jeremy walked through the bright green grass, passed the low, uneven bushes, and approached the front door.

Murray recognized something of himself there on the front stoop. Maybe it was the eagerness in Jeremy's eyes or perhaps the curiosity. It was Murray in his youth, before the bombs, before the train, before the camps. Before he decided to become invisible. He cleared his throat gruffly. "Did you bring your computer?" he asked.

"Yes, sir, right here," Jeremy said, lifting his bag over his shoulder.

"Good, good," grunted Murray, turning sideways, allowing Jeremy to pass by him. "We'll sit in the kitchen."

The two walked over the green shag carpet and into the small kitchen. Murray gathered up the day's newspaper from one of the chairs, folding it and placing it on a small pile of newspapers. "Please. Sit down. The event with the rabbi and the doctor did not go as I had expected," Murray said, rubbing his cheek and staring up at the ceiling.

"I think the doctor was lying," Jeremy said.

"Do you? Yes. Hmm. Well, in any case, they were crazy claims. But he did seem sincere, and he professed to have evidence for them."

Jeremy's forehead furrowed in confusion. "But do you think he was telling the truth? I don't understand. What he said must have been made up, for some reason, but why?"

Murray didn't answer his questions. He wondered how Jeremy would respond to the favor he was about to ask. "I reason I asked you to come... well, I'd like to check up on some of the things the doctor said. Would you be able to help me do the research on the Internet?"

"I don't see why not!" Jeremy responded, now sounding more encouraged. "Let's prove he was lying! Where should we start?"

"I don't know." Murray put his head in his hands. "I don't know. I have trouble remembering specifics. There was something about expulsions from Lydia."

"I thought it sounded more like 'Lida.'"

"Yes, that's probably correct. I think you're right. Can we start there?"

Jeremy opened his laptop computer and began typing. He stopped, read, scrolled down further, and then typed something different in the search bar.

"Here's a Wikipedia article on a place called 'L-y-d-d-a.'"

"Wikipedia?"

"It's an online encyclopedia. Kind of. It's not perfect, and you have to check sources, but it's a good place to start."

"What does it say about Lydda?" Murray asked, moving his chair around to better see the screen.

"Well, it says there were expulsions from the towns of Lydda and Ramle. Between 50,000 and 70,000 people were expelled," Jeremy mumbled as he kept reading. "An expulsion order signed by Yitzhak Rabin was issued to the Israel Defense Force..."

"What does it say there about an Israeli historian?" Schwartzman interrupted.

"Let's see. I'll look at the citations. They're down here. Benny Morris? Well, if we click on that, it will take us to his page. He's an Israeli historian born in 1948."

Jeremy clicked the link, and soon, they were scrolling through more information, much of it confirming what Dr. Friedman had been saying at the debate. Murray felt a pit gathering in his stomach, a kind of dread that much of what they both had condemned as lies was proving to be true.

"Can this information be trusted?" Murray asked Jeremy. "I hear about fake news and false information spread through the Internet. Are you sure this wasn't all written by some Palestinian with a grudge?"

"Yes, the Internet is full of misinformation, but all of this looks legit. They're citing Israeli sources. Actually, they're citing sources from all over the world."

Murray and Jeremy became caught up in their hunt for the truth, thinking back over all the things Dr. Friedman had brought up in the debate. They scrolled down page after page, Murray often pointing to the screen and asking Jeremy what this or that meant. Before Murray knew it, they had spent several hours online.

Everything they found matched up with what Dr. Friedman had said, and more, including the rapes committed at Safsaf.

Murray winced and went to the cupboard. He wanted to find Jeremy a snack, but he also needed a break from all this new information. Savage, all of it. He felt overwhelmed and unsure, even a bit dizzy. Everything he had believed about his people and about Israelis and Palestinians was crumbling in front of him, echoing that apartment building from his dream.

The shadows were returning, taking over. Too many memories, long buried. Too many old wounds he'd worked for decades to suppress. He'd come to America for a happy, productive life dedicated to God. But the past had followed him, been waiting for him, hiding in the dim recesses of his mind.

He handed Jeremy a plate of large dry cookies and a glass of milk. He chugged the water he'd poured himself, trying to settle his stomach.

"Thank you, Mr. Schwartzman," Jeremy said. "By the way, I found the Hamas Charter online. Friedman had mentioned it in one of his on-line posts. It does say, 'Under the shadow of Islam, it is possible for the members of the three religions—Islam, Christianity, and Judaism—to coexist in safety and security.' *Under the shadow.* That sounds ominous."

Murray nodded. Shadows. Always shadows. But these words danced in front of him with a new clarity. In black and white. How could he have been so blind?

"Jeremy, thank you for coming," he said abruptly. Then he realized Jeremy hadn't finished his cookies. Miriam would have chastised him. Such poor manners he had, the manners of a man who'd once had to fight for food. He regrouped and smiled down at this helpful, vibrant young man. "But first, tell me how things are going for you."

"Things are great. I just met a girl, and we're dating."

"Is it Adina?" Schwartzman asked, referring to one of the girls in the Jewish youth group.

"Uh, no," Jeremy said haltingly. "We are very good friends, but I don't think she's interested in boys."

"Oh. Yes. Well," Murray said, clearing his throat. "Is the girl you're dating Jewish?"

"Not exactly," Jeremy said, parceling out his words. "She's... not... Jewish, but she's in medical school, and she's very nice. You would like her."

"Not Jewish?" Murray couldn't help his judgmental tone. He felt personally rejected by this revelation.

This stirred up one of the areas where he disagreed with Rabbi Matt —the rabbi's willingness to perform interfaith marriage ceremonies, weddings where Jewish attendees at the temple married outside of the Jewish faith. Murray worried that intermarriage would bring about the end of the Jewish people. However, Murray also consoled himself— Jeremy would probably tire of this shiksa, come to his senses, and find a nice Jewish girl to marry someday. At least he could hope.

"Jeremy, before you go, could you find Dr. Friedman's contact information for me?"

"Sure," Jeremy said, seeming eager to change the subject. He googled Dr. Friedman, Dermatology, and Methodist Hospital. "Would you like his email address or phone number?"

"Phone number, please," Murray said, pushing a pen and paper toward Jeremy. "Thank you again for coming today. It has been very enlightening."

"My pleasure, sir. I'd love to meet up with you again. This has been very, uh, interesting. Not at all what I expected. I learned a lot today."

Murray didn't get up, leaving Jeremy to let himself out. He was exhausted. All this new information felt heavy, like a weight on his shoulders. Could it all be true?

Before he lost his nerve, he moved over to the phone and called the number Jeremy had written down.

"Could I have a word with Dr. Friedman?"

Murray listened for a moment.

"Yes, yes. My name is Murray Schwartzman. Could I arrange a time to meet with him? No, not for a medical appointment. Tomorrow? Thank you, yes, that works for me. I'll see him then."

15

The Next Journey Begins

Murray Schwartzman

Dr. Friedman's office was a small, windowless room. Two large filing cabinets lined one of the walls, and a low bookcase full of medical books filled the wall across from them. The desk, pushed against the third wall so there wasn't much space behind it, was immaculate. Murray frowned to discover such cleanliness—clearly, the doctor was neither a procrastinator nor disorganized. A large marker board was covered with scientific jargon that Murray did not even try to decipher. A large, framed picture of someone in a lab coat was on the wall behind the doctor's desk.

Oddly, there was also a framed picture of what looked like Dr. Friedman getting a haircut.

"What kind of a narcissist has a picture of himself getting a haircut?" Schwartzman said aloud. Innumerable plaques lined the walls and leaned against books on the shelves, all commendations touting Dr. Friedman's lectures worldwide.

With special thanks to Dr. Joseph Friedman for delivering the keynote address at the University of Riyadh.

This award commemorates the work Dr. Joseph Friedman has accomplished in the work of reconciliation (University of Belfast).

Dr. Friedman came bustling into the office, smiling when he saw Murray standing there.

"Please, please, have a seat," he said, motioning toward a plump armchair that had somehow been shoehorned into a small space between the door and the filing cabinets. "Thank you for attending the debate the other night and visiting with me today."

Murray sat down and began tapping his foot on the floor, then crossed one leg over the other to prevent unconscious fidgeting. He was uncomfortable in the academic world, and all the diplomas and recognitions only made him more so. He cleared his throat as if to speak but couldn't find the words. When he did speak, he could tell he was scowling, both from sheer concentration and his disapproval that this educated man could hold the views he had.

"I don't like you," he said in an even tone. There was no anger in his voice, only his normal grumpiness. "Before yesterday, yes, before yesterday, I hated you... with a passion."

Murray paused and looked at the doctor, but he didn't move to reply, so Murray continued.

"But you told me important things that I did not know. Things I have never heard before. Did you tell Rabbi Rabinowitz about these things before the debate?"

The doctor nodded. "I told Rabbi Rabinowitz all of those things. I even gave him copies of the supporting documents. But the rabbi wasn't prepared to hear them at that time. Simply put, when it comes to Palestinians, Rabbi Rabinowitz is a racist."

"Racist?" Murray erupted, unable to stay calm. "You don't know what you're talking about. Rabbi Rabinowitz is a good man, a great man!"

"You're right, Mr. Schwartzman," Dr. Friedman replied, holding up his hands in surrender. "Of course, you're right. There is much to like about him. The rabbi *is* a great man. A real mensch. Of the highest order. But it's only human to have some blind spots. The rabbi is a great man with a blind spot about this one great thing. So were many

Afrikaners, likewise wonderful people, warm and friendly. Yet, they were racist toward Blacks. Even here in Winston-Salem, not so long ago—as I'm sure you know—there was enforced separation, all of which was supported by Christian pastors."

Murray sank back in his seat. The doctor continued.

"I used to think the Southerners were awful, heinous people. Now, I live here among them and see that they are and have always been good, warm, caring, God-loving people who thought of Blacks like the rabbi now thinks of Palestinians. They believed Blacks were inherently violent and needed to be kept separate. Even the Germans, a country of poets and philosophers..."

"Do not talk to me about the Germans," Murray said, determined to pace his voice, although, in his mind, he could not help but see the eyes of the guards, the men whose gazes he had met, surprised to see that they were humans, just like him. "Do not talk to me about Germans. I know too well what they were like. You've shown me that we have done things to Palestinians. Yes. I see that now. But we were forced to do these things. Muslims hate Jews."

Friedman shrugged. "Given what we Jews have done to Muslims, I don't doubt that some do hate us now. But, if it were true that Muslims always hated Jews and wanted to throw us into the sea, how was it that Palestinian Jews lived peacefully alongside far, far greater numbers of Palestinian Muslims and Palestinian Christians for over a thousand years? Dermatology has allowed me to travel to Egypt, Kuwait, and Saudi Arabia, Mr. Schwartzman. I'm openly Jewish, yet I have had no problems in those places."

Murray's mind swirled with too many competing thoughts. "Hmph," he grunted. So the doctor went on.

"The Saudis named me Editor of the *Saudi Journal of Dermatology*. They don't appear to hate Jews. The dermatologists in Iran had me come speak at their national meeting. After speaking in Tehran, they took us foreign guests—I was the only American and only Jew among them—to Isfahan to see their fabulous sites. After spending the morning visiting mosques and palaces, they gave us time in the afternoon to go shopping in the bazaar. One of the Iranian hosts came up to me, pulled me aside, and whispered, 'Joseph, you are Jewish, right?'"

Murray thought that sounded ominous.

"I was upfront with him," Friedman said, "and I told him, 'Yes, I am Jewish.' Do you know the next thing he said?"

Murray shook his head, enthralled by the story and wondering what might be coming.

"'Joseph, there's a Jewish synagogue down the street. Today is Saturday,' he told me, pointing south. 'I think they are in prayers now. Would you like to go?' I told him, 'Yes, for sure!' and ran down the street, finding the synagogue with its entrance on the corner of an intersection. Do you know how many guards they had there?"

Friedman paused like he had in the debate, probably for dramatic effect or perhaps so Murray would take a guess and be wrong. Murray wasn't going to bite.

"None! If you go to my brother's synagogue in Cleveland, they have locked double glass doors with a security guard to protect people from anti-Semites. But in Iran, a Muslim country that supposedly hates Jews, there was no apparent need for such security."

Murray pictured the locked glass doors of Temple Shalom. "While you were there," he countered.

Friedman continued. "I walked right in and was welcomed. It was an orthodox synagogue like the one where I had my Bar Mitzvah, which my grandfather had helped build. Men on the ground level and women praying separately on the balcony. The prayer book was in Hebrew with the same prayers as in the siddur I used growing up. I felt quite at home. In Iran! I asked the man praying next to me if things were hard for Jews there in Iran. He told me they were. I asked him if it was because of religious persecution, and he looked at me as if I was crazy. 'Religious persecution? Hah! No! Things are hard here because of the American sanctions! Our economy is a mess. The value of our money is collapsing.'"

"Fine," said Murray, "perhaps you met some Jews in Iran who weren't persecuted so much, but Palestinian Arabs are violent. They despise Jews. They do not live in Iran. They live in the West Bank and Gaza."

"Okay," Friedman said. "How many Palestinians do you know, Mr. Schwartzman?"

Murray's gaze moved down to the desk and said, "It's not easy for Israelis like it is for us Americans. They have to be on the defensive morning and night."

"Who tells you this? Rabbi Matt? How many Palestinians does Rabbi Matt know?"

Again, silence was thick in the room. But the doctor didn't wait for Murray to grow too uncomfortable before continuing.

"Yes, I was taught they hate us, too. But then I went to Palestine and met Palestinian people."

"You went to Palestine," Murray mumbled. He couldn't keep the amazement from making its way into his voice.

"Yes," Friedman said. "I went to Palestine. Just this past summer. My heart told me not to go, that they hate Jews, that it would be dangerous for me, and that I would die there, but my brain said not to trust what I had been told. It was quite a surprising experience."

"Surprising?" Murray said. He felt an inexplicable softening in him, accompanied by something else he didn't initially recognize: curiosity.

"Yes, surprising. Even though many of my family in Israel tell me that Palestinians are all terrorists, I told myself to keep an open mind. So I arrived expecting to find that Palestinians would be nice people, just like us. I was wrong. They weren't like us. They were nicer! The nicest people I have met anywhere in any of my travels. It was what you might expect people to be like if they were the people walking the paths Jesus walked. Of course, Palestinians are those people."

Murray grunted. He wasn't convinced. Either Friedman didn't catch the sound, or he chose to ignore it.

"Our group ate meals in the homes of Palestinian families. We visited mosques, PLO headquarters, and refugee camps. We visited Bethlehem and Hebron. I found no one who said they hated Jews. Not one person.

I did, however, hear many people saying they hated what we did to them and what we continue to do to them."

Murray looked up and found himself staring directly into the doctor's eyes. Murray couldn't look away. In the past, he would have let his anger overcome him, giving him the momentum he needed to shout something or even simply get up and leave. But there was something about Dr. Friedman that he found compelling. Almost reassuring.

"The Palestinian people are so gentle," the doctor said, returning Murray's gaze. "It makes my blood boil to think of how Rabbi Rabinowitz defames them."

Those words hung in the air between them for several minutes. Murray had no need to argue, not anymore.

The doctor went on to say, "Well, there was one time, just one time, while I was visiting when a Palestinian held a blade to my neck."

Murray glanced up at Friedman with surprise. "Really?" *Palestinians were violent, after all!* "You see, you can't make them out to be good guys after all."

"Hold on a minute. I haven't told you my story. I thought I should get away from my tour group and, by myself, go out and meet Palestinian people. Real people, you know? But where to do it? I thought, a barbershop! That's a place where real people go to meet and talk. So I went to the barbershop and got a nice haircut and shave. So, the Palestinian barber was old school. He gave me a close shave with a sharp razor blade. There's a picture of it there on the wall. That's about as close as I've ever come to any kind of 'weapon' in Palestine."

Friedman chuckled at his own joke, pointing to the photo of him getting a haircut.

"I'm not here to joke with you," Murray said.

"I apologize," Dr. Friedman said. "I don't mean to make light of a serious situation. There's more."

Murray replied, "I know, but..." He sat motionless in his chair, wanting to stand up and go but feeling overwhelmed by all he had heard. "This is too much already. I need to think more about what you have told me."

Friedman smiled and clapped his hands. "I know the feeling! Listen, there's a group called Jewish Voice for Peace. Their annual national meeting is coming up. They are Jews who walk the talk of our principles. I think you would be pleased to see what's presented there."

Murray let out a small grunt. "Jewish Voice for Peace or JVP for short. I've heard of them. Of course, that sounds very admirable. On the other hand, it sounds like a group of tree-huggers."

Friedman laughed again, this time loud and joyful. "Let me make arrangements for you to attend the meeting."

Murray looked uncertain. "I don't know. Where is it?"

"Baltimore."

"Baltimore?" Murray exclaimed, relieved that it was so far away, which meant he couldn't possibly go. "I can't go to Baltimore."

"It's an easy trip," Dr. Friedman assured him. "I just need some information from you to book the ticket. I'll have drivers pick you up for the flight and at the airport in Baltimore. You won't have to lift a finger."

"I don't know. I'm not much for long trips. I went to Washington, D.C., recently, and it took a lot out of me. I'm not a young man anymore."

"I understand completely. Let me handle everything."

"You would do that for me?" Murray asked. Dr. Friedman had surprised him. He possessed a reassuring nature. The facts behind his beliefs were compelling if they were all true. And now he was paying to send him to Baltimore. What surprised Murray most was that he was considering the offer. He was willing to interrupt his comfortable routine for this man, this stranger, and travel to another city to attend a meeting where he knew no one. It was completely out of character for him. Miriam wouldn't believe he was the same man. He wished she could see him. What was happening?

"I'll make sure you get to the airport," Friedman said, standing up behind his desk. "I'll call you with all the details."

"I still don't like you," Murray mumbled as he got up to leave.

Friedman laughed a friendly laugh. "I'm looking for allies who will join me in pursuit of peace and justice, not for approval. My friends at JVP feel the same way. Just in case you don't like them, either."

Murray took the doctor's extended hand, and despite the hard front he put forth, he couldn't help but feel a kinship with the man.

16

Peculiar Allies

Murray Schwartzman

Murray arrived at Baltimore-Washington International Thurgood Marshall airport feeling exhilarated, not at all tired as he thought he would be. He felt a certain pride in this new sense of adventure. Who was he becoming? Calling up Dr. Friedman and meeting with him to confront his views? Flying alone to Baltimore to meet up with strangers? He felt himself walking taller. Renewed. More like his younger self. No, better than his younger self in ways. Facing things. All this exercise had helped his joints. Relying less on his cane, he felt healthier with each step.

As he came down the escalator to baggage claim, he saw a tall, African-American man in a dark suit and cap holding a sign that read, "Moses Schwartzman."

Schwartzman walked toward him carrying only his cane, and the driver said, "My name is James. Are you Mr. Schwartzman?"

"Yes, but call me Murray," Schwartzman replied. "Everyone does."

"You're traveling light. Did you check luggage?" James asked.

Murray nodded.

"Ever been to Baltimore?" James asked in a loud, friendly voice on the way to his hotel.

"No," Murray said.

"I think you'll like it here," James said without elaboration.

Normally, Murray would be content to let the conversation die at that point, but this new feeling rising in him couldn't be dimmed. "Why do you like it here?" he asked. It was so unlike him to engage strangers in idle conversation, but he found himself enjoying this new-found curiosity.

"Grew up here," James said as if that explained everything. "If you read the newspaper, you know we got problems. Doesn't every place? But it's a good city. It's a good place to live."

James pulled up to the hotel and helped Murray unload his luggage onto a porter's cart. He tipped his hat, smiled at Murray, climbed back into his car, and vanished into the city.

Murray could tell the lobby would be a beautiful place once all the construction was finished, but for now, it felt a little in between, some-what rough around the edges. Kind of like him. Scaffolding lined the main stairway, and the old carpet had been removed, revealing stark cement floors. But the front desk area had been completed, and it felt modern, very sharp.

After checking in, Murray headed toward the gallery, where the meeting was already in session. His courage dimmed as he stood in the long lines to sign in. He certainly stood out.

At the temple, he was one of many older people all dressed pretty much the same with white buttoned dress shirts and dark suits. At home, he was, well, by himself most of the time. A loner. But here, no one else looked or dressed anything like that. First, they were mostly young people, but unlike the kids he traveled with to Washington, these JVP members had long hair or even no hair, or worse, only half a head of hair, much of it dyed purple or green.

What a collection of misfits, he thought. There were people he imme-diately assumed were gay and others whose sexual status was entirely indeterminate. He noticed someone had placed paper signs on the walls beside the bathrooms: "This bathroom is for those who identify as male" and "This bathroom is for those who identify as female." The most conservative-looking people in the group were a few older women, but even they were wearing tie-dyed shirts and rainbow-tallit prayer shawls.

For a moment, a truly short moment, Murray considered turning around and making his way home. What was he doing there? Why had he let Dr. Friedman talk him into coming when he knew so little about this? When he didn't know a single person there? Did the doctor want Murray to be uncomfortable? Was this some cruel trick? But then he checked himself. He had once been an adolescent with no hair to speak of, tattered, ratty clothing, and thin as a skeleton. And the soldiers who rescued him had been kind to him. The displaced persons camp director had nourished him. And the homes he'd been welcomed into on his long journey to becoming a United States citizen knew no equal. Those helpers were all gone now, dead. But he needed to carry out the legacy they'd started, with him. He pivoted, looking around for someone who could direct him... somewhere.

As these memories swirled through Murray's mind, he was greeted by a short, energetic college student with long, thick, curly hair.

"You must be Mr. Schwartzman," she said as if she'd heard his thoughts. "I'm Sara! We're so glad you're able to be here. The Executive Director is excited to meet with you. Do you have time now?"

He smiled back at her. Her enthusiasm was contagious.

Relief flooded over him—meeting with a "grownup" would be reassuring. Plus, it was nice to have someone to talk to. Youthful exuberance was fine, but he had been hoping to find people a bit more, well, experienced. There's something to be said for maturity, a fully ripened mind.

Still bubbling with the energy of a spinning top, Sara led Murray to a small conference room adjacent to the registration area. Several people mingled around the room, apparently none older than 35, and all were casually dressed once again. Most of them were adorned with visible piercings likely meant to elicit reactions of either shock or awe, though these seemed moderate compared to some of the folks milling about in the registration area.

Sara reached back and took Murray's arm. He almost jumped with surprise when he felt her warm touch but quickly relaxed. The small, innocent gesture made him aware that he'd not been touched by another person in quite some time except for handshakes. Touch, even all these years later, startled him.

She led him to another young woman dressed smartly in a dark blouse and matching pants. She had light brown hair down to her shoulders, and while, at first, she seemed to blend in perfectly with the rest of the crowd, as she made eye contact with him, Murray got the feeling that she was a mature soul.

"Mr. Schwartzman," said Sara, "this is Becky, our Executive Director." Becky was probably only in her mid-thirties, but that was "senior" among this crowd.

"I am so glad to meet you, Mr. Schwartzman!" Becky said. She gave Murray a warm handshake and said, "Your friend Dr. Friedman told us you'd be coming. He's one of our more supportive members, not to mention a generous benefactor."

Murray mumbled a barely audible reply. "He's not really my friend. More of an acquaintance."

Becky didn't seem to hear him. "Let me introduce you to the rest of our executive team. This is Rabbi Amy. She leads our student recruitment efforts."

Rabbi Amy was probably in her late twenties. She had short, cropped blond hair with a subtle purple tone, except in the back, where it was much longer. Murray hadn't met a woman rabbi before but managed to hide his surprise. Today was packed with surprises.

"This is Ari," Becky said, pointing to the tall, handsome man with the multi-pierced ear who looked also to be in his late twenties. "Ari oversees our financial development efforts. He's our chief fundraiser."

"It's an honor to meet you, Mr. Schwartzman," Ari said. "I hope your travels here were smooth. Where's your home?"

Murray replied, "North Carolina. Winston-Salem."

"Oh. That's, uh, nice," said Ari as he turned to Becky and gave her a look that left Murray feeling like they were sharing some inside joke. "This is Rabbi Seth. He's from Chicago."

Rabbi Seth looked, well, "normal" to Murray. He wore blue jeans, a dress shirt, and a colorful yarmulke. Piercing-free, he looked like he might have been cut from the same mold as Rabbi Matt, only shorter and with a sharply receding hairline.

"My pleasure," Murray said.

"We were just finishing up our planning process for the year," Becky said. "We have new initiatives for growing our presence at colleges and creating more local chapters all around the country. We also have a few upcoming events where we will be protesting Israeli cultural events."

Murray felt the old insecurities and discomfort rise in his chest. Why would Jewish people protest Israeli events? Did these kids have any idea what their Jewish ancestors had been through? He sighed.

"You might enjoy this Haggadah we prepared last Passover," Becky said. "Putting Jewish holidays in the context of modern conflicts and Jewish values resonates with us, particularly with so many refugees suffering these days."

Murray began to look through the materials.

"Oops!" Becky said. "It's nearly time for the plenary session. Follow me. It should be quite full. Over 2,000 people registered to attend the meeting this year, and we couldn't accommodate everyone who wanted to attend. We're streaming the events online for those who couldn't come."

Despite being overwhelmed, Murray could see why they were doing so well as an organization—and why all these people were eagerly following such a young leader. It wasn't just Becky's charm. She had a way of walking her talk, showing him as a guest that their cause was worth examining twice.

A front-row seat had been reserved for him in the auditorium. Murray looked around in amazement at the crowd. The lights dimmed, and the program started.

Murray listened, intently searching for something that would alert him to any inaccuracies or propaganda the speakers might be promoting. Yet scouring the Internet with Jeremy and then meeting in person with Dr. Friedman had opened his eyes to things he had never known before. As each speaker gave their presentation, he became increasingly receptive to what they had to say and how they viewed the world.

First, he heard a detailed history of what Jewish forces had done to Palestinians, even more detailed than what Dr. Friedman had shared. The next speaker, a union organizer, described the history of the Jewish labor union in pre-Israel Palestine; the union eventually became a foundation of the Israeli government when the state was first formed. The speaker noted, on the one hand, the union's benevolent, socialist, idealistic beginnings and, on the other hand, what the speaker termed a "racist exclusion of Palestinians," even at the union's inception.

Another presenter described how American police forces were being trained in Israel, learning the techniques Israeli forces used to control the Palestinian population. The speaker noted that a JVP chapter in Durham, North Carolina, got their city council to disassociate their police force from the Israeli training program. This elicited enthusiastic applause from the crowd.

Just down the road from Winston-Salem, Murray thought with a smile.

Two speakers gave rather dry talks full of statistics and lists. Murray still found the information useful, but he worried that the young audience would not. An Israeli member of Btselem, an Israeli human rights organization, revealed that Israel had killed a hundred-fold more women and children than the Palestinians had. His mind wandered, listening to statistic after statistic, especially about the number of casualties. Something in that young man's eyes brought him back to his first days of freedom, after they'd liberated the few remaining in the camp. He'd kept hidden for at least two years, but he'd lost count.

In 1945, when an American soldier loaded him on yet another train, in a series of buses and trains, he was older, not so much in years, but in misery. He was short and squat, not having grown a centimeter, and his very bones ached so that he had trouble standing. This time, though, they allowed him to sit. He sat huddled in the corner of the long train seat, his body curled like a baby mouse, arms covering his head. Making himself invisible. Or so he thought.

Somehow, the men in uniforms and a few women beside them offered him food. They warned him not to eat too much, that it would be too much for his body to handle. He took a piece of bread, more than a crust, no mold on it all. Its scent alone made him faint. The smell of newly risen yeast. The texture soft. How he wanted to gobble it down, and there was no Uncle to advise him not to, no Uncle to share this celebration with.

Hunger overtook him, and the piece of bread was gone in a breath. And it stayed down. It hit a hard place in his gullet, and it opened him up, and tears ran down his cheeks for the first time since he became invisible. But then, he covered his head with his arms again, curled up himself up against what might happen next.

A dim light and a tap on the shoulder woke him, and the soldiers herded them all out, the men, women, and a few children who had been able to stand. Up toward the front of the train were the ones they'd had to take out on stretchers.

He looked around. This wasn't Poland. He looked up at the conductor with a big white mustache and an even bigger whistle. He didn't speak. He might be shot on the spot.

But this man did not look Polish or German or American. He said something in words like French. And the boy understood one word. He was in Paris. It was a gray day, but the trees were budding beyond the tracks, and everywhere trains came and went, people coming and going at leisure.

A soldier approached. This one seemed different. Smiling. No one smiled these days. It made Murray think the soldier might be a ghost.

"Come on lad," he said. Maybe he was from England or Ireland. When he touched Murray on the shoulder, guiding him, it was obvious they were both alive. Just very pale. Murray didn't understand his words, but he did understand his kind eyes. So he followed him. "We're going to take you to a resting camp," the man said. Murray understood one word, "Kampf," but he followed the soldier, too tired to protest. Another camp, he thought.

Maybe they will shoot me when I arrive. If not, I shall never be free again.

The soldier stood by him the whole way on a plane over a big body of water, perhaps an ocean, much larger than his hometown river. The soldier took him to many huge houses, not to a camp. He prayed that night in the place they put him, which was warm and well-lit, with crisp white sheets that felt like cardboard, though full of the dying and maimed. He prayed, not to God, because he wasn't sure God would hear him, but to Uncle and to Mother.

"Please help me stay invisible," he pleaded. "Please help me get to safety. And please, let me know what became of you both."

He received no answer. He hadn't expected one.

So many Palestinians had been killed. Why had no one told him that before? How many left alive were without their parents, just like he had been? Murray realized how invested he was in the JVP mission despite his misgivings.

"If Israel was truly trying to avoid killing civilians, they're doing a poor job of it," the speaker concluded grimly.

Why had Murray been told the exact opposite? He'd also been taught Israelis held human life to be so much more precious than Arabs did. But the rationale for that suddenly seemed questionable.

Is Jewish life the only valuable life? he thought. *Is one human worth more than another?*

A representative of Adalah, another Israeli human rights organization, described their work documenting scores of laws that discriminated against Palestinian citizens in Israel. The Jewish National Fund was just one example. It limited where Palestinian families could live. In the past, Murray had taken great pride in making modest donations to the Jewish National Fund to buy land and help Jewish families settle in the Holy Land. But now, he heard, *truly heard*, the opposite side of that coin, that the Jewish National Fund refused to sell or lease its land in Israel to non-Jewish families.

At the Q&A session afterward, he raised his hand. "These 'laws.'

How long have they existed? They remind me of the Aryan paragraphs that excluded Jews from clubs, organizations, and neighborhoods in Germany."

His hands trembled on his cane as all eyes turned on him.

"Land grants began as early as 1901," the speaker said. "They've increased since, as the organization became well-funded."

Was his support for the Jewish National Fund similar to a prominent Winston-Salem family's donation of land in the 1960s for a park reserved exclusively for white residents of the town? "For the good of the white race," according to the donor's last will and testament. It sounded so horrible, so inhumane. Murray had always thought the racists of the South were a little different than the German racists. Now he wondered. They all thought they were doing good for "their people," just as Murray believed he was doing good by giving money to well-established, well-meaning Jewish causes.

Murray found the entire event enlightening yet frightening. The solemn weight of his ingrained thinking bore down on him. He began shuffling through his memory, revealing snippets of the things he had said in his life, the money he had donated, the causes he had supported, so many of which now felt, at best, misguided and, at worst, completely harmful.

Sarah Briggs, a French-Jewish woman who had moved to Israel, brought him back to the room, his face burning bright crimson. She shared stories from her book, *A Revealing Look at a New Israel*.

"I was a single Jewish woman in a small Arab-Israeli town. My Jewish-Israeli friends warned me I'd be raped, kidnapped, or even killed. Instead, I found it was not a problem being a single Jewish woman living among the Arab Muslims. The Arab-Israelis I met were some of the most down-to-earth, caring people I'd ever met. They were as fearful of traveling in Jewish areas as my Jewish friends had been of traveling in Arab areas."

She described how difficult life was for Israel's Arab minority and the many ways Arab families were disadvantaged by the Israeli state.

"For more than a decade, the Israeli government has enforced a travel ban on Palestinians in the occupied Gaza Strip and sharply restricted the entry and exit of goods. These restrictions limited the two million Palestinians living there of their freedom to travel, to access to electricity and water, and devastated their economy. Eight percent of Gaza's residents depend on humanitarian aid. And that's just the Arab residents of Gaza. Israeli authorities demolished 568 Palestinian homes in the West Bank in 2020, displacing 759 people this year alone."

The next speaker, who seemed to be held in high regard by the audience, proclaimed that she was a proud Black lesbian academic and spoke on the forces of power and colonialism and of the parallels between Israel/Palestine and the mistreatment of gays, discrimination against Blacks, the emergence of the #metoo movement, and the treatment of the indigenous population in the United States. From her lecture, Murray learned a new word: heteronormativity. The Black Lives Matter material she covered would have been news to him if Rabbi Matt hadn't been such a big influence in his life.

It wasn't the first time that day that Rabbi Matt came to his mind. He felt an ache that he couldn't describe or explain, but he knew it had to do with wishing the rabbi was here beside him, listening to the same information. It didn't necessarily make him feel "good," all this new knowledge, but it felt *necessary*. It felt right. And he wished so badly that Rabbi Matt could feel the same freedom along with him.

What Murray found most interesting was the talk by a Palestinian from an organization called Badil about the practicalities of returning Palestinian families to their homes, how to address displacement of Jewish-Israeli families, and how to create a "truly democratic state" where all people, regardless of their religion, would be treated as equals.

Is that possible? Murray wondered. *Is that what Palestinians want?*

As the day wound down, Murray felt overwhelmed but energized by these young people and their commitment to Judaism and justice, though he thought creating peace was probably more complicated than the speakers believed. He still found their general left-wing mindset and aversion to what the speaker had called "heteronormativity" foreign, something that his 80-year-old mind had difficulty processing after so many decades of seeing things one way. In fact, Murray could think of only one person he knew who might feel entirely comfortable among this collection of far-left, peculiar young people.

How ironic, thought Murray, smiling to himself as he looked back over the auditorium while the attendees filed out. Here he stood, with nothing in common with any of these people except for their commitment to peace and justice in the Holy Land, while Rabbi Matt, having almost everything in common with these people, held views on Israel— and peace and justice—that were completely antithetical to those at the conference.

Perhaps even completely at odds with my own newly developing views. That thought was both sobering and thrilling.

17

A Serendipitous Adventure

Murray Schwartzman

Murray wasn't sure what to do with all his newfound knowledge and energy. His first thought was to talk to Rabbi Matt about it, but he felt that a meeting with the rabbi would lead to deep division and disappointment, and he wasn't ready for that. Not yet. So, he went to see Dr. Friedman to thank him for his generous gift and to share the enthusiasm and insight he'd absorbed in Baltimore.

Murray spoke without taking a breath. He praised the JVP speakers and leaders. He admitted that he didn't have a plan for what he'd learned but wanted one. When he finally finished, he could feel the peace that filled the room between them.

"Do you still dislike me, Murray?" Dr. Friedman asked.

Murray gave him the usual scowl, but there was the hint of a sparkle in his eye.

They continued their meetings. The get-togethers became more casual, taking place at coffee shops and in parks. Murray found his cynicism melting away, subsiding, his defenses lowered. He was not only entertaining new ideas, but he was also making a new friend. He wanted to believe in this idea that Jews and Arabs could coexist in peace. After what he'd experienced in his life, he knew peace was always the answer, the only answer. He didn't want any children, regardless of race or religion, to experience what he'd been through. He wanted to believe in a harmonious Israel.

Murray thought less frequently of Rabbi Matt and more of his new friend, Dr. Friedman. He'd become consumed with new ideas, a new way of thinking, a renewed hope. The positive energy had awakened his spirit and his lust for life. He truly felt renewed and owed much of that to Joseph Friedman's oddly charismatic nature. Their friendship gave him a purpose he never realized he needed.

"Murray, I have an idea. It's something I've been thinking about, and I want to get your opinion," Dr. Friedman said at their next meetup.

"Well, what is it? Don't keep me in suspense," Murray said as he sipped his coffee.

"I want to arrange another trip for you."

Murray's expression changed. "Hmm, I'm not sure, Doc. Travel is more difficult for me these days. Don't get me wrong, I appreciated the trip to Baltimore, as you know, but I'm pretty much a homebody. Venturing out for coffee with you is my adventure for the week."

Dr. Friedman nodded. "I know, Murray, but this is different. It's a long trip, but it's an important one. In fact, it's the trip of a lifetime. If you will let me, I'd like to arrange for you to accompany Joel and Henrietta Cadbury on their annual journey to Palestine. What do you say?"

"Uh, wait, what?" Murray stuttered. Talking about those faraway places was one thing, but actually visiting? He'd never even considered it a possibility, especially at this stage in his life. "Gee, Doc, I don't know. You mean go to Israel? It would be amazing, possibly life-changing, but that's quite a distance to travel. Not only that, but I also couldn't let you gift me such an extravagance."

"No, no, Murray. Please don't think of it like that. It would be an honor for me to make a trip like that a reality for you. If anyone deserves it, you do."

Murray realized that his protests were futile, and to be honest, it would be an amazing opportunity. Finally, he graciously accepted.

In the weeks leading up to the trip, Murray visited his medical doctor as a precaution. With the medical checkup completed, his anticipation began to build. He couldn't believe how fortunate he was, especially at his age, to travel, and to Israel of all places! It made him feel alive again.

***

The group flew to JFK Airport in New York and then on to Tel Aviv. As the smiling flight attendant placed food on his tray, Murray turned to watch the clouds dance by the oval-shaped window. Not a single bump in the sky. Murray found himself enjoying the experience, finding comfort in the chatter of the others, the hum of the jet engine, the feeling of adventure.

Once they landed, Murray was equal parts thrilled to be in Israel and afraid of what the authorities might say when they found out the group was there to aid Palestinians. But as the leader, Joel was well-practiced in the art of entering Israel, and he explained to the young Israeli border guard that they were on a service trip there to do volunteer work at the Quaker Friends School and Meetinghouse in Ramallah and to tour the Holy Land. The guard let Joel through, then spoke to the other members of the ostensibly Quaker group, all Christian, save Schwartzman. The guard didn't take long with them before motioning them through. Apparently, there didn't seem to be much risk in a group of Quakers.

Then came Schwartzman's turn.

The guard asked Murray what he was doing with this group and whether he knew what he was getting into. "I have a grandfather your age," the guard said suddenly in his Israeli accent. His face crinkled with concern. "It's not a safe place where you are going. Especially for a Jew."

Murray looked into the man's intense eyes, and something about them reminded him of the guard from all those years ago when he had boarded the train to hell.

We are, all of us, human, Murray thought to himself. "Yes, thank you, my son. I know where I am going."

The man stared at Murray for another moment, shrugged, and motioned for him to enter the State of Israel.

Aboard their large, air-conditioned bus driven by a Palestinian driver, he sat by the window, studying the landscape as it raced by. He could feel the heat working its way through the gaps in the window, but it only added to the experience. Everything was just as he'd imagined, yet so much more alluring in person.

He was navigating these various modes of transportation with ease. His new zest for life filled his spirit. Physically, he still had his limitations, but he felt stronger than he had since Miriam's death. He often had to remind himself to retrieve his cane when he stood up.

The group first stopped in the Arab-Israeli town of Ibillin, where Elias Chacour, an Israeli-Palestinian Arab Christian Pastor, had opened the Mar Elias School. Some 1,200 students from around Galilee —60% Muslim, 40% Christian—were enrolled there.

Murray walked the school's halls, one hand in his pocket, jingling keys he'd forgotten to leave at home, the other loosely swinging his cane, paying special attention to the student artwork displayed on the walls. He passed an open door and saw a class of children sitting at their desks, learning, no different than the school he had visited with Rabbi Matt. Murray thought of all the children studying in Winston-Salem, looked around at all the students in this school, and filled with joy. He'd never thought about where Palestinian children learned to read and write. His own studies had been cut short for him. Yet, despite the conflict surrounding them, these young ones could be in school, learning, making friends. At first, it seemed strange to him that he felt this concern toward the Palestinian children who attended the school, but it was there all the same.

He wondered if they often felt like they were in danger. He hoped they could live a peaceful life, but what would that mean for the Israelis? It was a strange place to be, surrounded by the children of parents he had considered his enemies for so many years.

The pictures on the walls also reminded him of the Temple Shalom students and their artwork. When he saw a watercolor of a dove with an olive branch and a tile mosaic of the yin-yang symbol, he felt a pang of homesickness. He hadn't gone back to the temple since the debate. Also, he hadn't yet returned any of the rabbi's calls, not because he was upset, but because he was unsure of how to proceed in that part of his life.

What struck Murray the most about the artwork was that none of it promoted violence. In fact, most of it focused on images of peace. Pictures of families in the marketplace, walking through the streets, eating a meal together. A group of people holding hands in a circle. They looked like they were singing. And the peace symbol, popular when he was a young man in the United States, appeared on many drawings, even if it was in the corner.

He walked around the room, taking it in, twice, then strolled out to see the rest of the school. He was particularly taken by a section of a speech by Father Chacour on display by the administrator's office:

"You who live in the United States, if you are pro-Israel, on behalf of the Palestinian children I call unto you: give further friendship to Israel. They need your friendship. But stop interpreting that friendship as an automatic antipathy against me, the Palestinian who is paying the bill for what others have done against my beloved Jewish brothers and sisters in the Holocaust and Auschwitz and elsewhere.

And if you have been enlightened enough to take the side of the Palestinians -- oh, bless your hearts -- take our sides, because for once you will be on the right side, right? But if taking our side would mean to become one-sided against my Jewish brothers and sisters, back up. We do not need such friendship. We need one more common friend. We do not need one more enemy, for God's sake."

Murray and the rest of Joel's Quaker group ate dinner in the school's modest cafeteria, a delicious meal of chicken, rice, hummus, and what Murray thought was "Israeli salad" prepared by two older Palestinian women who seemed friendly, though they kept mostly to themselves since they spoke little English. The entire time he ate, he found himself in awe that he had finally come to Israel after all these years.

At dinner, the group learned about the success of the school's students and the esteem in which everyone held Father Chacour. They also learned that retaining faculty at the school was getting harder because Israel's government funding of schools for Arab students was considerably lower than for Israel's public or religious schools for Jewish children. The teachers had to find higher-paying jobs to survive.

They all spent the night in the Mar Elias School dormitory. Before retiring for the evening, Murray climbed the stairs to the building's roof and looked out over the Israeli skyline. He could barely make out Tel Aviv and the Mediterranean Sea beyond the hills. The air was dry and pleasantly cool. All was quiet and still. The sky was peppered with brilliant stars. A nearly full moon and a large neon cross on one of the adjacent school buildings provided enough light that Murray could see his way back down to his room. It felt peaceful here in the Holy Land. It felt like home.

The next day, they traveled to the Sea of Galilee, touring a convent on the Mount of the Beatitudes, where Jesus gave the Sermon on the Mount. At first, Schwartzman took in this part of the trip without great enthusiasm, but he understood it meant a lot to the Christians in their group.

However, he soon found himself reveling in the location. It was steeped in history, having been a commemorated site for more than 1,600 years. It also fascinated him that the peak was more than a hundred feet below sea level. Walking along the Mount's paths, he stopped to read small signs, each with a line from Jesus' sermon. While the sermon was unfamiliar to him, the words touched him. "Blessed are those who mourn, for they will be comforted." "Blessed are the peacemakers, for they will be called children of God."

Next was a visit to a kibbutz, spending time with a man named Noam and learning his perspective on Palestinians. Noam greeted the group in the kibbutz playground and motioned everyone to sit on the well-manicured grass in the shade. It was a warm, sunny, exceptionally pleasant day and setting.

"We don't hate them," Noam said, referring to Palestinian Arabs. "We just don't want to live with them. They want to live with other Palestinians, and we want to live with other Jews."

In Noam, Murray saw a man much like himself. While a bit younger, Noam had a similar build, short and stocky, with light brown hair and strands of gray that caught the sun. He was tanned and somewhat wrinkled, probably from years of working in the unforgiving sun.

At first, Noam's opinions sounded reasonable, but then he heard Friedman's voice in his head saying that those arguments were a lot like the justification southern whites had probably used for not wanting to be neighbors with Blacks. That brought Murray's thoughts to Rabbi Matt's perspective. He wondered if this was anything like the kibbutz the rabbi had grown up on with its bountiful crops, groups of giggling children, and free-range fowl darting at the ground.

Over lunch in the kibbutz cafeteria, the group met with Jackie Sosnowick. After growing up in what she described as a Zionist home in a suburban New York Jewish community, Jackie had made Aliyah and joined the kibbutz thirteen years ago. She was forty-one years old and wore a scarf over her hair in typical Orthodox Jewish tradition. She had three children, two of whom were currently in the Israeli Defense Force. In her thick New York accent, she described how wonderful it was to be in a land where everything was Jewish. She loved that having Jewish holidays off from work here was normal.

One of the Quakers asked about the recent violence the IDF had inflicted on Palestinians. She hesitated, then answered. "Look, I feel bad about what is happening to Palestinians. But the IDF did what it had to do. We made some mistakes. We did our best. The IDF is keeping us safe. If Palestinians were the majority here, they would treat us much worse. They would throw all us Jews out."

Another Quaker asked Jackie what it meant to be Zionist. "Did it mean something about a Jewish homeland, or was it about expelling non-Jews from the land?"

"What a question!" Jackie exclaimed. "Of course, it is only about returning to our homeland. We don't want to expel anyone from their homes. Look, I wish all kids were taught not to hate. I heard my own kids say some racist things when they were young, but we don't teach our children hate the way Palestinians do. Palestinians learn hate in school."

Murray grimaced. That's not what he saw going on, but perhaps they had staged the place for his visit, like the Nazis had for Red Cross delegate visits in the German camps.

When asked if she knew any Palestinians personally, she replied, "Yes, well, at one time, I knew a friend's gardener. He was a Palestinian." Jackie seemed like a bright, warm, caring person, but Schwartzman wondered if, with such little contact with Palestinians, Jackie understood anything about what Palestinians wanted or what they taught their children in school. He had seen only love, not hate, being taught at the Palestinian school they'd visited.

After visiting the kibbutz, the group boarded the bus to their next destination, Jericho, crossing the border into the West Bank. They traveled past working farms along the Jordan River, fertile green oases in the desert with bountiful pineapples, other fruits, and vegetables. Murray couldn't take his eyes off the lush landscape rolling by. Joel explained that even though this was the West Bank, ostensibly Palestinian territory, these were Israeli settlement farms.

"Cultivating water-intensive crops like these types of fruit is possible on the farms because the Jewish settlers have access to plenty of water. In fact," Joel went on, "the West Bank water table has dropped considerably due to the removal of so much water by Israeli settlers."

The settlers had installed deep wells providing continued access to water, while the Palestinians weren't allowed to have deep wells and suffered from water shortages at home and drought in their fields.

"You can always tell a Palestinian home from an Israeli one because the Palestinian homes have a water tank on the roof," Joel explained, gesturing out the bus windows. "They don't have access to piped water and rely on intermittent water delivery services."

Murray stared through the window, searching for such a water tank, found one, and thought about his kitchen faucets at home, where he had access to water whenever he wanted. After the way he'd grown up and the harsh conditions he'd experienced, he had learned not to take such conveniences for granted.

Murray surprised himself by donning a bathing suit at an Israeli beach resort on the Dead Sea and joining the others to float there. His more adventurous companions also covered themselves in the sea's healing mud. Then, after getting cleaned up and changed, they went on to Ramallah. Dropping their bags at the Friends school, they walked through town toward the Friends' Meetinghouse, where they would do their service work.

A man came running up to the group and grabbed Joel from behind. It gave Murray a start, and he felt nervous for the first time on the trip. Why was this dark-haired, dark-skinned man grabbing their guide?

"Joel, habibi, welcome back to Ramallah! It's so nice to see you again! Can you and your group come to my house for dinner tonight? I will call my wife and tell them you are coming!"

Joel replied, "That is so nice of you, Amir. Thank you. We can't tonight. We've already made arrangements to have dinner at the home of the parents of one of the students at the Friends school."

Amir persisted for several minutes before Joel could pull the group away and continue to the Friends' Meetinghouse. But Murray looked back over his shoulder as he walked away, struck by Amir's welcoming and insistent hospitality.

They walked down a crowded commercial street. It could easily have been any major city's downtown, save for the signs, most of which were in Arabic. On many buildings, posters showed pictures of young men and boys along with Arabic writing that Murray couldn't understand. Joel explained that the young men pictured in these posters were *shuhada*, martyrs, people who had either been killed by Israeli forces or who were currently held in Israeli prisons. A sense of shame sat in Murray's stomach. Even though part of him wanted to know what wrongs these boys had committed to get themselves killed, he also realized that his people had done it. His people had killed them, and some of the boys were hardly more than children.

Still on their way to the Friends' Meetinghouse, the group was swarmed again, this time by three energetic children, perhaps ten years old. They were smartly dressed in dark pants and light-colored, buttoned dress shirts. They appeared to be helping a parent sell wares from one of the tables that lined the street. The children were full of questions.

"Where are you from?" they asked in English.

Joel replied, "From the United States."

"Oh, from the United States! We love the United States!" they cried. They approached Murray. "Welcome to Ramallah, Uncle! We are glad you are here."

Murray was taken aback. His eyes filled up, and his breath caught in his throat. *Uncle. They'd called him Uncle.*

He reached into his pocket, pulled out some hard candies, and shared them with each child. They gazed up into his eyes and thanked him with smiles. "Thank you, Uncle!" The eldest grabbed a gorgeous small trinket box and handed it to Murray. Murray assumed the child wanted him to buy it, so he reached into his other pocket, the one full of change and keys. But the child waved his money away. "No, it is a gift."

This was not the picture of Palestinians presented at their temple. Not even close! These kids were beautiful. Inquisitive. Respectful. They were no different than the young Jewish boys at Temple Shalom.

We are, all of us, human.

***

Over the next two weeks, Murray and the rest of the group painted and cleaned at the school and meetinghouse and spent much of their time touring and meeting Palestinians. Each day after work on the meetinghouse, a lovely old stone building that had hosted over 100 years of people meeting for the cause of peace, the group had lunch in the common area. The common area was also used as a library and a playroom with children's books on a shelf, including books about Martin Luther King, Jr. and Nelson Mandela.

The Clerk of the Friends Meeting, Jean Zaru, hosted them after they finished one day. She was roughly Murray's age. While Schwartzman carried the scar of having lived through the Holocaust, Jean Zaru carried a scar, too, her childhood marked by having lived through the Nakba, the expulsion of Palestinian families from their homes. She, too, was held in similar reverence and respect by all who knew her. She was petite, old, and yet still bursting with energy.

If she were to attend a prayer service at Temple Shalom, Murray thought, *no one would guess, not even for a moment, that she was Palestinian. They would hold her in esteem because of her age. And they would love her because of her personality. Then what would they do when they learned about Jean Zaru's heritage?* Murray didn't have an answer to that question.

He'd always been welcomed in the synagogue when he arrived in America, but finding his way in other areas of life wasn't easy. He spoke little to no English. He looked like a child, even though he was sixteen. Most people laughed and pointed at him or shook their heads as if they had no idea what or who he was. He got used to the derogatory names he was called, just let it slide off his shoulders, and hid away in his memories of his mother's deep brown eyes, looking toward him and his brothers as she watched them leave.

What would he have done without the sanctuary the Jewish place of worship and community had given him? They'd provided food and clothing, sometimes even a place to sleep, as he learned English and looked for work, any work.

He was going to leave with more questions than answers.

Jean told the group her story, too, how, during the Nakba, her father and other Palestinians in Ramallah's Friends Meetinghouse took trucks with food and water to the refugees and how they took refugees into their homes, over fifty refugees in the case of Jean's family home. Some refugees lived with Jean's family for two years before they were able to find other housing.

After that, Jean began a lifelong effort to bring peace and justice to the residents of Israel. Murray was amazed by many things about Jean, but none more than that she harbored no will to commit violence toward the Jews of Israel, or toward anyone else, for that matter, even after steadfastly working to promote the return of Palestinian refugee families to their homes for over sixty years. She did so locally and internationally, having served as a member of the International Council of the World Conference for Religion and Peace, vice president of the World YWCA, and a consultant to the Middle East Council of Churches.

"I would have welcomed anyone who was hurting into my home," she said. "Jew, Muslim, Christian. It didn't matter their religion. It mattered that they were in pain." Schwartzman saw a lot to respect in the views of Quakers, at least as evidenced by this incredible woman.

By the end of the day, Murray was exhausted, but not from the physical labor. His emotions were running high, and memories came to visit during his sleep that night.

18

I'm Sorry You Were Tortured

Murray Schwartzman

After completing their cleaning assignments the next day, Murray and the rest of the Quaker group visited Bethlehem. It was a bright, sunny, hot day. Murray, having already walked far enough and, unlike the rest of his group, having no enthusiasm for visiting the place of Jesus' birth, waited outside the Church of the Nativity alone, leaning on his cane. Two Palestinian strangers approached him, and Murray felt himself tense up. What could these young men want? Why were they approaching him?

"A'me, Uncle, are you alone here?"

"Well, um, yes," Murray replied hesitantly. That was the second time someone had called him "uncle." He would have liked to have said no, but he was obviously alone. "I am with a group, but I'm waiting for them to return from inside the church."

"It's hot today, A'me. Would you like some water?" one of them asked, offering him a bottle. "There's more shade and a bench on the other side of the church. We will keep you company."

The other added, "The church's exit is near the bench, too, so your friends should be able to find you easily there."

Murray realized he was staring at them. He nodded his head. Yes, he would like some water. He took the bottle from them, and the two Palestinians accompanied him to the shaded bench on the other side of the church, one of them guiding him by the arm as they walked. He wasn't sure where this situation was headed. Would they rob him? They waited with him once they reached the bench, just keeping him company. Murray felt comforted by their hospitality, and sitting here in the shade was much more comfortable than standing in the sun's heat.

"Have you been to Bethlehem before?" one of them asked Murray.

He shook his head. "I've never been to Israel before."

"This used to be a very busy place," one of the men lamented, gesturing toward the thin crowd of people wandering around the famous birthplace of Jesus.

Murray grunted. "What happened?"

"The Israeli occupation happened," the other man said, and all three grew quiet. When they saw the rest of Murray's group approaching, the two young Palestinians said farewell and walked away.

Joel came over to Murray with a smile on his face. "Did you make new friends?"

"They saw me standing in the heat and just wanted to help me. They gave me water and brought me to this shady spot."

"Were they Muslim or Christian Palestinians?" Joel asked.

Murray paused. He shrugged. "I don't know. Didn't think to ask."

Later, at the Al Aida refugee camp's Al-Rowwad cultural center, dedicated to teaching "beautiful non-violent resistance," they heard about the occupation.

"We are dedicated to shared respect of human rights and values," the center's director said. "We are resisting occupation through education. We teach our children to be proud of their culture." As in most places they visited, stunning graffiti murals of flowers graced the stone walls of the narrow passageways in the refugee camp. Then, the children flowed out and performed a dance for their guests.

Upstairs in the library, young children played on computers and read books at low tables. Seeing the children at play gave him a sense of déjà vu. At first, he couldn't place it, but then he remembered. These children reminded him of the ones he had helped Rabbi Matt teach about Passover.

The next day, the group visited the Jalazone refugee camp, where they met with camp leaders, learned of refugee family origins in the expulsions from Lydda and Ramle, and heard of the camp's overcrowding and stressed infrastructure. The camp seemed somewhat self-contained, with its own schools, sanitation services, and even a medical clinic and pharmacy. It was clean, but some buildings needed a big facelift. Most of the residents appeared to be young adults, and there was no shortage of goats and sheep.

Khalid Zaid served as the camp's Executive Director, and in his modest office (which also served as a conference room), Murray saw a familiar picture on the wall. It was one he would see in offices all around Palestine: a photo of Yasser Arafat. Below that was a picture of a young man.

"Who is he?" Murray asked as he pointed at the young man.

"That is my oldest son," Zaid said with pride as his eyes moistened. "His name was Abdul. He was killed by the Israeli occupation forces."

Murray was speechless. He hadn't expected this and didn't know what to say in response that wouldn't sound trite. He reached down and rubbed the series of numbers tattooed on his arm. He took a deep breath, thinking of how many lives had been snuffed out for no reason during the World Wars. And now he was discovering that his own people had done the same. It made him ache.

He was relieved when Joel came over and shifted the conversation to the medical needs of the Jalazone refugee community, which Zaid described as desperately inadequate, much like all the other infrastructure needs of the camp's burgeoning population.

The next day, the group visited a mosque for prayers and to meet with its imam, Sheikh Faisal. Mohammed, a Muslim Palestinian who was one of the teachers at the Friends School, had arranged the visit. At the mosque entrance, the people in Murray's group were separated by gender since women worshiped in a separate area of the mosque, away from the men. The separation seemed archaic to most of the group members—especially to the very liberal young women in the Quaker group—though they went along with it. But it seemed rather normal to Murray, who had, over the years, visited Orthodox Jewish synagogues in which men and women worshiped separately.

Mohammad asked the men to remove their shoes before entering the mosque, then led them to a colorfully tiled room with faucets. He directed them through the Muslim ritual of cleaning their feet, hands, and face before praying, then guided them inside the mosque and oriented them to the place. Since it was Friday, the expansive room rapidly filled with men in preparation for the late morning prayer. Mohammad explained that in Islam, all people are equal, both the rich and the poor, and that all pray side by side, the banker together with the beggar.

The men in Murray's group tried to follow the lead of the imam and the Muslim men, participating in the prayers. Too late, Murray realized the pattern of lines on the mosque carpet helped organize mosque attendees into regular rows when, during the prayers, with everyone bowing deeply in unison, Murray accidentally kicked the head of the Muslim behind him. He turned, embarrassed, giving the man an apologetic expression, but the man just smiled at him and gave him a nod.

The prayer service was a powerful, moving religious experience, intensified by the sense of community, of people side by side praying in unison. Murray had never been interested before in interfaith events, unlike Rabbi Matt, who participated in them frequently. How would Rabbi Matt feel about worshiping in a mosque, and if he did, would he be so quick to condemn Muslims if he had experienced this prayer service alongside them?

As prayers ended and the crowd dispersed to return to their jobs, chairs were put into a circle for the Quaker group so that they could meet and talk with Imam Faisal. Murray took a seat, listening to everything going on around him. His back ached from the day's walking, and he shifted to one side in his chair, hoping to ease the pain. But it was the pain of physical exertion, of muscles gone unused for too long, not the ache of a lonely heart. From the outside, he must still look like the grumpy old man, but inside, he felt enlivened, both invigorated and curious.

The imam was in his early fifties but looked much older, with his thick white beard and weathered, wrinkled complexion. Though he spoke English well enough, Mohammad didn't feel he could translate adequately for the imam, so he introduced Murray and the group to Rima, a young Muslim woman who spoke Arabic and English fluently. Rima was about twenty, with long black hair, and looked like any of the young women at Temple Shalom. She had graduated from Ramallah's Friends School and was now a student at Guilford College, another Quaker-founded institution near Winston-Salem. She was home, here in Ramallah, for the summer.

Rima introduced the imam to the group as both an imam and a former Hamas representative to the Palestinian legislature.

Hamas? A terrorist? Murray tensed.

With Rima providing the translation, Imam Faisal proudly described the basic tenets of Islam, including faith in one God, praying, giving charity, and living one's life in accordance with God's will. Murray was surprised but put at ease by the imam's calm demeanor and the degree of similarity between Judaism and the Islam the imam described. The imam didn't seem to be a violent man at all.

Murray listened to him intently as the imam went on to describe what living under occupation was like and what it was like to have been tortured in an Israeli prison.

"It got worse for us after the war in 2014. It destroyed existing infrastructure, and we had little to repair the buildings with. Not to mention the bombings of homes and the fractured families they left. We face violence every day. Misunderstandings at checkpoints. Coming too close to Israeli settlements. Even being too friendly, speaking to an Israeli. Our parents warn us not to look at them too closely. We can no longer get to the sea, so our food and water sources have literally dried up."

"I'm sorry," Murray said quietly, without even thinking. The imam looked at him with a questioning look.

"I am Jewish," Murray muttered, looking away. "That's all. I'm sorry you were tortured."

The imam smiled and slowly replied in his gentle yet authoritative Arabic so that Rima could accurately translate each word. "We do not hate Jews. Islam teaches us to love everyone. Jews are people of the Book. We hate being made refugees. We want to return to our homes. The foreign Jews will have to leave because they will not let us return."

"Why don't the people go to other countries?" one woman asked.

Rima gave a sardonic chuckle, as did Imam Faisal when she translated. "It's even worse in Lebanon right now," he explained. Rima added, "My cousin Fatima just lost her seven-month-old daughter, Sadia."

She dug in her wallet and handed Murray a photo of the family.

"They didn't have the money for surgery. Lebanon's economy is worse than ours right now, and over 200,000 Palestinian refugees still live there, as well as 1.5 million Syrian refugees. For a country smaller than your American state, Rhode Island, one wonders how they sustain this housing, such as it is, and the assistance. But the Arab people are generous, and three-quarters of us live below the poverty line no matter where we are."

Murray stared into the huge ebony eyes of the children, eyes that could have been his at that age. They had big smiles on their faces, but their bodies were skinny. "Where is their father?" he asked.

"Their father lost his life to Covid-19. He worked in a scrap yard, and he couldn't see what he was touching during the electricity outage. Their mother, Fatima, has diabetes, but she does her best for them."

So many families in so much misery. "What if the Israelis did let you return?" Murray asked.

Rima translated the imam's response. "They would never let us return. They want *all* the land."

That's exactly what the Israelis would say about Palestinians. Murray was disappointed that the imam hadn't really answered his question. How would Palestinians react if they were allowed to return? With violence? Or peace? The Palestinians Murray had met seemed to all be such extraordinarily gentle, peaceful people. So many of them held their faith very dear, and whether Christian or Muslim, peace was central to their lives.

From there, the group had a trip to PLO headquarters. There, they met with Salem Barahmeh, PLO International Affairs Advisor, a young Palestinian man who had gone to college at Lawrence University in Wisconsin and who had played on the school's varsity basketball team.

"He must have been a guard," Murray thought, since Salem was not particularly tall.

While Barahmeh spoke, Murray noticed the ubiquitous picture of Arafat hanging on the wall, as did the other Quakers.

"Do you think that having a picture of a terrorist on your wall is consistent with the message and image the PLO is trying to convey of itself?" asked one of the Quaker women. Murray couldn't help but agree.

Before Barahmeh could respond, one of his assistants replied quietly. "You should be asking why Israelis celebrate terrorists like Begin and Shamir and why the United States celebrates a genocidal slave owner by putting his face on $20 bills."

A tense silence fell. Barahmeh looked at his colleague with pity mixed with consternation, then turned to the rest of the group. "He speaks out of turn. You must understand that Yasser Arafat was a beloved leader who dedicated his entire life to the pursuit of peace and justice, fighting for the liberation of Palestinians. He is not unlike Nelson Mandela, who was also portrayed as a terrorist before people came to love and respect him."

Murray was amazed at this perspective. He found it difficult to comprehend—after all, he had spent most of his life thinking of Arafat as a Middle Eastern Muslim terrorist. But here were people who saw a different side of things. He wondered whose truth was real.

Besides eating out at a falafel joint once, the group took most of their meals in the homes of Palestinian families, both Christian and Muslim. Murray found it heartwarming to watch the families interact, the children being silly, and the parents loving and protective. Their walls were lined with textiles, and back home, the Jewish families he knew would have had abstract paintings. Otherwise, he could find little difference in their homes, or in them. No matter where he went, homes had one thing in common: refrigerators covered with photo after photo of children who were the apples of their parents' eyes.

Murray didn't hide the fact that he was Jewish, and yet no one seemed to care. They all treated him with warmth, friendship, and respect. While there was no mezuzah on their doors, the word "Peace" was displayed in one language or another in all the homes, just as it was in Rabbi Matt and Rebecca's home.

After long days of service and touring, Murray had no trouble falling asleep at the Friends School... except for two occasions. One night, he heard shouting and what he was sure was the sound of gunfire and stones being thrown, followed by the buzz of helicopter blades overhead. It all sounded awfully close, and the next morning, he learned there had been a brief incursion by the Israeli Defense Force into Ramallah, attempting to arrest someone whom the IDF deemed to be a Palestinian terrorist.

The next night, he was awoken well before dawn by the painfully loud sound of the muezzin from a mosque minaret near the back of the school. When Murray first woke, he thought it would last only a few minutes and that he could go back to sleep. But it continued for over an hour.

"How do people stand this?" he wondered, turning over and putting the pillow over his head. He later learned this was a special call for prayer. The month of Ramadan was ending.

The streets became more festive. It was obvious families congregated at night, moving from prayer to breaking their fast. Their laughter echoed around the town, and Ramadan tents dotted the street corners for people to celebrate together. Murray began to look forward to the setting sun to see what new adventure and delicious meal the evening would bring. He watched from the roadside outside the Friends school as a parade went by, led by Muslim imams and Orthodox Christian pastors. He was starting to like it here.

Their two-week trip was ending, though, and the group headed from Ramallah for a tour of the city of Hebron by way of Jerusalem. The bus arrived at a checkpoint to get into Jerusalem from the Palestinian West Bank. Outside the bus, a long line of people stretched as far as the eye could see, standing in the heat, waiting, Murray was sure, to try to cross the checkpoint.

His thoughts drifted to memories of waiting in lines at the concentration camp. Everywhere, barbed wire, closing them in, closing them off from his country, his people, the world. One night, a man had dug a hole out and escaped, only to be captured a minute later. Young Murray watched as they kicked him in the gut, sliced his arms, shot out his kneecaps. Only then, when he had escaped into unconsciousness, did they shoot him dead. Murray clinched his fists as he saw again and again the man as he lost his kneecap, collapse to the dark earth, silent, without a sound. Lost, worthless in their eyes, totally expendable. That's what they'd been to Hitler and his band of inhuman humans.

He shifted in his seat. Three Israeli soldiers were boarding the bus, heavily armed and covered in protective gear. As they approached, they looked imposing, but once they got close enough for him to see their faces, it was clear that they were mere boys, probably hardly out of their teens. The soldiers were curt but not disrespectful. They spoke with the Palestinian driver, checked everyone's passports, and dismounted the bus, allowing the group to pass.

The bus stopped in Jerusalem to pick up four passengers. Two were former Israeli soldiers who were now working for Breaking the Silence, an organization working to expose the Israeli public to what Israeli soldiers were doing in the occupied territories. These soldiers would be the group's guides in Hebron, and they took seats at the front of the bus. The two other new passengers, young men, boarded the bus and sat by Murray. One was Jeremy, fresh from his Birthright trip.

19

Under the Shadow of Islam

Murray Schwartzman

"Jeremy!" Murray said with surprise. The others in his group looked up, shocked, probably because they hadn't seen Murray this animated all week.

"Mr. Schwartzman!" Jeremy replied with equal surprise. "How wonderful to see you! The last time I saw you, we were sitting in your kitchen surfing the net. "

"That's true," Murray said, smiling. Jeremy looked tanned and happy.

"What are you doing here?" Jeremy asked.

"I've been touring Palestine with Christians," he said, his voice returning to something close to his normal growl but ending in a chuckle.

Jeremy laughed, too.

"In fact, it was you connecting me with Dr. Friedman that has led me all the way here, Jeremy," Murray said. "Why have you come?"

"I'm here on my Birthright trip. This is my friend, Barry. He's also here on his Birthright trip—he's from New York."

"It's a pleasure to meet you, Mr. Schwartzman. This wasn't a scheduled part of the Birthright trip. Going into Hebron was Jeremy's idea.

I'm still a bit nervous about it. I haven't told my parents. They would worry too much," Barry said.

"I wanted to see for myself if what we found on the internet is true," Jeremy said.

"I think we'll be fine," Murray said. "We should be in good hands with these IDF soldiers leading us," he added.

The bus entered Hebron from Kiryat Arba—a modern, exclusively Jewish settlement nestled in the mountains—and stopped. They exited the bus into another clear, hot Holy Land day. Their guide, Avi, walked them through Kahane Park, a white sand and stone-covered square. The park was named after Rabbi Meir Kahane, founder of a banned far-right Israeli political/terrorist organization. Kahane had argued that a Jewish state and a democracy were incompatible, that Arabs should be paid to leave Israel or be forcibly expelled, and that intermarriage between Jews and non-Jews should be banned. Murray wondered, *Was this the Jewish KKK? How is restricting marriage between Jews and non-Jews any different from restricting marriage between Whites and Blacks?*

They walked past the park to the grave of Baruch Goldstein. On the grave, in Jewish tradition, were both stones and flowers.

"Goldstein was born to an Orthodox Jewish family in Brooklyn, New York, and pursued a medical career," Avi said. "He wanted to help people. After receiving his medical degree from the Albert Einstein College of Medicine, he emigrated to Israel, settled in Kiryat Arba, the Jewish settlement bordering Hebron, married and had four children, and worked as a physician."

Avi paused.

"Goldstein was also a mass murderer."

Murray was captivated. Avi was a compelling storyteller.

"Hebron was the first Jewish real estate bought by Abraham," he continued. "Here in Hebron is the Cave of the Patriarchs, holy to both Jews and Muslims. There is a mosque here, built at the site of the cave where Abraham, Isaac, and their wives Sarah and Rebecca were buried. In 1994, Goldstein went into that mosque and started shooting as many Muslims as he could, killing dozens and wounding over one hundred.

He was stopped by the survivors, beaten to death, and buried here. His grave is venerated by some Jews. They make pilgrimages here to place small memorial stones or flowers on his grave."

Avi looked down at a few stones placed on the grave. Then he bent down, cupped his hand, and swept them off in one quick motion.

A few other graves stood out in this small cemetery, and Murray walked around to each of them. They weren't any more ornate than the others, just larger. He stopped in his tracks when he saw the name on the second one. It was "Schwartzman."

"Do you know who this was?" he asked Avi.

"No sir, I do not. But it must have been a person who was admired, a crucial part of the community."

Murray squinted, looking closer. "Noah Schwartzman," he said under his breath. "1927 – 2003." The common Hebrew epitaph: "May his soul be bound up in the bond of eternal life." But then underneath, in smaller script: "Tell my brother the greatest gift he gave me was his love." Shock waves coursed down Murray's spine.

"Are you okay, Mr. Schwartzman?" Jeremy asked, reaching out to steady him.

"I think... I'm nearly sure..."

"Let me get you some water," Avi said.

"No, no, it's not that. I believe this is my brother's grave. It means... it means he lived! He lived long and came here. All along, he's been here." Murray couldn't stop the tears from flowing. He picked up a stone, then every Quaker picked up a stone, and single file, they placed the stone on Murray's brother's headstone.

The groundskeeper walked past. "Oh, you knew Noah Schwartzman," he said. "He did great things. He always spoke of his time in Poland during the war. He said he never wanted any other Jew to suffer as he had, as his family had. He worked his entire life for the Jewish people."

After they all absorbed the import of Murray's discovery, sitting in the shade sipping water, they continued walking deeper into Hebron, its streets baked in sunlight; Avi wiped the sweat from his forehead and explained how this empty street was once a bustling center of business.

"Now, few people come here, mostly just Israeli soldiers whose mission is to control Hebron and protect the few Jews living here. Do you see the iron doors of these businesses? They have been welded shut by the Israelis." Avi showed the group a picture of the street on which they were standing—Shuhada Street. It had been a bustling market full of people.

Murray was overwhelmed by the silence. His brother had lived here. Especially after his recent discovery, the deserted street felt scary, like a ghost town. Like a town he once knew well.

"Hebron was holy to the Jews," Avi explained, "so Jewish 'extremists' wanted to have a Jewish presence in this city of over 100,000 Muslims. The Jewish extremists established a foothold by squatting in an old Hebron hospital and eventually obtaining protection from the government. These settlers began complaining of harassment at the hands of the Palestinians, hoping the government would create a sterile buffer zone that Palestinians would not be allowed to enter."

He paused, looking up and down the street. Murray followed his gaze. Still, he saw no one but soldiers.

"Once buffer zones were established, Jewish settlers would expand into them, again complain that adjacent Palestinians were harassing them, which led to further expansion of the buffer zones."

Murray studied the street around him. On the buildings, there were pictures of families with writing underneath. In English and Hebrew, they described how specific Jewish families had been killed by Palestinian terrorists not just in Hebron but throughout Israel. The signs were very moving, Murray thought, but they didn't mention the names of any of the far greater number of Palestinians who had been killed, here and elsewhere. There were stone walls and a few guard towers overlooking the streets. Coiled barbed wire blocked the alleyways. Murray saw an Israeli flag fluttering in the breeze, far up a large hillside. Hebron reminded him of the ghetto where the Jews had been forced to live, perhaps where his family had been forced to live, and even die. His mouth suddenly felt dry.

Advancing up the hill toward the flag, they passed two young girls, thin with long dark hair and dressed in school uniforms. The girls walked toward a gap in a fence topped with barbed wire beside a guard box staffed by two heavily armed IDF soldiers. The soldiers wore flak jackets, carried automatic rifles, and had extra ammunition on their belts. Avi explained that such a scene was just a normal day for the Palestinian children of Hebron and that passing such checkpoints on their way to school was routine.

Passing the guard box toward the top of the hill, the group reached a spacious crossing with another street. "This place looks familiar to me. Did something happen here?" Murray asked.

"Yes, I'm surprised you know of this place," Avi said in his thick Israeli accent. "This is where a Palestinian, I don't know his name, stabbed an Israeli soldier. The Palestinian was shot, and as he was lying on the ground, wounded, Elor Azaria, an Israeli soldier, walked up and calmly shot the Palestinian again, in the head. There was a video of it, and it circulated on the Internet. It caused quite a stir. Azaria was convicted and served some time in jail. But Palestinians get longer sentences for throwing a stone that hurts no one. It is typical of what happens here."

"That's not fair," Jeremy said softly. His friend nodded in agreement.

Avi shrugged. "There are different rules for the Jews and the Muslims. If a Jewish child throws stones at Palestinians, we are told to do nothing. If we see a Muslim child throw a stone at a Jew, he is to be taken to military court and given jail time, perhaps up to twenty years. This is how it is here. We Israelis are in control."

"How is this justified?" Murray asked, his voice a low rumble, still thinking of his brother. Everyone in the group looked his way. When he spoke, his voice was like thunder. Perhaps he'd start speaking up more often.

"Israelis are treated under civil law," Avi explained, "while Palestinians are subject to martial law. Israel demolishes the homes of Palestinian suicide bombers' families. The Israeli government wouldn't even consider doing that, not even for a millisecond, to Goldstein's family."

Jeremy nudged Murray in the arm, looked at him, and shook his head in disbelief. "I wish Rabbi Matt could hear all this," he whispered.

"I joined the IDF," Avi said, "to protect the State of Israel. My first assignment was here in Hebron, where I would participate in 'mapping.' They tell us that we are collecting information in the mapping operations to help keep Israel safe. In the middle of the night, we would enter random Palestinian homes, wake the entire family, and search their homes. This was done with the clear purpose of instilling fear, of reinforcing our control over them. I doubt any information we collected was ever used for anything. You see the children, terrified, some wetting themselves. The children see their parents are powerless. The fathers are humiliated. I took no pleasure in it."

"But aren't there terrorists hiding among them?" one group member asked.

"The way we treat them, it's a wonder more of them don't turn to terrorism," Avi replied in a weary voice.

Avi walked the group past the homes of some of the settlers. A Jewish woman came out and started yelling at Avi in Hebrew. She seemed to be cursing him out.

"Don't mind her," Avi said. "That's Shoshana Cohen. She's all bluster. She came to Israel from Brooklyn. She's one of the extremist settlers here who harasses Palestinians. When new IDF soldiers come here, she bakes cookies for them, treats them very well, and tells them how important they are, protecting her and the other settlers from what she tells the soldiers are evil, violent Palestinians."

They reached the yard of an old stone home on which "Youth Against Settlements" was spray painted in several places. A makeshift conference room with a mix of cheap plastic lawn chairs was arranged in a circle under two large trees whose gangling limbs provided a welcome relief. Shade. Murray gazed at the light and shadow play, more dazed than he'd been all day. He shouldn't, couldn't go there, into that locked box of memories. He felt dizzy. Then he remembered, "Under the shadow of Islam, the members of the three religions: Islam,

Christianity, and Judaism, can coexist in safety and security," the Hamas Charter had said. Maybe some shadows were good.

He plopped into one of the lawn chairs. "I'm sorry, I'm a bit dehydrated," he said. One of the group members went to find some more water for him. The others seemed to welcome the break and stood under the long limbs, getting to know one another better in this place where so much tragedy had happened.

Murray's thoughts drifted despite his efforts to control them. He'd lost all sense of time when he'd been in Hitler's clutches. He couldn't tell how long it lasted, how long he'd had to stay out of sight and sound. He'd only been beaten once, along with every person in the crowd he'd gotten caught up in. He'd managed to escape with just a black eye. He was never caught stealing food. He was quick as a rabbit, stealthy as a fox, and tiny as a mouse. Most were not so lucky. He saw many beatings in the camp, and many people were killed right before him. Men and women were shot in the head or pounded with rudimentary clubs until their faces were unrecognizable.

Worse still were those taken from their side of the camp, brown and muddy, even the grass having been eaten by the starving prisoners, to the other, greener side, where the smokestacks were always churning, where the smell of burning flesh rose. They never returned, but there were always more trains, more Jewish passengers to take their place. Yet somehow, during this entire time, Murray was never singled out, never approached. He was, in fact, eventually the only child left in the camp, but no one paid him any mind, not the guards or the other inmates.

No one, that is, except Uncle, who continually promised him the feast was just around the corner, as was the next train ride that would take them to the South of France, where they would lie on the beach and share apricots, dates, and juice and eat exquisite sides of lamb. Having prepared the feast for them, Murray's family would be there, and Uncle would see his wife and children, possibly his grandson, all again in a reunion to surpass all others.

"We're nearly there, Murray," the man said, his voice weaker every day. "We're almost there."

One day, filled with a drenching rain, Uncle was gone, vanished when Murray went back for his few hours' sleep after another day of filth, sweat, and labor. As soon as he heard the snoring of the other prisoners, he searched the camp, skirting around its perimeter, taking risks crouching, then standing, so close to the barbed wire. He continued to search for days and weeks.

But Uncle, just like his family in Poland, had vanished, evaporated, into the rain. The shadows had returned, never relenting, even after he'd met Miriam, until now, until today. She had diminished them, not banished them completely.

Now, only the sun cast shadows, beckoning him toward a new day.

That's interesting, Murray thought. *While "shadow" sounds ominous, here in this hot, sunny, dry land, a cool shadow is probably a welcome respite in the same way warm sunshine would be to northern Europeans. Perhaps a better translation of the Hamas document, one less literal, would have been, "Under the sunshine of Islam, the members of the three religions: Islam, Christianity, and Judaism, can coexist in safety and security."*

He took a deep breath. No more shadows. Not here.

Avi and two young Palestinian men, barely more than boys, chatted briefly as the group mingled. A group member brought bottles of sweating cold water, and they all gulped them down.

Murray noticed surveillance cameras on the top corners of the building. "What are the cameras for?" he asked Avi.

"The Palestinian youth put the cameras there to record all the interactions between the young Palestinians living in this home and their adjacent Jewish neighbors," Avi said. "Shoshana and the other Jewish settlers would complain to Israeli soldiers in Hebron of these Palestinian youth being violent when the reverse was true. So, the Palestinian youth, actually subject to violence from the Jewish settlers, had no recourse other than to document with the video cameras that they were the ones being harassed by their Jewish neighbors. Even with the videos, the Palestinian youth are at risk of being jailed under Israeli martial law."

"One of their projects was to get worldwide support to force the

Israelis to reopen Shuhada Street," one of the Palestinians said. "But we're hoping to do it with non-violent measures, putting pressure on the Israeli government to dismantle the settlements."

Avi introduced him as a YAS leader, Issa Amro, a plump Palestinian, taller than most and probably in his late twenties. "We Palestinian youth would peacefully resist the occupation, and we'd immediately be arrested," the boy said. "I've been arrested by the Israelis more times than I could count."

It reminded Murray of the oppression he'd faced. *How can we treat these good people like this?* he wondered. The walls, the deserted streets, the storefronts welded shut. Barbed wire and guard towers. Heavily armed soldiers patrolling over young children. *Have we become like the Germans were to us?* It sickened him to his core. He felt a sudden kinship with Amro, his Youth Against Settlements comrades, and all Palestinian families living as refugees.

"I wonder if you knew my brother, Noah," he asked, but Amro shook his head.

"I'm sorry," he said. "I don't know many Jewish people."

Jeremy leaned in close again. "This is nothing like what Rabbi Matt described. Why are we treating them like this?"

Murray just shook his head.

When they rose to leave, he heard Amro calling out. Turning, he saw he was handing him another water bottle and some bak'lava. "My mother made it," Amro told him with a smile. "Take good care, sir; it is easy to be overcome by the sun on a day like today."

Murray thanked him with a smile. *Overcome. On a day like today. Yes, that is exactly how he felt, with the sun pouring down on him, opening his eyes.*

***

Jeremy and Barry accompanied Murray and the rest of their group back to Jerusalem, where they found a coffee shop just a few blocks from the Old City. Exhausted, having witnessed apartheid in Hebron, the group found a coffee shop near the Old City in Jerusalem to de-stress. There, they met Bassam Aramin, a Palestinian man, and Rami Elhanan, an Israeli man, both members of the Parents' Circle, or what

Rami lightheartedly called "the only association in the world that does not wish to welcome any new members."

"The Parents' Circle," Rami explained, "is an organization of parents of children who have been killed in the conflict between Palestinians and Israelis." He gestured to the other man. "Bassam's daughter, Abir, was ten when she was killed. My daughter, Smadar, was fourteen when she was killed by Palestinian suicide bombers in the busy Ben Yehuda Street pedestrian mall."

Bassam didn't interrupt as Rami did most of the talking—in a careful, measured monotone that couldn't hide his underlying emotions as he described his precious daughter, how she was killed, and its effect on him. "I ran to her, but she was already—gone," he said, bowing his head.

Rami spoke for Bassam, too, describing how Bassam had been arrested by the Israelis many times, how he had participated in violent demonstrations in his youth, and how, while in prison, he first learned about the Holocaust, seeing a movie about it.

"He knew nothing about the Holocaust. He couldn't believe what he was watching. It explained so much about the Jewish people, to see what we had gone through," Rami said. Then he explained how Bassam's daughter was killed, shot in the back of the head while walking home from school by an Israeli border guard. He told the story in a few sentences, much like the other stories Murray had heard today and earlier that year at the Holocaust Museum. The story he had experienced himself as a child. Alive and vibrant one moment. Shot dead the next.

His words hung in the air. What words could match this kind of story, happening over and over? What words could explain violence against children?

Rami spoke again. "This conflict," he said, "is not worth the life of one more child. The only way forward is to talk to one another, to understand one another's point of view."

Murray looked at his companions. Everyone, including Jeremy, appeared to be fighting tears. How Rami was able to speak without weeping was beyond him.

"We don't tell these stories to persuade you for one side or the other.

We don't want you to be pro-Israeli or pro-Palestinian," Rami said. "We demand of you to be pro-peace, to be against injustice, and against this ongoing oppression in which one people is dominating another. It must be changed. It's the essence of evil, and it must be stopped.

"I am a Jew with the utmost respect for my people, my tradition, my history, and my religion. And I will tell you that ruling and oppressing and humiliating and occupying millions and millions of people for so many years without any democratic rights is not Jewish, period, no two ways about it, and being against it is not anti-Semitic. It is human."

20

An Unpopular Stand

Murray Schwartzman

Murray left Israel with a determination to end his silence. People couldn't change what they didn't know about. He invited Jeremy and his girlfriend Katie over to form a plan of action. They all thought the temple youth would be a more open audience at first.

"Mr. Schwartzman, Katie is the medical student I told you about. She studied dermatology with Dr. Friedman up at the Methodist. Can you believe that?"

"What a small world. It's nice to meet you, Katie." Murray said, smiling. Dr. Friedman seemed to be showing up in many people's lives.

"Jeremy has told me a lot about you, Mr. Schwartzman. He has a lot of respect for you and what you're doing," Katie said in a slight southern drawl.

Murray replied that he had tremendous respect for Jeremy, too. He could tell that Katie was a warm, sweet human being. She radiated quiet confidence as she peered at him through delicate wire-framed glasses. Not only that, but she would soon be a doctor.

Times were certainly changing. His trips first to Baltimore and then Israel were a testament to that, and maybe Murray was changing too.

At one time, his first thought would have been, *but she's not Jewish*. Now, he found himself more impressed by the young couple's unwavering enthusiasm and positivity.

Murray proposed that he and Jeremy pen an opinion piece for the *Winston-Salem Journal* as a testament to their Israel trip. They pored over every sentence, every word, until, at the end, Murray sat back in his chair, took a deep breath, and sighed. Jeremy rubbed his own shoulders and moved his head from side to side, trying to loosen up.

"Well," Murray said, but he had no words remaining. Everything in his mind had been transcribed into the letter. Jeremy nodded.

"I think it's perfect," Katie said, smiling.

As Jeremy and Katie prepared to leave, Murray pulled Jeremy aside and said, "Jeremy, can I talk to you alone for a moment?"

Jeremy went over to him and, perhaps trying to preemptively ward off potential criticism, quickly said, "Mr. Schwartzman, I know she's not Jewish, but..."

Murray held up his hand, cut him off, and said, "No, you've got the wrong idea. I wanted to tell you how happy I am for you both. Katie seems like a genuine, caring person. That's what's important."

The Journal printed their letter in its online edition, though not in its print newspaper.

On the Ground with Israelis and Palestinians

As American Jews, having lost family in the Holocaust and having loving family members in Israel, the Holy Land is deeply important in our lives. We just returned from visiting Israel and Palestine, where we saw incredible achievements of the Jewish people there. Yet, we were saddened by the treatment of Palestinians suffering under Israeli occupation. A former Israeli soldier, proudly Jewish, took us to Hebron and described how if an Israeli throws a stone at Palestinians, nothing is done; if a Palestinian responds with a stone, he or she is sentenced to years in prison.

We witnessed "sterile" zones from which Palestinians are forbidden to enter but where new Jewish settlements spring up. Formerly vibrant parts of Hebron, a holy city of over 100,000 Muslims, have become ghost towns, Palestinian businesses closed, the iron doors of people's homes and businesses welded shut. In their defense, Israeli settlers would point out that the patriarch Abraham bought the land of Hebron for Jewish people and that what the settlers are doing is not nearly as bad as what was done to Palestinian families in the founding of Israel, when hundreds of thousands of Palestinian men, women, and children were forcefully expelled and made and kept refugees from their homes and villages. But the Palestinians have been swept out of the area, nonetheless.

What surprised us most during our trip was that Palestinians were kind to us, among the nicest people we have ever met. Israelis told us that we would be taking our lives in our hands if we entered Arab-controlled areas, but the biggest hazard we experienced was all the stores selling ice cream, doughnuts, and other sweets. In Ramallah, home of the PLO and Palestinian Authority, people warmly greeted us wherever we went. It was a friendliness we had not experienced anywhere else, not even in Winston-Salem. The warmth and kindness of the Palestinian people was what you might expect people to be like if they were, as Palestinians are, people who walk the paths where Jesus walked.

People who have not had the firsthand experience that we have had may tell you, based on the violence that they have seen in the media or heard rumors of, that Palestinians must be violent people, but they aren't. Peaceful Palestinian people suffer from far more violence meted out by good Jewish Israelis. Israelis are pained by the violence they commit but believe—quite wrongly—that the only way Jews can secure their children is through their oppression and dispossession of non-Jewish Palestinian families.

We've supported Israel. We still support peace and security for Jews in Israel. But let us work together to end the segregation and separation of Jewish and non-Jewish families in the Holy Land and work toward peace and security for all the people living there.

Having broken bread in the homes of Palestinian Christian and Muslim families and having met Palestinian workers, teachers, children, religious leaders, refugees, and legislators, we are convinced that there could be peace and security for Jewish people if Israel would repatriate Palestinian families, enforce law by equal measure, and treat everyone with justice. This Holy Land demands no less.

The article caught the attention of Robert Anderson, a local businessman. He called Murray and invited him to speak to the Rotary Club about his experiences in Israel and Palestine. Murray shrugged off any reluctance. He could reach a broader spectrum of the community if he spoke at such a place. He agreed to speak.

First, though, Murray visited with the local Jewish youth group where Jeremy was a member. Murray started by describing his experiences without making any judgments or criticisms. He simply talked about what he had seen and done, much as he had related his experience in Poland to the children at The Holocaust Museum.

The teens, including Rabbi Matt's son Asher, listened without interrupting, at least until the end, when Sam Weisblatt's son Aaron spoke up.

"You're wrong," he said to Murray. "The wall, the different laws, all of it is something we do only for peace. We wouldn't do any of that if Palestinians didn't make us. They are the violent ones."

"I won't tell you what to think, just what I saw. I only ask you to remember the lesson of the Holocaust: act to protect all people from injustice. *All* people," Murray's words came out gentle, but strong. "Please know I am only telling you what I witnessed."

Murray thought the time had come to talk to Rabbi Matt. He'd thought of the rabbi so many times while he was on his trip. He hoped and fully believed that the rabbi would understand his new views if he could only find the right words. Everything Dr. Friedman had said was true. Everything. Murray was sure that Rabbi Matt would learn to love Palestinians the way he had learned to love gays, Blacks, and other oppressed minorities. They'd be a team again, explaining the reality of what was happening in Israel to the entire local Jewish community.

On a whim one evening, Murray got in his car and drove to the bungalow he used to frequent. He hadn't given it much thought. Maybe it would have been better to meet on neutral ground, like the temple. Yet, he somehow felt that a more informal visit would be best. He liked how spontaneous he had become.

It was still warm as he came up the shady walkway. The yard was immaculate, a lush green, and the glow of lights from the windows was as welcoming as always. Murray knew that at this time of year, Rebecca kept flowers in pots to add color to her family's home. Amazingly, she could find the time to maintain such an impressive home while doing so much for the Jewish community.

As he approached the house, he passed a small, colorful sign placed next to the walkway:

WE BELIEVE
BLACK LIVES MATTER
NO HUMAN IS ILLEGAL
LOVE IS LOVE
WOMEN'S RIGHTS ARE HUMAN RIGHTS
SCIENCE IS REAL
WATER IS LIFE
INJUSTICE ANYWHERE IS A THREAT TO JUSTICE EVERYWHERE

Murray smiled as he read the familiar sign that said so much about the couple's philosophy and what they taught their children and the community. He rang the bell at the door, and Asher greeted him.

"Hi, Mr. Schwartzman," he said brightly. At the sound of Murray's voice, Miri came running, wrapping Schwartzman in a tight hug.

"Hello, kids," he said, his eyes watering noticeably. They were like grandchildren to him. It had been much too long.

Rebecca swept into the foyer. "Asher, Miri, go upstairs to your rooms. I need to talk to Mr. Schwartzman." Her voice sounded sharp, and Asher and Miri complied, giving furtive glances to say goodbye.

As the children headed upstairs, Murray asked Rebecca, "Is Rabbi Matt here?"

She stared hard at him, her arms folded. Her voice came out in a low hiss. "No, he isn't. Mr. Schwartzman, I saw your letter to the paper and heard you have been telling our kids even more lies about Israel. I've also heard that you have taken up with Dr. Friedman—that you are on his side, even! You know I have family over there. You know they are under constant threat. How could you?"

Murray was taken aback. He had not expected this. "It's not like that, Rebecca. Palestinians are—"

But before he could finish, Rebecca interrupted him. "They are animals, Mr. Schwartzman! Animals! They've killed Israeli children! Children! People I knew! You have no idea what damage you are doing. Those pigs are using you, Mr. Schwartzman. You've become a traitor to your people."

He stood frozen. He'd never seen this side of Rebecca, the caring, compassionate wife and mother. Murray was sure his shock showed. He had anticipated some misunderstanding, perhaps, but nothing that could not be overcome with a sensible conversation about his trip. What he had seen, with his own two eyes!

"Please, leave *now*. You are not wanted here." As Murray backed away, Rebecca slammed the door in his face. The old Murray might have fallen backward. Even now, he clutched his cane to stabilize himself.

Murray could feel the heat of her rage, far worse than any words she expressed. He felt a punch to the gut, an awful, empty feeling, and he quickly turned and left. He wondered what he should do. He could see how wrong she was but also that changing her mind wouldn't be easy.

Would there be any way to reach her or, for that matter, Rabbi Matt? When Murray was in Israel and Palestine, he had been so excited about what this new information might do for the Jewish community in Winston-Salem.

Murray knew from his own past how passionate people felt about Israel. Having a new perspective himself, he had been certain his stories would be what was needed to show them the truth. But he had encountered the reality there on the rabbi's doorstep. Changing minds and hearts would take more than just presenting facts. Even that might be daunting.

Murray drove home, consoling himself that he could still reach people in the greater community. After all, he had the big event coming up at Rotary.

Or so he thought.

Late the next week, Murray received another call from Robert Anderson. "Mr. Schwartzman," said Anderson, "I'm calling to let you know we have to cancel your talk at the Rotary meeting. I was truly looking forward to hearing about your experiences, but it's not going to work out after all."

Murray waited to hear the rest. He had a few guesses as to why his talk had been canceled.

After an uncomfortable silence, Robert continued. "To tell you the truth, the leadership of the Rotary received messages that your presentation wouldn't be balanced, that it would be too political. I'm so, so sorry to have to tell you this."

Murray, while disappointed, was not entirely surprised. He knew that people, friends at the temple, would perceive his new attitude in a negative way. They held a lot of sway with others, and they were well-organized. His interaction with Rebecca had made all too clear what they now thought of him.

When Murray didn't say anything, Anderson went on. "Mr. Schwartzman, if you are willing, I want to hear what you have to say. Would you be willing to come to my home and share your experience with me? I would invite some colleagues to attend, too. As far as I know, most are not Jewish, so it could be interesting for them. However, I can't promise how many, if any, will show up."

"Gladly," Murray replied. Even if he could reach only a few more people, even one more person, it would be a step in the right direction.

On the night of his talk, Murray arrived early at the Andersons's home on a street of grand homes on large lots thick with trees. It seemed desolate. The streets were empty, with only an occasional car and nobody out walking. Most houses stood quiet and dark. Empty like Hebron, but full of darkness instead of sun. It was a world away from the hustle and bustle of downtown Ramallah. No one to rely on for help.

Murray parked and walked up the circular driveway to the front door of the Anderson home. Robert met him there. "Please come in, Mr. Schwartzman. You're early."

Anderson walked Murray into a large living room furnished in a traditional style. Murray was offered a seat in a large leather chair in the corner, and Anderson left to get him a glass of water. The doorbell began to ring, and soon, the room was full, even cramped.

Not only did Murray have many of the people who would have been at the Rotary meeting, but he also had many of their spouses in attendance.

"Thank you very much for coming, Mr. Schwartzman," Robert said with a smile, looking out over the crowd. "As you can see, many of us here are very interested in what you have to say."

Murray nodded his thanks and took a deep breath.

21

A Traitor to His People

Murray Schwartzman

Murray's colorful stories brought the crowd along with him—from his arrival in Israel to multiple border crossings, back and forth, from Hebron to Ramallah to Jerusalem. He described the warmth of the people he had met, how they had welcomed him. Most of all, he explained how they made him feel. With tears in his eyes, he told the story of Rami and Bassem and how they had each lost a child to the conflict.

"So you can see I felt that people in Winston-Salem ought to know about my experience," Murray concluded, looking around the room, meeting each guest's gaze.

After a few minutes, Anderson moved over closer to where Murray sat, and he talked for a moment about how Murray's witness resonated with him.

"I've seen over and over in my business the many needless misconceptions and conflicts that often develop between my marketing and sales teams. I've also seen how easy it was for one side to see things very clearly one way while the other side saw things equally clearly, but through a completely different lens."

When he finished, Anderson asked if anyone had any questions for Murray.

Receiving none, Anderson said he had a question. "What would you have us do, Murray? We're so far away. How can we possibly help the situation?"

Murray nodded and cleared his throat. "I know so many Jews and so many Israelis. They are all good people. But what they are doing to our Palestinian brothers and sisters is terrible. American communities have to help our Israeli friends see that what they are doing is wrong. We have been their enablers. We have to stop. The only way I see to get Israelis to stop is to peacefully boycott Israel, as we did with South Africa."

An uncomfortable blanket of silence coated the room. Finally, one of Anderson's colleagues asked, "Wouldn't that make things worse? Wouldn't it be better if we used business to bring people together? Help Israeli businesses work with Palestinians?"

In that moment, Murray realized he had come a long way. Back when he thought that all Palestinians were evil terrorists, he used to hear leftist Jews at the temple argue that Jews should be encouraging more business interactions with Palestinians. He had thought those liberal Jews had been naïve and a danger to the Jewish people, that whatever resources Palestinians had would be used to kill Jews. Now, he found himself on the other side, even further to their left, arguing against those business ventures for an entirely different reason.

"I spoke to many Palestinian businesspeople. They told me that such business ventures just further entrench Israel's occupation and bring Palestinian families no closer to full equality. It would be," Murray paused, realizing how much his perspective had changed, "like supporting some business among Blacks in South Africa during apartheid. Sure, it would, obviously, make a few people's lives better, but it wouldn't solve the problem. It would build up a privileged few, not solve apartheid. It would make apartheid last longer."

A young woman spoke up. "Thank you so much for being here, Mr. Schwartzman. We need to foster peace and justice, and your words are so moving. It seems to me our government has given up on supporting the two-state solution. Is there something we can do to address that?"

Murray thought, but didn't say out loud, that what this young woman was asking for sounded fine on the surface but was no different than Afrikaners wanting peace between a white South Africa and Black Bantustans. He gathered himself and said, "Israel controls everything in the country from the Jordan River to the Mediterranean Sea. It is one country split in two by apartheid. The solution is to treat everyone as equal. One state, two states, that doesn't matter."

"But if you don't have two states, then there won't be an Israel," she said, sounding slightly panicked. "If, if, uh, if it were one state, that would mean the end of Israel. There wouldn't be a Jewish state. There has to be a Jewish state. There has to be a land for the Jewish people," she said.

Murray shrugged. He had come so far in his thinking that he had no desire to have an intense argument with this woman. He had presented his side. But she couldn't let it go.

"Shouldn't we support a real peace between a Jewish State of Israel and an Arab state of Palestine?" she asked.

Many in the audience nodded their approval.

This young woman and other young people like her were the future. How idealistic she was. And yet also morally blind when it came to Israel, supporting a Jewish state the way the white nationalists supported a white state.

He tried to respond gently. "We have to have a *morally* Jewish state," Murray said. "If there's one thing that Judaism has taught me, one thing that the Holocaust has taught me, it is that we have to treat everyone as equals. Separation and segregation were wrong here in the South. Today, the idea of institutional segregation of Blacks and whites, separate water fountains and bathrooms, and separate business districts and neighborhoods is anathema to us. The idea that we have to separate ourselves from our non-Jewish brothers and sisters is... please don't take this as an offense against you... absolutely abhorrent to me. I'm sure you, too, would find it horrifying to hear someone say, 'We need to have a white state. We need to separate ourselves from Blacks.' Saying we have to separate Jews from our non-Jewish brothers and sisters just doesn't resonate with me anymore, certainly not by making and keeping Palestinian families refugees, separated from their homes."

Murray paused to gather his thoughts again.

"Israel is a state run by Jews for Jews in a land where non-Jewish people were the majority; that isn't a *Jewish* state, not in any moral sense. A democracy that guarantees Jewish control is not a democracy. We all want Israel to be a democracy, but it isn't. Not now. But it can be."

Murray, who had always cringed when anyone suggested that Israel's behavior was like the Nazis, thought for the first time but didn't say aloud that the idea of creating a state run by and for Jewish people at the expense of non-Jewish people was about as kosher as Aryans trying to create a state for Aryans in Germany by getting rid of anyone they saw as non-Aryan people.

An older woman, clearly upset by everything Murray said, leaped from her seat. "I don't know about the rest of you, but I've heard enough of this drivel. The Palestinians are full of evil and hate," she spewed. "They kill Jews for fun, and they want to destroy Israel. You single out Israel for condemnation when other countries are so much worse. You are an anti-Semite! Israel does what it does only to protect itself. You should be ashamed of yourself, Mr. Schwartzman. Rebbetzin Rebecca told us you've lost it, that you've become a traitor to your people. She couldn't be more correct."

"Sister," Murray began, but the woman interrupted him.

"I am not a sister to you. Have a nice life," she said as she stormed out.

The group was quiet. The words that had been spoken were probably similar to what others had been thinking, but to say it to Murray's face, this survivor of the Holocaust, had seemed beyond rude.

Murray let the woman's words sink in. "You are a traitor to your people." That sentence could have come from an Aryan German to another Aryan German who stood in defense of Jews, or by a white North Carolinian to another white North Carolinian who stood in defense of Blacks here in Winston-Salem only a generation ago. Had the others heard the words the way he had? "I understand where she's coming from," Murray said, shrugging. "I would have said those same things not so long ago. But I have seen the truth, and I have come to realize that when we speak out for justice and equality for all people— for Palestinians and for Israelis—we are being Jewish. We are standing for the principles of our religion. Let us not single Israel out as the one and only one country that we will allow to do bad things.

"You Christians, if you feel guilty about the Holocaust, don't let us Jews mistreat Palestinians. Speak out against all injustice! That is the lesson of the Holocaust. Let's not forget. Never again. Not 'Never again should Jews be mistreated.' No. Never again should *anyone* be mistreated, certainly not by us Jews. We should know better. We Jews know suffering and injustice."

He felt only sadness, not anger, at the woman who had left. He felt passion taking anger's place. He felt fresh, alive, and free. He felt this passion for peace and justice out of love, not out of anger or hatred. He harbored no hatred of her, or for anyone.

He could see now that his old passion was dark, born out of a misguided hatred of certain other groups like the Palestinians. He recognized the same darkness in Rabbi Matt. A blindness of sorts. Tunnel vision. Matt felt a passion for peace in the Holy Land. Matt was a man infused with love for everyone. But he meant everyone except for Arabs. He could see it in Rabbi Matt's dear wife Rebecca, lovely Rebecca, sweet, caring Rebecca, who exuded warmth and love for her children, who gave from every pore of her soul to everyone in their community, yet who, on more than one occasion, had referred to Palestinians as cockroaches and their children as "little snakes," eerily similar to the way some had referred to the Obamas as apes and monkeys.

Was Murray now thinking like a Christian, he wondered, loving everyone as Jesus would, but as too few so-called Christians did? Was this what Judaism was really about, what Rabbi Hillel said, to truly love your neighbor?

People began leaving in ones and twos. Several stopped to ask if he would be willing to speak to their church groups. One of the last to leave was Pastor Johnston. Murray had not noticed him in the crowd.

"Mr. Schwartzman," Pastor Johnston said, "you know I am good friends with Rabbi Matt. But I can see you are right. My greatest regret growing up here in the South is that I saw the mistreatment of Blacks and did nothing. I was raised in a segregated environment, which was all I knew. But I still knew, somehow, that it was wrong. My religious beliefs won't let me stand by and do nothing again. I once gave a sermon about how we must step in when we see one of our friends, big and strong, harassing someone weaker. You've helped me clearly see the need to do that now. Thank you."

Murray felt a chill run up his spine, half gratitude, half awe that his words were making a difference. It was a sensation that became common in the ensuing days, as Pastor Johnston and several other pastors reached out, asking him to speak at their church men's groups and social action committees. Murray agreed to every request. When a church put out the message that Murray was going to speak, calls came from temple members urging the pastor to cancel the "anti-Israel," "anti-Semitic," and "unbalanced" presentation.

No pastor did.

The pro-Israel supporters tried arguing that Schwartzman's presentations would impede dialogue and make Jewish people uncomfortable or threatened. But even Pastor Johnston, who had a strong personal connection to Rabbi Matt and whose congregation had such close ties to Temple Shalom, held steadfast in giving Murray a podium to speak. Even though, Murray suspected, Rabbi Matt had urged him to cancel. They held such awe and respect for Murray that they did not succumb to the pressure to censor him.

22

The Tide Is Turning

Murray Schwartzman

Since Rabbi Matt was no longer an option for advice, Murray turned to Pastor Johnston, whom he discovered to be a reliable source of comfort and guidance. Their sporadic phone calls evolved into weekly debriefing sessions.

"Ah, Gerald, how are you today," Murray said on one such occasion.

"Not as busy as you've been lately, Murray

Murray laughed, something he found himself doing more these days. "That is quite accurate, Pastor. Before all of this happened, I had never stepped foot inside a church, never wanted to, and never needed to. Now, I almost feel like an expert on the various denominations. It's been quite an unexpected education."

"I can only imagine," the pastor said. "I'm encouraged by the groundswell of support from so many houses of worship." Murray turned off the TV to better focus on the call. "I've been so pleased by the positive reactions, Gerald. I've even reached out to a wide range of Christian denominations on my own. Can you imagine?"

The pastor chuckled. "You've certainly changed, my friend. I'm sure most churches would be eager to have you attend. With their peace-seeking orientation, I bet Quaker groups would be most inviting."

"I haven't had time to focus on Quakers; they seem to already understand anyway. Visiting other churches has been such a blessing. The people have been so warm and welcoming that it makes me look forward to the next event. While not every Christian I've met agrees with me, at least not yet, everyone seemed passionate in their desire for peace and justice. It's motivating. I'd never imagined my life would have such purpose at the stage."

"Murray, that's God's work in all its glory. Everything you've been through has led to this moment. Your words are so impactful because of your past. Have you had any luck with Jewish synagogues?"

Murray had difficulty speaking.

"Murray? Are you still there?"

He felt that now-familiar chill spilling down his spine. "Yes, Pastor Johnston, I'm here. Just needed a minute. I haven't had much luck with Jewish temples and synagogues since they seem to insist on inviting other panel members to speak on the topic 'for balance.' The problem is that there's rarely a non-Jewish Palestinian voice included at the synagogues, just speakers who hold misconceptions of Palestinians, who haven't had any firsthand experience getting to know Palestinian people as I have."

"That's a shame. But things are headed in the right direction. Are you speaking to any other groups?"

"Indeed! Young Jewish people have been receptive; God, I love talking with them! I've been invited to national events hosted by Jewish Voice for Peace, and I loved the Open Hillel events."

"Murray Schwartzman, I'm so pleased with how you're handling everything. Watching you grow into such an influential community member for all faiths has been a joy."

"Thank you, Gerald. I appreciate that, especially coming from you. I guess you can teach an old dog some new tricks. Talk soon, my friend."

Maybe Pastor Johnston was right. Everything had fallen into place so effortlessly that it felt predestined. And it wasn't just local. Murray heard that Israeli national papers were writing stories about the Jewish Holocaust survivor in America who was speaking out on behalf of Palestinians. Depending on the bent of the paper, he was described as either a leftist (which he found ironic) or a traitor. American national media didn't seem to take notice at all.

The phone rang again. "Pastor Johnston, you just can't get enough of me, can you?" Murray said with a belly laugh.

"Is this Mr. Schwartzman?"

"Oh, yes, I'm sorry. I thought you were someone else."

"No worries, sir. I'm calling from U.S. Representative Georgia Jones's office. Ms. Jones heard from many constituents who have attended your presentations. They have clearly followed your advice to speak to their Congressional representatives in support of peace and justice for all the people of the Holy Land. As you know, no one is a bigger supporter of Israel in Congress than Representative Georgia Jones, and she would like to meet with you to discuss a matter of some importance."

"With me?" Murray asked.

He immediately felt anxious. He thought back to his brief meeting with her and Rabbi Matt. When his friends at Jewish Voice for Peace learned that Murray was from Winston-Salem, they asked, "Isn't Winston-Salem in Georgia Jones' Congressional district?" About the best thing that folks in Jewish Voice for Peace had to say about her was that she was an "evil, hateful bitch." As chair of a House Commerce Committee, she blocked all efforts to support worker rights and facilitated new laws to weaken unions. She was pro-NRA. She was against everything that the Jewish Voice for Peace stood for.

Perhaps Rabbi Matt and other temple members enlisted her to stop me from speaking, Murray thought. But he understood that it often takes many people to effect change. People like him and the congresswoman. Just because their ideologies didn't align didn't mean they couldn't help each other. If the result was the same, it would be worth it.

"I'd be happy to meet with the representative," Murray said. Yet his voice held no enthusiasm.

A few weeks later, he was greeted by the congresswoman's well-dressed staffer, who introduced himself as Jules Brown. He offered Murray a seat next to a table full of North Carolina snack products, including peanuts, Moravian cookies, and bottled water. Georgia Jones appeared just a moment later.

She greeted Murray enthusiastically and took him to her office. He wondered if she knew how far his stance had changed since his first visit with her. He couldn't imagine she would welcome him with such excitement if she did.

"Thank you so much for coming in today, Mr. Schwartzman," she said. "I need your help."

That got Murray's attention. But he still said nothing, curious to see where this conversation would lead.

She described her most recent trip to Israel, funded by the Israeli government. It was a lot like her previous trips to Israel, though she marveled at all the development that had occurred since her last visit.

"I was amazed by the technological discoveries being made at Technion, the development of new molecular biology-based pharmaceuticals. Have you been there recently?"

Murray nodded with pride.

"Whenever I go there, I am amazed by how God has given that land to the Jewish people. Their accomplishments in such an arid wasteland are astounding. I tried to arrange business collaborations with the people here in Winston-Salem. I think we could really benefit each other."

Was this it? Was this the reason she had asked him to come to her office? To facilitate business? After all that he had learned, he didn't think he wanted to help with that, not if it was simply going to strengthen the existing systems of segregation.

"This latest trip to Israel was a bit different from the others. One of my staffers who attended Guilford College got to know several Palestinians also studying there."

Ms. Jones stopped for a moment. Murray smiled at how she pronounced "Palestinian" with her southern accent.

"This staffer took a class on the history of the Holy Land and learned about the expulsions and massacres that Jewish-Israeli historians had documented. When he arranged the trip, he had added Palestinian-held areas to our itinerary. I thought that was crazy at first, perhaps some kind of mistake. But he said I would get to go to Bethlehem, and I was excited to see where Jesus was born! How could I pass that up?

"I have to admit, I was afraid," she said. "But I felt better after I met our Palestinian hosts. They were so warm and kind. They weren't what I was expecting. We went through all of these checkpoints."

She paused and shook her head. Murray could see this last trip had affected her greatly.

"On our way to the Church of the Nativity, we saw the security wall around Bethlehem that cut into Palestinian-held territories. I decided to ask some people while there how things were. The main problem at the moment seems to be the lack of water. I met people who suffered from water shortages, but in the distance, I could see the blue water of Israeli settlement swimming pools."

She adjusted some things on her desk, then looked up at Murray.

"None of this changed my view of Israel, you understand. Shortages exist everywhere, including in our country. I still believed, at that point, that everything Israel was doing was for peace and that Palestinians would have a better life if they would just give up their hate. If they put down their weapons, they could fill up their water containers."

Murray nearly replied, but he didn't want to send her off track.

"The guide asked if I wanted to see a Palestinian school. I guess he'd heard that I had been a teacher long ago. He handed me a picture of a small but functional schoolhouse built with funds from the European Union. He said it wasn't far. I told him I'd love to go see it. We drove a short distance and stopped by a pile of debris. I remarked how emblematic it was of Palestinians' failure to keep house.

"My guide said nothing, and I asked him if the school was within walking distance. 'This is the school,' he said. 'It *was* lovely. It was a clean and safe place where our children could learn. The walls of the school were decorated with the children's art. But the Israelis destroyed it. The debris you see around us is all that is left.' My guide shrugged as if it were a normal occurrence. So I asked him if it was, and he said, 'Of course it is.'"

Murray nodded. "I saw many places like that during my trip."

"I got out and briefly picked through the debris. I found a child's drawing. It was tattered, but I could make out the image of a sweet little blue bird," she said, her voice breaking. "Then I noticed mothers had gathered nearby, holding their children's hands, and one of them came up to me and spoke very quickly. I couldn't understand a word she said, but her tone was emphatic. Somehow, I still knew what this mother was saying. Her children wanted to go to school; her children *needed* to go to school. Education was the only way forward, and Israel was denying even that to their children.

"That's when my view was transformed. How is destroying a children's school helpful for peace and security? I realized, in that moment, standing there with those mothers, that I was supporting apartheid."

That was the word he'd thought of the first time he saw Palestine buildings in ruins.

"Mr. Schwartzman, I want to help you," Ms. Jones said. "I've read about your efforts to change Americans' perspective on what's happening in Israel. I *need* to help you. Would you consider testifying at a committee hearing I am running?"

She explained to Murray that Congress was considering a law that would make it illegal for Americans to boycott Israel. Even though Jones loved the idea of supporting business development between her district and Israel, after what she had seen, she realized that passing a law that would restrict people from peaceful actions in support of Palestinian families was a bad idea. The bill would come through her House Commerce Committee, and she wanted Murray's help to derail it. She wanted to use this bill to help people see what she had seen. She wanted Murray's voice to gain national attention.

"You're the person to champion this cause. You're Jewish. You're a survivor. You have nothing to gain financially or politically. And I want to help you do it."

He tried to shake the sense of shock from his system.

"Will you speak at my committee?" she asked again.

"Of course," he said, feeling his emotions rise.

"My apologies, I have another meeting I need to get to," she said.

She came around the desk, and Murray hugged her, knowing she'd had the same change of heart he had experienced on his own trip. He hadn't hugged a stranger in a long time, not even his tree-hugging Jewish Voice for Peace friends. Going into this meeting, he certainly had not expected he would end the meeting by hugging Georgia Jones.

"My staffer will make arrangements for your committee appearance," she said, leaving him with Jules.

"You know," Murray said to Jules, "my Jewish Voice for Peace friends are not fans of Representative Jones. I hope they get to know her like I just did."

Jules smiled. "Despite the impression of many people on the left, Ms. Jones is a fair, caring person who takes her responsibility to her constituents seriously. I'm not a token Black in this office; Representative Jones respects hard workers, regardless of their skin color. She deeply loves all children, even those that haven't been born yet. She's against certain gun control laws because she wants better laws that will protect children from getting shot. She blocked recent minimum wage legislation because she feared it would result in job loss for people at the bottom of the pay scale."

"Yes, but what about her homophobia?" Murray asked.

Jules smiled again.

"Representative Jones knows that I'm gay. She isn't homophobic. She just believes that marriage is between a man and a woman. I think she would support equal treatment of gay couples as long as the word 'marriage' isn't used. Now, I think it would be better for me to be able to marry and have my marriage treated like any other, but I also understand that it's hard for people to change how they see the world. When you are brought up seeing the world one way, it's hard to see it any other way. Plus, I'm only one constituent she represents. Her loyalty to the North Carolina voters doesn't make her a bad person. It means she listens to them and represents them."

Murray felt a strong respect for Jones and her staffer, Jules Brown. He wished Rabbi Matt could meet Jules. But he doubted he ever would.

23

Change Happens Slow, Then Fast

Murray Schwartzman

Murray looked at the calendar on his refrigerator and realized it had been a year since his revelatory trip to Palestine. He also saw that Yom Ha'atzmaut, the Israeli Independence Day, was coming up next month. He'd heard that Rabbi Matt, Rebecca, and many temple families were preparing for the celebration. However, Murray had a separate, burgeoning life of his own. Today, he was meeting with Dr. Friedman, Jeremy, and Katie to talk about a social engagement the old Murray would have rebuffed.

The taxi dropped Murray off at a charming bistro on Main Street in the city's historic downtown district. He immediately saw Katie's hand waving in the air.

"Mr. Schwartzman," she said as he approached the table, "it's so good to see you in person and not just on TV."

Jeremy laughed as Murray turned his attention to Joseph. "Ah, Dr. Friedman, it's been too long. So nice to see you."

"And you as well, Murray. I agree with Katie. We see you in the media more than we do in person. We need to fix that."

"I couldn't agree more."

"And thank you for fitting us into your schedule," Jeremy interjected.

"Murray, I realize we are making light of things, but you've impressed all of us with your unwavering commitment. It's inspiring to watch," Dr. Friedman said. "I was pleasantly surprised when you testified before the U.S. Congress. If Representative Jones had invited you months earlier, she probably would have suffered heavy backlash, but the landscape had changed so much."

"It really has," Jeremy agreed. "Jewish youth groups at colleges and high schools all across the country have started to ask whether unquestioned support for Israel was a good idea. Students for Justice in Palestine groups, with Jewish kids frequently joining, are proliferating at universities across North America."

"Well, they have you as much as me to thank for it. You got me to look at the world from an entirely different perspective. But for this groundswell to last, younger generations have to embrace peace and justice for all people," Murray said.

"I've heard of churches across the country hosting Palestinian refugees and encouraging them to share firsthand accounts of their experiences," Friedman added. "All denominations. That should educate all ages."

'The church I attend hasn't gone that far," Katie said, "but some of our members are beginning to question how Palestinian families are being treated."

"I was moved when the Pope wept openly with the families of Palestinian children, Christian and Muslim, who had been killed by Israel," Friedman added.

"It hasn't all been good news," Murray said. "Awareness often followed tragedy. Rachel Corrie, a beautiful young woman from Olympia, Washington, devoted to peace and justice, was killed and buried alive by an Israeli bulldozer as she tried to protect a Palestinian family's home from destruction. But her death moved another American, Anna

Baltzer, a Jewish woman who first appeared with Jon Stewart on *The Daily Show* and then as a pundit on several news programs, to describe her own personal experiences in Palestine and the oppression she had witnessed. But these sad stories were creating awareness now that they were getting airtime. One of the regular Fox News pundits, a Jewish one, spoke about his observations of Palestinian families' terrible conditions under Israeli occupation. It was starting to be a subject creating some buzz in Congress.

"Every day, the newspaper revealed some new, high-profile individual who was publicizing their support for Palestine and peace in the Middle East. The changes in media that continued to contribute to this astonished him, even taking the 'radical' step of having actual Palestinians on air to present Palestinian perspectives. An array of newspapers began carrying the editorials of Israeli writer Gideon Levy. 'The killing of Palestinians is accepted in Israel more lightly than the killing of mosquitoes,' he'd written."

Dr. Friedman placed a hand on Murray's shoulder. "Thanks to you, while opinion toward Israel is still generally positive, the foundation of that opinion is eroding. It will be interesting to see what happens in the planned Land Day protests."

Jeremy asked, "Land Day?"

"Yes," Dr. Friedman said, "It's a Palestinian holiday commemorating the lives of six Palestinians who were killed and the hundred wounded when peacefully protesting to stop Israel from further expropriating their land. This year's Land Day march is planned for next week. It could be violent."

"I hope not," Murray said. "I plan to be there."

Friedman, Jeremy, and Katie looked at Murray with a momentary sense of incredulity. Friedman then said, "Of course you do.

"I'm coming with you," Katie said.

***

The marches began with a thousand men, women, and children honoring Land Day and would continue intermittently for two months. Worried about Murray's wellbeing, Katie wouldn't leave his side. The

Israeli Defense Force was well-prepared to stop the marches—they had orders to fire on protesters if they even approached the border.

"Jeremy!" Katie exclaimed in a quick phone call home. "It's horrible! The marchers approached the separation fence. Many of them recorded the event on their cell phones, broadcasting it on social media. Israeli soldiers are firing on the marchers. I'm sending you my own footage. Reports say they've killed three and wounded twenty already. None of the Palestinians have weapons. I haven't even seen a pebble. I saw Palestinians being shot in the back as they ran away from the fence."

"I'm uploading it to Instagram right now," Jeremy told her. "And Katie?"

"Yes?"

"Please stay safe and come back to me."

Katie wasn't sure Jeremy had seen her smile of reassurance because their connection was cut.

Later that day, she watched her footage. It was going viral. Katie wasn't the only one moved; the whole world wept when they saw the carnage.

"CNN is reporting that in the U.S. Congress, Representatives Omar and Lewis gave speeches supporting the non-violent marchers and decrying Israeli violence, hearkening back to the days of the Civil Rights movement in the United States," Jeremy texted her the next day.

"In the 1960s, John Lewis was there on the bridge in Selma, walking with Martin Luther King," Friedman said when Jeremy spoke to him.

"I remember Rabbi Matt teaching us that we Jews were there with them, literally and figuratively," Jeremy replied. Then he paused, as if trying to get a grip on his emotions. "I hope they're both okay."

"They're as safe as they can be since they're with Representative Jones and several North Carolina Christian pastors. But you should be so proud of them. I know I am," Friedman said.

***

The next day, Murray called Friedman from Gaza City to update the doctor and to ask him to reassure Jeremy that they were both okay.

"Jones was adamant that we join the marches instead of sitting idly on the sidelines. Of course, I knew she was right, and I was excited for the experience. My only trepidation was the travel. I'm not a young man anymore." Murray laughed before his face grew somber.

"The travel turned out to be the least of my worries. Once there, it was amazing to see such support, but the danger was still very real. By sheer happenstance, Katie and I met two brave Palestinian women and found their unwavering commitment encouraging. The one with a white lab coat was probably in her mid-twenties. Her name was Maryam, and she was some type of medic or technician. I'm not sure if it was her occupation or an interest that grew out of necessity, but she seemed well-versed in first aid, particularly in trauma situations. When I told them that I was looking forward to a peaceful and productive event, Maryam surprised me."

Friedman seemed to be absorbing every detail of the story.

"Then there was Mila, her younger sister, who was not as talkative, but seemed just as committed to the cause. 'I'm glad to have someone well-versed in medicine,' I told Maryam, 'because I'm not a young man.' She nodded but didn't smile. She said, 'Mr. Schwartzman, I insisted to my sister that she could only attend if I accompanied her. Unfortunately, I fear violence.'"

Murray paused for a moment.

"That took me by surprise because everything I'd heard, all of the talk leading up to the march, stressed a powerful but peaceful protest. So, I shared that with her, that we'd anticipated nothing but peace. 'I hope you are right,' she said, 'but I fear violence from the Israeli side.'"

24

Look for the Helpers

Katie Summers

The call of the muezzin woke Katie early. She looked out of her window. A slip of sun was just showing itself above the horizon.

The crowds were getting larger and more vocal. Maryam's words yesterday had caused her to toss and turn all night. "Stay away from the outliers," Maryam had warned. "Look for the helpers."

Katie had promised Jeremy she'd get back to him all in one piece. Plus, she had to make sure Murray came back that way, too.

The call from the minaret calmed her, and she closed her eyes. "God," she said, "please keep us all safe today. We are just trying to save lives. And I know you love us all. You want us to be safe. You want us at peace. Thanks, God. Amen."

It all began pretty much the same as the day before, only bigger.

"They say we've got 30,000 strong marching today," Murray told her as they joined the throngs of people, banners, and calls for peace. Only today, few children marched. Katie looked wide out over the crowd, searching for a single youngster, but could see none.

"Do you notice? No kids here today?" she asked Murray.

"They're absolutely right to protect them," he told her. "Children needn't be out in a protest."

Katie noticed Murray was limping. "Where's your cane?" she asked.

"Don't need it. I'm a new man." His eyes twinkled at her. "See?" He pinched his forearm. "New purpose. New cells."

She laughed. "Whatever gets you going." Still, she watched him out of the corner of her eye. She feared he might have strained a tendon, or worse, that he was developing a blood clot. They went on that way for what seemed like a couple of miles.

The fighting began when they got to the Gaza border. What had once been a peaceful, if vocal crowd now rippled with screams. People began to run toward them, like a huge human boomerang, the lines rippling against themselves. Katie's eyes began to sting. That's when she saw it.

Hidden behind riot gear and barricade posting, Israeli soldiers pummeled them with tear gas. Smoke filled the air now, sinking into every crevice. Katie took a deep breath and pulled the bandana over her nose and mouth. She looked over at Murray. He looked pale. She fished another handkerchief out of her pack for him. When she looked up, the smoke had created a fog that nearly obscured everything. She was frantic.

"Murray!" she shouted. "Murray!

She found him. He had fallen to the curb and was clutching his chest. "Don't mind me," he gasped. "I'm okay. Been through worse."

"Nonsense," she said. "We need to get you to safety. But first, here, put this visor on, shut your eyes, and follow me. There's a cafe over there that looks open."

When they got inside, she poured her bottled water over his head, then hers. It still stung, but at least she could see better. "Can you see, Uncle Murray?" she asked.

He patted her on the arm. "I'll be fine, fine." But he didn't look fine. He looked frightened, as frightened as she was. His eyes teared up. "These are real tears, not from the toxins," he told her. "Maryam's prediction came true."

"Let's return."

"I wouldn't go out there," the café owner warned them. "Looks like it's getting worse."

Shots rang out just beyond the doorway. Everyone but Murray and Katie fell to the floor. The cafe owner pulled them down. Murray groaned as he hit the tile floor.

Sirens sounded next, and an ambulance with a big red crescent zoomed past. A couple of protesters carried a motionless body inside. "They shot a medic," they cried.

"I'm a doctor," Katie told them. "Let me help." She pulled the mask off what had been a beautiful young woman minutes before, ready to assess if she needed to perform CPR. She only had to look at the face to see it was useless. Part of the face was gone, and the other half—

"Oh no! It's Maryam!" she cried. "It's Maryam!"

Murray crawled over. He looked on in horror, weeping in earnest now. "It's Mila," he said, closing her eyes.

Lifeless. "No, no, it's Maryam. She has her crescent pin on her lapel."

Somehow, Maryam, who'd come to help Mila, had been shot.

Mila appeared at the door now, screaming Maryam's name. "No! No! No!" she cried when she saw the covered body with blood seeping beneath it to the floor. "She was trying to help a wounded man. Why would they shoot a medic?"

Mila was understandably hysterical. "How can I help you, Mila?" Katie asked.

Just then, military planes roared overhead, and everyone ducked again. A loud explosion sounded, and Katie's ears began to ring.

Murray was muttering something about shadows. "They are coming for us!" he cried. "They're coming to finish the job."

An American representative entered the building. "How did this happen?" he asked them. "How did I lose you? You were both right beside me."

"We lost Maryam," Katie said in response. "That's just as important. We've lost her forever."

***

"All I could see was the dirt before me as the chaos swirled around. Scores of people ran by, and I closed my eyes tightly and opened them, hoping it was all a horrible nightmare. Just then, I felt a tug on my arms as two men lifted me up, brushed me off, and pulled me to the curb so I wouldn't be trampled," Murray told Joseph and Jeremy as they leaned in close over the computer screen.

"That's when I found him." Katie's voice still sounded triggered. She had been terrified Murray had suffered a stroke, but after she had evaluated him, it was just a sprained ankle.

"And wouldn't you know, I sprained the same ankle as my bad leg," Murray chuckled. He seemed to have recovered.

"You scared me, Uncle Murray," Katie said, trying not to sound like she was scolding him. No, just the opposite. She was in awe of this heroic man.

"I tried to locate the sisters but couldn't find them anywhere. They'd been close by us. Maybe Maryam had been gurneyed out of the melee. I couldn't fathom the pain Mila must have felt during the chaos, especially when her sister insisted on coming along as a protector," Murray said. "Later, I met up with Representative Jones, but it was all so horrific and unfair to those women who just wanted to march for peace. Ultimately, Maryam was one of twenty people killed and over a thousand wounded, and in fact, there had been a few children there because they killed one. It was just tragic, Joseph. Just tragic," Murray said.

"I'm sorry, Uncle Murray," Katie said when they signed off the computer.

"For what, Katydid?" Murray asked.

"I didn't protect you."

"But you did, Katie. You did. You got me to safety."

"But not Maryam."

"No, not Maryam. We lost her, just like we lost my mother."

"My prayers didn't work."

"Sometimes they don't." He thought of all the times he'd prayed the Germans would leave their town by the Bzura River alone. And they'd come anyway. "But look at what did happen as a result."

"I guess so." Katie shook her head. "So much death, though. Needless."

"I agree, my dear," Murray said as Katie hugged him. "But we must have hope. That's the gift Maryam gave, the gift my brother gave me. They left us a legacy of hope."

"I'm so sorry. I've walked around numb from grief all day." Joseph replied. "We were so worried you'd gotten caught up in it all. I did see videos of people, including you, Murray, and Representative Jones, in that chaos. I noticed the Israeli media were filled with praise for their valiant Israeli Defense Force, though. They called their response 'restrained," blaming Hamas for provoking it. How could it have killed so many then?" He held up a photo for Katie and Murray to see.

Yet another tragedy occurred, captured in a photo. U.S. Representative Georgia Jones was screaming in despair, splattered in blood, and holding a wounded Palestinian child who had died in her arms. The captions beneath the images of Murray and Representative Jones compared the event with the scenes of violence at the Selma March and the Black Lives Matter movement.

"Just another photo op," Murray said, shaking his head.

"No, Murray," Friedman continued, "You can't think all of this was in vain. Countries in Europe, Latin America, Africa, and Asia have called for an end to the mistreatment of Palestinian families. Finally, people here in America seemed to have lost their will to support what they now recognize as apartheid. The talking heads on television have stopped discussing two-state solutions and, thank God, have focused on equal rights for Palestinians. The former Israeli Ambassador to the United States, the ever-eloquent Michael Oren, tried to stem the sea change in public opinion, but he was met with a tidal wave. Our friend Rami Elhanan is being given far more airtime, emphasizing what Americans have finally grown to appreciate: it is time to end the violence and occupation."

Murray's pessimism boiled up in rebuttal. "I wouldn't get too excited yet."

"It's been world-changing! At the United Nations, I saw that the Israeli ambassador ranted that all the attention on Israel was a manifestation of people's anti-Semitism. No one paid him any attention other than to take offense at the suggestion and at Israel's refusal to take responsibility for its actions.

"In fact, the United Nations passed a resolution declaring Israel's treatment of Palestinians apartheid. The resolution specified that the apartheid wall had to come down. It also called for specific economic sanctions. But countries are already enacting economic sanctions and boycotts. Major airlines aren't flying to Tel Aviv. India and Pakistan announced they won't buy Israeli weapons. Several Latin American countries have canceled their Israeli security contracts. I think Europeans have even stopped buying Israeli avocados. In truth, the Israeli economy is still strong. But with fears of a dip in economic activity, this has enormously affected the Israeli psyche. This is the best hope we've ever had for peace. Peace for Palestinians. Peace for Israelis. Peace for the state of Israel."

"Dr. Friedman," Murray said, "Did you hear that talks were held between the Israeli leadership and Hamas? Israel announced it was prepared to end its blockade of Gaza and, to the shock of Israeli citizens, remove all the Israeli settlements internationally recognized as illegal from beyond the Green Line, the 1948 Israeli borders. That means they'd establish the Green Line as the recognized international border between Israel and what Israel would agree to recognize as the Nation of Palestine."

"I did see that," Dr. Friedman replied. "That caused some pushback from Israelis. I heard they declared that 'The entire Holy Land was given to us by God,' and they were not going to leave willingly."

"As I'd expected," Murray began, "Hamas said no to the 'generous' Israeli offer, instead insisting on equal treatment for all the people of the Holy Land—Jews, Christians, Muslims, whoever—and the return of all refugees to their homes. One truly democratic country from the Mediterranean to the Jordan: one person, one vote. Hamas leadership recognized that the sensibilities of Israelis were forged by the Holocaust and couched its demands in the context of those sensibilities, telling Israelis that two states would not bring justice or peace, much less defensible borders. Without allowing refugee families to return to their homes, there would be no justice and, therefore, there would be no peace. The religious Jews, Hamas said, would be welcomed to stay in Hebron, or anywhere else in the Holy Land for that matter, as long as all refugees were allowed to return to their homes and live together in peace."

"Now, the call for one state seems not only moral, but sensible and inevitable," Dr. Friedman said.

"I'm getting a bit tired. It's time for me to call it a night, Joseph. I have a big day planned for tomorrow, too."

Murray joined in the final day of the Gaza Land Day marches, mere weeks after Representative Jones became an international social media meme. He had to use his cane, but he could tell he might walk without it again soon. Three hundred thousand Palestinians came out, joined by Representative Jones, Murray, and a host of other foreign nationals. Murray was given the honor of standing at the front of the march. They approached the security fence, expecting it to be unassailable and fearing it to be staffed by armed soldiers. But as they got closer, they saw that an entire section of the fence had been somehow miraculously parted just in time for their escape from Gaza bondage, an opening for their return home.

And for the first time, it felt like he'd come home.

Murray looked back at the crowd behind him, smiled as he raised his cane high in the air, and signaled for them to proceed with a sweeping motion. They marched peacefully toward their homes in Israel. It was Independence Day.

25

Making Things Right

Murray Schwartzman

Determined now to walk without a cane, Murray began his mornings with a brisk walk. He'd started slowly, careful not to let exuberance eclipse physical ability. In a few short months, he was traversing streets he'd never noticed and waving at ambitious gardeners and those bound up in robes for a quick dash to retrieve the newspaper.

Returning home, he'd get cleaned up and indulge in a thoughtful breakfast. The new routine caused him to dig out colorful suspenders and leather belts that had long been packed away. It had been years since he'd consciously tended to his own health with such focus. He especially savored the moments when he could leave that cane dangling on a hook by the door, and soon, it was most of the time.

With his morning routine complete, Murray would settle in for a dose of morning news. He was careful to sample them all, even turning in to the BBC's world news for yet another point of view.

According to the news, hundreds of thousands of Palestinian men, women, and children had peacefully marched back into Israel. There was no blood bath, not a single Jew tossed into the sea. Newspapers did report three Israeli deaths, one from a drug overdose and two in a tragic car accident. People soon realized that their worst fears, being overrun by a horde of angry Arabs, were without merit.

Murray smiled as he saw Israeli officials invite Hamas leaders to join them in Jerusalem to make immediate plans for the repatriation of Palestinian families. In truth, several Israeli army and government officials had already been making contingency plans for repatriation. When, for the first time since Independence, Jews were outnumbered by Palestinians living under Israeli rule, even Israeli officials realized that the world would, with considerable justification, eventually judge a minority of Israelis ruling over a majority of Palestinians as a form of apartheid.

The phone rang. "Yes?"

"Mr. Murray Schwartzman, please."

"This is Mr. Schwartzman. How can I help you?"

"I represent the newly established Israel-Palestinian Repatriations Committee," the deep voice said.

Murray's mood lifted. "Yes, I saw something about that initiative on the news."

"Ah, well, then, I suppose I can get right to the point then. You've been selected as a potential committee member, and I'm charged with determining your interest in such an offer."

Murray was speechless for a moment, his mind swirling. "I'm honored."

"There is but one caveat, and it's a requirement for the position, I'm afraid."

"And what is that?"

"It will require your presence in Israel. The committee is intended to be a hands-on, fully immersive vehicle for change. The operating by-laws require those who serve to reside in the immediate area. Is that a possibility, Mr. Schwartzman? You will, of course, be compensated, and we will assist in your relocation."

The old Murray would have hemmed and hawed, turning it over in his mind until he talked himself out of it. The new Murray eagerly accepted. He felt it was a sign of a higher purpose for him and still more for him to accomplish on this Earth. He had a chance to make a lasting impact on the lives of his people. What a marvelous opportunity to help families find the peace and stability that was taken from him so early in life.

Most things in his house went in storage, and a neighbor he'd met on his walks agreed to manage the property as a rental.

This time, Murray didn't allow himself to worry about the 6,000 miles he'd travel. His focus remained on the end goal, and stretches of discomfort were a small price to pay. He kept his cane by his side just in case. Once he landed in Tel Aviv, a driver took him to a temporary rental until he could find his own place.

As soon as he arrived, the committee got to work, putting together a broad outline that both sides considered generally acceptable: a standard package would be offered to each Palestinian refugee family. If their former home had been destroyed, they would be offered a new home in a rebuilt village or cash compensation; if their former home was still standing but was occupied by an Israeli family, the Palestinian family would be offered a new home and cash compensation or their original home; if the Palestinian family wanted the original home, the Israeli family living in it would be given the new home and the cash compensation, or if feasible, additional stories would be built atop the original home so that both families' desires to be in the home could be realized.

The groundwork for the process had already been laid by Badil's plans for Palestinian repatriation. A large majority of Palestinians to be repatriated would be returning to villages that had been destroyed in 1948 and replanted with trees. Rebuilding those villages would not displace Jewish families. Conflicts not easily resolved would be addressed in an arbitration and appeals process.

Having outsider mediators was dismissed as completely untenable. One of the Hamas committee members made the offhand suggestion that members of the Parents' Circle would be the only people that everyone would trust, the only people who commanded enough deference and respect. Therefore, two mediators from that group would handle all arbitration and appeals, one Israeli and one Palestinian. Few cases needed to be appealed. While conflicts over homes were emotionally charged, those feelings felt small compared to what Parents' Circle members had suffered.

Finding financial resources was a non-issue. So much money would be saved by ending the occupation and the resulting disarmament that there would be sufficient resources to repatriate all Palestinian families desiring to return home. The economic boon that was expected with peace would be gravy.

Enlisting the advice of South Africans and Germans who had been through similar unification processes, the Repatriation Committee determined that achieving economic justice would be essential. If people had jobs, there would be peace. The Hamas leadership, which was now fully integrated into the PLO, gave major high-tech Israeli industries assurances that they could continue to function, though they would need to integrate Palestinians into their workforce. Plans were made to put some type of manufacturing facility or other labor-intensive business into each rebuilt Palestinian village. With the integration of Palestinian Arabs throughout Israel-Palestine's government, businesses, and society, relations with neighboring Arab and Muslim countries would dramatically improve, opening many new export markets. Saudis, Kuwaitis, and Iranians would join the Europeans in buying Israeli avocados.

The employer benefiting most from all of this change would likely be the burgeoning tourist industry. With peace, Lydda-Tel Aviv airport was projected to grow to be among the world's largest. Plans for a second, even more modern airport in Gaza were initiated. More tourism meant more jobs. Restaurant work. Transportation work. Construction work. So much had changed in the world. It was astounding.

The evangelical Christian community extended a generous hand of cooperation. Murray, Katie, and Jeremy spent hours discussing plans on their computers. There had been so many Christians who had avoided visiting Israel simply because they were afraid. Now that the area was peaceful, Evangelical Christians flocked to the Holy Land, eager to visit the places where Jesus had walked. They created new partnerships with locals for tours of varying lengths and intensity. And as the Christians spent more time in Israel, they, too, saw firsthand that Palestinians were wonderful people.

During one of the meetings, Murray brought up something to consider.

"This tourism growth will be invigorating," he said, "but I remember my first visit and how important it was to have a guide. I think many well-educated tour guides will be needed. That means not only job training, but also language training."

The committee wholeheartedly agreed. They devised a simple plan that caused an enormous increase in the number of Israelis and Palestinians who spoke both Hebrew and Arabic. Schools providing free language education were opened throughout the country. In addition to Arabic and Hebrew, other special language programs were set up for those in the tourism industry.

There was general agreement that all secular schools would serve people of all religions. Religious schooling would not be discouraged; however, those schools had to ensure that students had extensive, intensive exposure to children of other faiths, and all school curricula had to include the history of both the Holocaust and the Nakba.

It's so important for the children to be a priority, Murray thought. Painful memories darted through his mind whenever the topic arose. Of his family. Of himself and Uncle. Of Miriam's family. Of Maryam's and hers. Was it God's plan for Murray to help ensure that no more children were subjected to the conditions he had to endure?

Murray met with a wealthy Jewish-American couple from Las Vegas, who had previously been funding a Jewish-only settlement in the West Bank. They agreed to provide funding for a model program to reward children for coming up with new ideas to reduce barriers between Muslim, Jewish, and Christian children and to fund the implementation of the best of those ideas. In addition, integrated sports leagues and arts programs for boys and girls would be expanded. Religiously segregated teams were not permitted.

Murray's life felt full. He found living in the Holy Land suited him, too. It hadn't taken long for Murray to find suitable accommodations, a Jerusalem apartment with a central location so he could walk everywhere.

Returning from one of his walks, he saw some familiar faces waiting for him.

"Jeremy? And Katie!" Murray said to the young couple.

"Mr. Schwartzman! So glad to see you. Katie and I have been dying to see you."

"Oh, Mr. Schwartzman, seeing someone from home is so exciting! We've been following your work here, and it's most impressive. We are thoroughly enjoying our visit!"

The three chatted, and Murray discovered they were quickly assimilating to life in the Holy Land. Jeremy, having had experience with the temple's Habitat for Humanity efforts, had joined one of the Israeli and Palestinian teenager groups that specialized in construction, building new homes. Katie had just joined the staff of a new infertility clinic in Ramallah. "I'm going to see to it that it becomes the center for reproductive health for the whole country," she confided.

"There have been so many positive changes that it's almost too much to keep track of," Murray told the couple. "For example, teenage Israelis, male and female, had been required to perform compulsory military service. Now, the Army is being integrated, and the bulk of its service has shifted from upholding the occupation to building the country's infrastructure. Most 'soldiers' are assigned to integrated Peace Corps units that focus on bringing basic infrastructure—water, electricity, roads—to Gaza and underserved West Bank communities and the Palestinian villages within the Green Line."

Murray smiled with pride as he continued.

"The Repatriation Committee also addressed elections for a new government. Initially, we proposed that Palestinian refugees of voting age would be allowed to cast two votes in parliamentary elections for the next ten years because they had been disenfranchised for so long. But in the end, all agreed that it would be one person, one vote. To ensure fair elections, voter ID will be required, and a system was put into place to assure that all eligible voters have appropriate photo IDs."

"It's wonderful to see you so involved and, I don't know, influential, I guess," Katie said. "Not that I expected anything else. But what about those who have committed acts of violence? How are they being handled?"

"That's a good question," Murray responded. "Frankly, it was a key sticking point. According to the Israeli peace group B'tselem's statistics that the committee reviewed, Israel had killed 10 to 100 times as many Palestinians as Palestinians had killed Israelis, and that included women and children. It was quickly agreed that those guilty of past violence, whether Israeli or Palestinian, would be treated similarly. Then, it was easy for all to see that they had to forgive, though not forget. Israelis would have loved for Palestinian *terrorists*," Murray said, using air quotes, "to be punished, but not at the cost of punishing Israeli pilots. Many Palestinians would love to see their Israeli torturers suffer, but not if it meant that even one more Palestinian *shuhada* would be imprisoned."

"To keep Palestinians who had committed a violent act from being imprisoned, they were willing to forego punishing the Israelis who had mistreated them so terribly for so many years, even the Israeli pilots who had dropped bombs on apartment buildings. Instead, a truth commission was put in place, led by two members of the Parents' Circle, and a thorough documentation of all that had been done by both sides was made available publicly. Israelis, who had been so enraged about Palestinian terrorists with blood on their hands, finally realized that the IDF had spilled far more blood and were grateful that Palestinians were so willing and able to forgive."

"It's just so much to take in," Jeremy said with a shake of his head. "How do you keep track of everything at your—uh, I mean—"

"And where's your cane?" Katie asked with glee. "Come on, Jeremy, he can run circles around us both."

Murray held up his hand. "I understand, Jeremy. I'm not a young man. There was a time when I didn't even know how to find my way around the Internet, if you recall." They both smiled. "But this work has somehow recharged me. It's given me a noble purpose I'd never dreamed of. For me, it's simple because I just think about how I'd want to be treated and how I wish Jews had always been treated, and then I work with the committee to make it happen.

"Here's what you won't believe. The only problem we encountered was that some Jews had issues with the early morning Muslim call to prayer, particularly at those times of the year when the call would drone on for well over an hour. An enterprising Israeli technology company found an engineering solution to the problem, developing and marketing muezzin-call canceling earphones that proved popular. They'd expected Jews to be their main customers, but the device was even more popular among Muslim families in Israel-Palestine and other predominately Muslim countries."

"Well, I'll be," Jeremy said. "All that ingenuity freed up to pursue innovation and peace."

"Katie, let me tell you something else I learned from one of my Palestinian friends," Murray said. "In the Jalazone Refugee Camp in the occupied territories, one of the first places I visited in Palestine, there was an Israeli Defense Force colonel, Ezra Barzilai, who had been in charge of keeping the territory around the camp under control. When the occupation ended, he sent a message to the camp's director, Khalid Zaid, asking Zaid to meet the colonel in Zaid's office. On my first trip to Palestine, I visited that camp myself, that very office. Zaid was asked to bring his children, too. Zaid felt uneasy. What did the colonel intend to do, he wondered? One of Zaid's children had already been killed during the occupation. Zaid worried the fall of the occupation had left the colonel angry. Still, Zaid complied.

"The colonel entered Zaid's office with his 11-year-old Zalman son at his side. Zaid rose nervously from his desk, his two boys standing behind him, the picture of his beloved dead son on the wall looking down on them."

"What happened next?" Katie asked inquisitively.

"The colonel approached Zaid and laid his weapons on Zaid's desk.

'The occupation is over,' the colonel said. 'What we did was horribly wrong. I'm sorry. I hope you can forgive me. We will do everything we can to make things right. And I know there's no way to completely undo what we did.'"

"Zaid looked at Barzilai, picked up the pistol, looked at it for a moment, and set it back down. Then he walked around his desk, hugged Barzilai, and began to cry. Zaid's children, who had watched their father be humiliated by Israeli soldiers in the past, could see how their father's strength and commitment to peace had overcome their enemy. They could not have been prouder. I couldn't be prouder."

"Wow, Uncle Murray," Katie said.

"Forty years in the desert. 60 years as refugees. From the passion of hatred to the passion of love," Murray said.

Jeremy squeezed Katie's hand. "It's changed so much. It's a miracle."

"And we were here to watch it happen," Murray said. "Let's get together again soon. Come over for dinner sometime. I know a little place."

Katie gave him a knowing look. "The café on the West Bank?"

"You know of it?" Murray gave her a sly wink. He couldn't wait to show her what they'd done with the place.

26

Miraculous But Inevitable

One story can change things. What became known as "Maryam's Story" did just that. But one story doesn't always change everything.

It was Passover Season once more. Five years had passed. Back in Winston-Salem, Rabbi Matt swung past Temple Shalom with its message. The remaining temple youth had used spray paint to change the sign to read "We Stand with Israeli and Palestinian Families" from "We Stand with Israel." The congregation had been held together by pride in their social justice accomplishments in their community, by Rabbi Matt's charisma, and by Rebecca's indefatigable planning, organizing, and encouragement. When Israel suddenly ended the occupation, tensions within the community flared. The temple youth had learned the lessons that Rabbi Matt and Mr. Schwartzman had tried so hard to instill in them. The sign reflected that.

At first, Sam and other senior temple members were not amused and quickly replaced the defaced sign with a new one with the original wording. But the spray paint returned.

It wasn't long before the discouraged younger families in the temple left to form their own congregation. What once had been a vibrant temple with people of all ages became old and stale. Rabbi Matt was dejected about the breakup. However, many of the older and more conservative temple members didn't mind that the gay members of their congregation left and thought it was for the best. Except for high holidays, many of those older members never attended services anyway, so they didn't much notice the dramatic change in attendance at Saturday services. It was a fractured congregation, and that hurt Rabbi Matt's heart.

A new temple started up in a former tobacco warehouse in the downtown area near the neighborhoods where the hip, young families lived. The new congregation put up a sign in front of their building saying, "We support peace & justice for all the families of the Holy Land." They centered their youth activities on a Jewish Voice for Peace model that stressed *Tikun Olum* even more fully than Rabbi Matt had.

Rabbi Matt would have been a natural fit for this young congregation, but he stayed with Temple Shalom. Rabbi Matt missed the former joyous, energetic atmosphere of well-attended Saturday prayer services, the Bar and Bat Mitzvah classes full of teens, and the frequent social justice outings that the remaining older population could not, or would not, endure. He also missed seeing and shaping the future of the Jewish people represented by the many children who used to be a part of the congregation.

The new temple, short on funds, began without a rabbi. Instead, a young, Unitarian lesbian professor in the religion department at the local university led their Saturday services and their active social justice agenda. Her Jewish partner joined her, and the new temple enthusiastically responded to her leadership.

Rabbi Matt began to realize how inflexible he had been with his ideology. It didn't take a rocket scientist to see that his impressions of Palestinian families were, as Friedman had tried to tell him, as wrong as those held by white supremacists were of Blacks. Still, despite the changes, he could never fully embrace the new Israel-Palestine because Rebecca didn't. She thought it was horrible that the Jewish state was no more. While she remained ever-loving and supportive of her Jewish community, her ill feelings against Arabs and her rabid anger at Murray Schwartzman were never resolved. Whenever National Public Radio discussed the new peace, Rebecca would spit out hateful words in Hebrew that Matt had never heard her speak before.

Rebecca changed and retreated more into herself as the children grew older, though she kept the temple humming.

Matt was looking forward to the Seder as he drove home. They would have once prepared together, but this Passover, Rebecca had told him not to bother if he was too busy. He'd worked in his temple office until near dark.

Earlier that week, Rabbi Matt visited the Jewish schools by himself, using Legos to represent the Red Sea. At home, he spoke ("zoomed") with his parents and Rebecca's parents, promising they'd come visit soon. It was so nice that they could at least see images of one another as they spoke. That wasn't an option when he and Rebecca left for the States. They ended the conversation by agreeing to meet again to light the first candle in their menorahs together. Rebecca's mom blew good-night kisses to her grandchildren.

Rebecca asked the kids for help with cleaning up the meal. Matt was about to offer, too, then said, "I'd like to just have a few minutes with your father, Rebecca."

She arched her eyebrows but left with the children.

"Adam," Rabbi Matt said, "I'm not sure how to ask this." He paused. "It's been troubling me since Rebecca told me the story— about the Palestinian men who pulled a knife on her."

Alarm crossed his father-in-law's face. "When did that happen?" he asked.

"Oh, long ago. I'm sorry. I should have told you that first. It's just not an easy subject. I'm sure you'd rather forget about it, and I'm so proud of you for standing your ground and sticking it out in our homeland through the violence. Remember? It happened one day when Rebecca was a teen going for a jog outside the kibbutz gates."

Adam looked back and forth, as if searching his memory. "Oh. That day."

"I am so grateful you saw her leave, that you followed her."

"Just being a good dad. You would have done the same."

Rabbi Matt smiled. Yes, he would have. "But do you know what they said? Why did they try to attack her? Why weren't they imprisoned on the spot?"

"Rebecca doesn't know that I returned after taking her home. The men were still sitting there as if they'd done nothing wrong. But they had. They had insulted my daughter, just a child. I gave them a good talking to. They would have never treated their daughters that way. They might have killed me if I had done so."

"What did they call her?"

"They called her *habibi* and *malika*. They were too familiar with her. They weren't much older than she was, and they claimed their friend who didn't work in the gardens started it, pressured them into speaking to Rebecca."

"Were they going to abduct her? Assault her?"

"What are you talking about? Their words were offensive, a verbal assault, of course. They should have never spoken to a Jewish girl. Ever. But abduct her?"

"Yes. Yes. She said one pulled a knife."

Adam scratched his head, visibly confused. "No. No, I would remember that."

"She said she saw it glinting when he pulled it out, right as you came around the corner."

"I don't think so. Maybe she saw the trowel. He'd accidentally put it in his pocket from the garden. He was handing it to her to give back to me. When I confronted him, at least, that's what he said he did. He hung his head and apologized, asking for his god's forgiveness and mine. And then he handed me a trowel. Said he'd 'accidentally' taken it from the gardens. Was just asking her to take it back in."

"And you didn't call anyone?"

"Those were early times, son," Adam replied. "Maybe today I would have. I had anger about it for a long time. Told the man he no longer had work with me. I told him never to show his face again after he exposed my innocent little girl to such sleaze. And I never saw him again. Nor the other two. But no, I didn't report them. We were trying to be at peace back then."

Rabbi Matt went to bed that night with a heavy heart because even if Adam's version of the story were true, he knew it wouldn't change Rebecca's memories. She would tell him she saw what she saw. She'd rage not only at him but at her father. But the rabbi was a loyal man. He couldn't back away from his congregation or his marriage. Leaving Rebecca was never an option, yet he often pictured what it would be like to go and experience the new Holy Land. She and Matt never discussed it, their views about the end of the occupation being so divergent, but this unexpressed tension left their marriage a listless, empty shell of its former self.

Asher and Miri didn't talk about it either, at least not while their parents were in the same room. The children stayed at Temple Shalom, though it had lost much of the joy it had when more children of their own age had been there. Even so, they'd internalized their parents' Jewish moral values and actively participated in a new Israeli-Palestinian youth movement, including online activities designed to foster the relationship between Israel-Palestine and diaspora Jewish and Palestinian communities. A cool fad was to wear Birthright T-shirts inside out to this movement's meetings.

Rebecca, who would comment on how disgusted she was with the movement whenever she read about it in the papers, didn't ask her kids about their participation in it, and they did their best not to volunteer information about it to her.

One day, when Rabbi Matt drove into the parking lot at the temple, the sign was gone altogether. He left it that way. Along with "Maryam's Story," it had done what it needed to do.

Murray, however, was completely unaffected by the changes at Temple Shalom because he spent the remaining years of his life living in Jerusalem. He felt genuinely happy, fulfilled, and at home there, perhaps the first time he felt truly at peace since being a young child in Poland. He had never considered himself a Zionist—when he had escaped Europe as a teenager, it was to the United States, not to Israel. Yet, there he was.

He had many friends— Jewish, Muslim, and Christian—whom he cared about and who cared for him. His favorite activity was his walks through the narrow streets of Jerusalem's Old City, where he would watch the throngs of humanity from all over the world flowing into Jerusalem for religious pilgrimages and sightseeing vacations. Over time, Schwartzman became friendly with many Old City shopkeepers on his walks. Gradually, his strolls in the Old City took longer and longer, even while the distance he walked grew shorter and shorter. It wasn't that he was slowing down; it was just that so many of the shop-keepers of the Old City—Christians, Muslims, and Jews— stopped him and shared a conversation over tea or Arabic coffee heavily flavored with cardamom.

When Murray died, he was honored as one of the righteous. The country unveiled a large commemorative stone in Hebron in the park containing Goldstein's grave. The new stone dedicated to Mr. Murray Schwartzman stood in stark contrast to Goldstein's. Goldstein was from an old, narrow-minded world. Murray had been, too. So had his brother. But Murray had been blessed enough to have his blindfold removed. Murray was buried near Noah, finally together again.

"A Holocaust Survivor who walked the talk of the lesson of the Holocaust in support of Palestinian people," the stone said. "He shall not be forgotten. We shall never forget."

The dichotomy of the markers served as a reminder of how good, smart, and deeply religious people full of righteous indignation and prejudice can do so much good or so much harm. The stones and flowers that would be left on Schwartzman's grave were in direct con-trast to Goldstein's unadorned stone.

27

Finally Home

Years later, Jeremy and Katie visited a memorial celebration honoring Schwartzman's memory. They revisited all the places Jeremy had seen on his Birthright trip and took in the many changes that had taken place since then. They visited Yad Vashem, which commemorated and served as a permanent reminder of the horrific Jewish experience in the Holocaust—and which had been updated to also include the history of the Palestinian experience of expulsion, torture, and death, a history that was in large part a sad consequence of the Holocaust and a final chapter to the horrors of World War II and the biases of the 20th Century.

They both teared up as they toured the memorial.

"I can't believe Mr. Schwartzman endured these atrocities," Katie whispered. "We knew a man who survived the Holocaust."

The words hung between them as they walked along the aerial photos of Auschwitz, Treblinka, and then a virtual Palestinian Nakba exhibit. "Imagine, whether you were a Jewish or Muslim child, being woken at night by heavily armed soldiers who ransacked everything you owned. And then took your family members away, never to be seen again," Katie said, gripping the small hand that held hers.

"Or any child whatsoever," Jeremy replied.

The couple also visited Bethlehem, the Church of the Nativity, and the last remaining section of the apartheid separation wall, which had been saved as a reminder. The wall, just outside Bethlehem, was still covered with some of Banksy's famous graffiti, a painting that made it look like there was a giant hole in the wall with blue skies on the other side.

"I can't believe Banksy has been here." Jeremy laughed as they picnicked in a nearby park that had been converted from a former checkpoint.

They ended where they began, at Hebron. The family walked down Shuhada Street, now bustling with Muslim, Christian, and Jewish shoppers sprinkled among the many tourists who came to see not just Abraham's tomb but the people now living peacefully together in a place where so recently they had been sworn enemies separated by walls and barbed wire. Far more Jews lived in Hebron now than during the apartheid period, and they did so in peace with their Muslim neighbors. The Hebron tour guides no longer showed pictures of crowded Shuhada Street to tourists standing on a desolate road; instead, they showed pictures of desolate Shuhada Street to tourists standing in a crowd. Up the hill from Shuhada Street, the Youth Against the Settlements house was still there, next to the homes of religious Jews. Only now, Shoshana and her children would bring the cookies she baked to the Youth Against the Settlements house and share them with Issa Amro and Shoshana's other young Muslim Palestinian neighbors.

It almost felt like Murray was there with them, his strength of character and sturdy gaze looking at them. The world had changed so much because of him.

Ten years after their first visits to Israel-Palestine, they were now looking at their friend's memorial, and only steps away lay his brother, whom he'd lost as a child. All around them was the hustle and bustle of a city in stages of urban renaissance. Yet they brought back memories of a special time with their friend Murray in Israel. They'd always remember the place, but more importantly, the man who had brought them together.

The next day, a plane would take them back to Winston-Salem, where they always knew they'd migrate back to. But they were glad their son had seen this country as it rebirthed itself. Who knew what it would look like, what progress would have been made when he was in his 30s? The young couple was also proud their son would never know the Holy Land as anything but a place of peace and that, as he grew older, he would wonder how it might have ever been anything else.

Jeremy took Katie's hand, and together, they looked down the hillside at their son with curly dark hair and green eyes, running free, singing a song, then went to join him.

"Come back, Murray!" he called to the boy. "It's time to go home."

"Just a little while longer?" he asked.

"We've got a plane to catch to get home," Jeremy reminded him.

"But *the world* is my home, Dad!" Murray shouted back.

About the Author

Dr. Steven R. Feldman grew up in Washington, D.C., attending the Hebrew Academy of Washington and Beth Sholom Congregation, institutions that his grandfather and father helped to found and lead. As a child he collected dimes to help plant trees in Israel. Like many young Jewish children, he believed that Jews had come to an uninhabited land of deserts and swamps and made the land bloom. But as an adult he saw United Nations data that showed that about 700,000 Palestinians became refugees during the fighting of 1948. *That seemed odd*, he thought. *If we Jews had come to a land of empty swamps and deserts as I had been taught as a child, how did so many Palestinian men, women and children become refugees?*

Professionally, he received his M.D. and Ph.D. from Duke University in Durham, N.C., in 1985, then he completed his dermatology residency at the University of North Carolina at Chapel Hill and his dermatopathology residency at the Medical University of South Carolina, in Charleston. He is a professor of Dermatology, Pathology, and Public Health Sciences and the Director of the Psoriasis Treatment Center at Wake Forest School of Medicine in Winston-Salem, N.C.

Dr. Feldman leads the Center for Dermatology Research, a health services research center whose mission is to improve the care of patients with skin disease. Dr. Feldman's chief clinical interest is psoriasis, a chronic, physically & psychosocially disabling condition. His passion is to help guide how patients with psoriasis receive treatment. He serves on the Medical Board of the National Psoriasis Foundation, was awarded the Foundation's 2019 Outstanding Educator in Psoriatic Disease Award and directed psoriasis education programs for the American Academy of Dermatology. Feldman has also done groundbreaking work on addiction to tanning beds (and was interview by Diane Sawyer on *Good Morning America*) and on patients' adherence to their medication treatment regimens. The website Expertscape.com has ranked him as the #1 expert in the world on dermatology and on psoriasis, and the #2 expert on acne.

Feldman's work in psoriasis led him to an interest in patient satisfaction. Feldman created the www.DrScore.com doctor rating/patient satisfaction website. He analyzes data from that website to better inform doctors on how to enhance their care of their patients. He has given more than 700 invited lectures to dermatology groups and organizations around the world including the Pan Arab Dermatology Meeting held in Riyadh, Saudi Arabia, the Iranian Dermatology Society meeting in Tehran, Iran, and the Pan Asian Dermatology Meeting held in Seoul, Korea.

Published Works

- A Jewish American's Evolving View of Israel published by the American Council for Judaism (http://www.acjna.org/acjna/articles_detail.aspx?id=529)
- A Doctor's Prescription for Peace with Justice published by Americans for Middle East Understanding (http://www.ameu.org/uploads/vol43_issue2_2010.pdf).
- Practical Ways to Improve Patient Adherence
- The Magic Tongue Depressor